Undiscovered Angel

by

Sharon Saracino

Earthbound Series, Book 1

Undiscovered Angel

Cover Art by *Tamra Westberry*

The Wild Rose Press, Inc.
PO Box 708
Adams Basin, NY 14410-0708
Visit us at www.thewildrosepress.com

Publishing History
First Faery Rose Edition, 2014
Print ISBN 978-1-62830-401-5
Digital ISBN 978-1-62830-402-2

Earthbound Series, Book 1
Published in the United States of America

Jerry held the car door as Kassian ducked into the back seat settling Kat on his lap. The door slammed behind him as soon as he pulled his legs in, and the tinted windows shielded them from the trailing photographers and curious onlookers. He pulled a blanket from under the seat and tucked it around her as he realized he hadn't thought to see if she had a coat and the November evening was chilly. The atmosphere still felt heavy and oppressive with something dark, though it was less pronounced now. He tucked the blanket more closely around the motionless woman in his arms. In sleep, she looked like a child, young and defenseless, her fisted hand resting quietly on his chest, her thick lashes forming dark crescents against her pale skin. Her intricate hairstyle had come loose and wisps of spun silk tickled his neck as Jerry cranked the heat and opened the rear vents. He absently stroked the softness of her cheek, his long fingers brushing a wayward strand of hair behind her ear and she curled into him like a lost kitten. He felt something heavy settle in his chest, a temptation in the air that had nothing to do with evil, but everything to do with sin. Damn, this was so not on his agenda.

Dedication

For Vince, my own personal angel

Prologue

London, November, 1888

On the corner of Commercial and Fournier, a faceless, cape-shrouded prowler of the night lounged against the cold stone pillar of Christ Church, indistinguishable from the shadows that concealed him. His attention remained firmly fixed on the ribald jocularity emanating from the Ten Bells, directly across the road. Closing his eyes he inhaled deeply, filling his lungs with the sweet scent of sin and fear, reveling in the wretched despondency of desperation swirling through the alley, as thick and choking as fog on the Thames. Misery slinked among the rag shops, pubs, and poisoned human lives, like a malignant shadow. He depended on the power of desperation, and this squalor spawned many bleak souls ripe for harvest, like juicy plums hanging from a tree. He hoped the whore would be leaving soon; he had other matters to attend to this night. As if in answer to his silent wish, the increased volume of slurred shouts and laughter across the way heralded the opening of the door. His red eyes narrowed to speculative slits. Finally! He pushed all other thoughts aside, growled in satisfaction and anticipation...and faded into the shadows.

By the time winter's weary sun stretched tentative fingers across the cobbled courtyard outside Number 13

1

Miller's Court, little of the mutilated remains in the small, cold room bore any resemblance to the young woman who had sheltered there. When the Metropolitan Police arrived from Scotland Yard, few of those gathered in the curious crowd remembered anything particularly unusual about the previous night. Someone thought they'd heard Mary singing, some described seeing her with one man, some another. In the end, no one could say for sure. There was little love and even less trust between the East Enders and the police. Few would mourn the unfortunate girl; and fewer would remember the shouts of battle and the clashing of steel in the fetid courtyard outside Mary's room following her death. No, those memories had been carefully and deliberately erased.

Chapter 1

November, Present Day

The evening was an exercise in endurance, at least from Katrina Shephard's perspective. She detested the wall-to-wall people in the pub, and was uncomfortable in the large crowd. She concentrated on ignoring the passions and emotions swirling through and around her, craving her solitary living room with the overstuffed armchair and the pile of books awaiting her attention.

"Having fun yet, babe?" Elle's blue eyes flashed with excitement that was nearly palpable. Her short red wig was fashionably layered and spiked, and her heart shaped face bore little make-up, only enough to enhance her lapis eyes and full, pouty lips. The accordion pleated skirt of her sapphire halter dress ended slightly above her knees, swirling seductively with every twist and turn, and the high, strappy Jimmy Choo's made her legs look longer than they actually were. With eclectic elegance, she always managed to pair upscale designer with funky downtown chic. Kat shook her head in affectionate wonder. Elle could wear anything well and was frequently reinventing herself. Tonight she looked to be channeling a mischievous and sultry pixie chick.

"Just living the dream." Kat rolled her eyes and laughed while Elle stuck out her lower lip in a mock pout and linked her arm through Kat's. Kat stiffened only slightly, comforting herself that she was suffering for a good cause; her best friend would have been crushed if she hadn't at least put in an appearance at the party celebrating her latest book release.

"You really need to learn the meaning of the word fun, Kat," Elle complained giving her simple black sheath and understated accessories the once-over. "This is your success too, you should be enjoying it."

"I do know the meaning of the word fun; we just use different dictionaries! You know this is your scene, not mine. I'm more of a hover-in-the-background kind of girl. Besides, I didn't even think you should do this book…I only came for the food." She snatched an appetizer from a passing tray to punctuate her point.

"True, but you got right on board once I convinced you I was right, as usual…hence the reason I'm not saying I told you so." Kat nearly choked on the shrimp toast she'd just swallowed. Elle pounded her between the shoulder blades until her breath and natural color began to return. "Well, okay, maybe I said it once or twice, but I didn't rub it in or anything. And by the way, in that outfit you will not only hover in the background, you'll blend right into it!"

"Good, then my evil plan is working…and thanks for the ego boost." Kat bumped her hip against Elle's, pushing her away. "Go…your adoring public awaits," she urged with a laugh. "I'm going to find a quiet spot to hide until I can decently make myself scarce. I am so proud of you, sweetie."

Elle looked around at the milling crowd and squeezed Kat's shoulder in a quick hug.

"Hey, good luck with that quiet spot thing…I know

you hate this stuff. You really are the best, you know."

"Yeah, yeah…. preaching to the choir. Now get out of here and enjoy yourself."

Kat continued to count the minutes until she could make a graceful escape. When Elle Gates, one of McAllister Publishing's premier romance authors, had initially pitched a dark, gritty, investigative piece about Jack the Ripper, Kat did everything but turn cartwheels and spit wooden nickels to discourage her. The genre was the complete antithesis of Elle's established market. But she refused to be dissuaded, and her previous sales record and reputation got her a reluctantly tentative go ahead. Not only an outstanding writer, Elle was also an excellent judge of her fan base, and initial sales figures indicated that Ripper-mania was still alive and well over a century after the murders. Kat was more than happy to have been wrong. Elle never did anything by half measures; the book was incredibly well researched, tight and well written, and included new, never-before-published details. It ultimately stopped short of drawing any concrete conclusions, allowing the reader to draw their own. It was guaranteed to provoke discussion and debate.

Kat surveyed the crowded room and silently congratulated whoever had made the decision to host the party in an English style taproom rather than the usual upscale venue. Finley's had always been one of her favorite places, and with a little research, a competent decorator, and the enthusiastic cooperation of the pub's owner and staff, the interior now bore a strong resemblance to a late Victorian establishment. Cunningly fashioned arrangements constructed from reproduction prints of the East London Observer articles chronicling the Ripper's bloody nineteenth century rampage centered every table. The wait staff and bartenders wore costumes reminiscent of working class London in the 1880's, and the dark, wood paneling and flickering oil lamps contributed precisely the right touch of ambience. The overall effect was intimate, elegant, and a tad mysterious. A continuous hum of conversation punctuated by laughter mingled with the tinkle of fine glassware as strains of the Bare Naked Ladies played inconspicuously in the background. The music, along with a faint, but pervasive odor of sterno, provided a jarring element of modernity, but Elle loved the band and her agent decided it was a little enough concession; especially when she'd had to veto the fog machine. Kat could appreciate the authenticity of the décor as she had accompanied Elle on her London research jaunt.

The long hours in the close confines of the plane had been a challenge, but she'd managed with her iPod blasting five hours of music into her ears at top volume. Once there, she found herself fascinated by the research process, though the actual evidence was gruesome. Kat's own writing was confined to poetry and didn't require such meticulous research and adherence to fact. By the time she finished reading Elle's final draft, Kat knew that she'd be eating her words. Despite her initial misgivings, the book was a winner, one that was going to rocket right to the top.

Kat finally found herself a relatively uncongested corner and tuned out her surroundings. She concentrated instead on building a symphony in her mind to block out the cacophony of feelings bombarding her as she sipped at the fluted crystal of lukewarm ginger ale that she had opted for in lieu of champagne. The throbbing in her head was still dull, but she knew from experience it wouldn't stay that way long. She estimated she could disappear without provoking comment in another thirty minutes, or so.

Kat made people uncomfortable. And the feeling was mutual. She was well aware that spiritual metaphysics were controversial at best. The world at large is dependent upon that which is perceived and received through one of the five senses. There is simply not enough hardcore evidence for the majority of mainstream society to accept psychic and empathic abilities as a real possibility. Of course, there were exceptions, like Elle, who Kat suspected might still believe in the Tooth Fairy, but the world at large regarded abilities like Kat's with suspicion. Kat was different. Her different was twisted in the strands of her DNA. Her different was balancing on the blade of a double edged sword, alternately blessed and cursed, two things that were not mutually exclusive. Hardwired at birth, she couldn't change it any more than she could change the length of her legs, the cleft in her chin, or the brilliant pewter sheen of her thickly fringed eyes. But she had learned to control it. Mostly. The alternative was existence in a state of constant exhaustion being knocked around by other people's karma. Different was not always easy, but it was the only reality she had.

A sudden flurry of activity at the rear exit of the pub caught her attention and she felt the almost painful spike of excitement move through the crowd despite her best efforts to block it out. Across the room she saw Elle's face light up in nervous expectancy. Her eyes met Kat's, bright with anticipation as she mouthed "McAllister." Kat nearly choked for the second time that evening. Honestly, Elle must be trying to kill her. Everyone who was anyone had heard of the elusive Kassian McAllister, but few knew him personally. He kept a very low profile, surrounded himself with a few trusted assistants, and as far as Kat knew, had not attended a public party in all of the time Elle had been affiliated with McAllister. Members of the press gleefully punched their speed dial and chattered a mile a minute into their cell phones. Any appearance of Kassian McAllister guaranteed a media frenzy.

From her vantage point, Kat watched over the rim of her glass as he worked his way toward Elle. Tall, broad shouldered, and slim hipped, McAllister moved with a casual elegance and lithe grace that hinted at controlled danger. He had classically chiseled features, full sensual lips, and long, dark hair which he'd pulled straight back and secured with a leather slide at his nape. Much younger than she would have expected, he certainly wasn't the stereotypical business magnate. The man was a knockout and coupled with a net worth reportedly well over a billion, Kat wasn't surprised to see that half of the women in the room nearly drooled outright. They monitored his progress through the room as though he was the last drop of water in the middle of the Sahara at high noon. On his part, the disinterest was almost palpable.

McAllister reached Elle's side, brought her hand to his lips, and bent to say something in her ear. Kat had never seen Elle blush like that and curiosity trumped caution. What could he have said? She avoided touching individual minds as a rule, avoided invading privacy whenever she could. But it couldn't hurt, just this once, could it? Elle wouldn't mind and the suspense was killing her. She took a deep breath, dropped her shields, and sent a gentle push into the mind of Kassian McAllister and found... nothing? Impossible! People, in general, were an open book to Kat, usually way too open. Occasionally she encountered someone with some degree of natural ability to block their innermost thoughts, but she had never come in contact with a person she could not at least get something from. Worse, McAllister's head whipped around immediately, his eyes scanning the crowd then locking on her in the corner; he knew exactly what she was doing. Her heart raced with excitement and fear in equal measure. Though people claiming to be psychics could be found flipping tarot cards and gazing into crystal balls behind thick, velvet curtains all over the city, Kat had never encountered anyone else besides her mother that could actually do any of the things she could. Apparently that had changed, in the middle of a crowded cocktail party, of all places. She really needed to find a new hobby; being the poster child for Murphy's Law was exhausting.

Kat glanced down at the slender gold watch that had been a sixteenth birthday gift from her mother and checked the time. She needed to get out of here. Her head truly pounded now and she began to mentally recite Longfellow's Evangeline to drown out the overwhelming rush of impressions that had assailed her from every direction when she'd opened herself seeking McAllister's thoughts. Hopes, dreams, disappointments, despair, guilt, lust. Dumb, dumb, dumb! Now she was distracted and having trouble re-establishing her shields and there were some things she really didn't want to know about people. In fact, she grimaced at a few particularly vivid impressions, there were a whole lot of things she really didn't want to know about people. And wow, she would never look at Bernice Perkins quite the same way again! Kat had always been unwittingly privy to more information about the people around her than anyone should have to endure. Since childhood, words and music had been one of Kat's few escapes from the continual stress of sensing and taking in the pain and emotions of other people. Words gave her peace and music took her to a quiet place where her thoughts and feelings were her own. Eventually, she learned to control and block the endless stream of information coming at her from all directions, but it took a great deal of effort and concentration on her part, and, like now, left her with a screaming headache. It was exhausting in a crowd this size. It was so much more restful to embrace the welcome serenity that a quiet room and a good book, or a blank page and a soothing symphony could provide.

She glanced around and noticed to her dismay that Elle was leading McAllister in her direction. Fudge! Kat was happy for Elle; McAllister's appearance at the party would garner an enormous amount of attention. It implied he was giving his personal seal of approval, something that was unprecedented. That would no doubt provoke an increased interest in the book. Elle deserved the success and this unexpected recognition by someone with McAllister's cachet. This might be her biggest blockbuster yet. That being said, she was one of the only people to whom Kat was truly close. Kat would miss her after she was gone, since she fully intended to kill her at the first opportunity! Elle knew better than anyone what a struggle crowds were for Kat. What was she thinking dragging the CEO over to add to her stress level? It was sad, but she was really going to have to kill her.

Her mouth felt suddenly dry and she immediately downed what remained of her lukewarm drink, looking for a passing tray to deposit the empty glass. She formulated a quick plan; go in the opposite direction, make short work of the inevitable farewell tour, and slip out quietly. But, before she could make any headway in the crush, she found herself captured by the darkest eyes she had ever seen, obsidian eyes that hinted at a thousand secrets locked behind thick inviting lashes. And they were only inches away. Kat loved words, words were her friends, and words were her salvation. Now, when she could have used a bit of back up from the little buggers, for the first time in her life, words failed her miserably. She felt a flutter of awareness, a gentle push of his mind touching hers... and she was slightly irritated to find that it felt more like a caress than an invasion.

McAllister fixed his gaze on Elle. He blinked, once, twice. Then he turned his attention back to Kat. Elle flushed and looked from one to the other as if suddenly confused.

"Um, yes, right...Kassian, this is my friend, Katrina Shephard...oh, I guess I told you that already...Kat this is Kassian McAllister." Beautiful, eloquent, always in control, Elle was nearly babbling. "Kassian is...oh, right, you know who Kassian is......okay, gotta run...later, gator." She smacked an air kiss in the vicinity of Kat's cheek and squeezed her hand in encouragement, or maybe apology?

Kassian raised Elle's fingertips to his lips, gazing directly into her eyes. "Miss Gates, it has been a pleasure. The book is outstanding. As usual, you've done both yourself and McAllister Publishing proud."

His voice was low and hypnotic, as dark and smooth as warm, melted chocolate. Kat couldn't quite put her finger on it, but she sensed he was saying far more than the gallant words tumbling off of his tongue indicated. Elle appeared caught in a spell. As he released her hand, Elle mumbled something that might have been thank you but sounded more like "take me" and beat a hasty retreat to the bar at the far side of the room. Thanks a million, pal, Kat thought sourly. You are *so* going to hear about this. She noticed McAllister's lips twitch and wondered if he'd caught her thought.

The heat in the room felt suddenly oppressive and Kat found her heart racing far too fast. A flock of butterflies seemed to have taken flight somewhere in the region of her stomach and quickly rose to clog her throat with furiously beating wings, stealing her breath. She instinctively took a step back, but the wall brought her up short. McAllister moved forward at the same time, bringing her nose-to-incredibly-well-muscled-chest with him, and forcing her to tilt her neck back painfully to meet his gaze. Kat's few awkward and painful forays into the world of men could never have prepared her for Kassian McAllister. She guessed he didn't spend an awful lot of time languishing behind a desk. He exuded power and a dark, volatile appeal that was impossible to ignore. Kat knew in a single heartbeat that she was out of her element. She sensed darkness in him, not evil, but more a weary resignation. His features appeared cool, controlled, and expressionless, and she recognized so much more simmering below the surface, but she couldn't quite touch it no matter how hard she tried. She wanted to ignore the width of his shoulders; the thickly bunched biceps moving under his sleeves, and the flat plane of his stomach accentuated by the tight black tee he wore under his jacket, and concentrate on wondering why his mind remained a blank test pattern to her. But she found the total package difficult to ignore and totally mesmerizing. When he quirked a dark brow and his very defined, very masculine lips curled in amusement, she wondered if he had caught that thought, too. The mortification was just enough to penetrate her momentary stupor. For the love of Pete, she needed to get a grip! Appalled to realize she was standing there in a room filled with people, press, and professionals ogling the man like some half-witted groupie, she glanced around nervously. More than one person was fixated on their exchange and McAllister had no way of knowing how completely out of character this behavior was for her.

"Was that really necessary?" She licked her lips and nodded toward Elle who watched from across the room, still looking a bit foggy. Kassian followed her gaze, and then looked back to her, his expression unchanged.

He arched a dark brow. "I have no idea what you're talking about."

"Oh, please." Kat rolled her eyes. "If you knew Elle, and believe me, I do, she doesn't rattle easily...and she doesn't babble, *ever,* so I am guessing that little display was your, um, influence?" She arched a delicately winged brow, proud that her voice remained cool and firm, as though she encountered psychics with mind control abilities every day.

He assumed a look of feigned innocence and shrugged slightly. Her gray eyes narrowed suspiciously. He was lying. Why? Lying was careless, and he didn't have a reputation as a careless man. He must realize that she was nervous. She supposed she should be nervous after her amateurish attempt to read him. She wondered if he was having any success trying to read her as clearly he was capable of it. Still, it didn't look like he was going to admit to anything. She maintained eye contact and waited impatiently for his response. She suspected there weren't many people who could stand toe to toe with him and stare him down without flinching. Well, she might be wary, she was definitely curious, but unlike the rest of the women in the room, she wasn't in awe.

****

Kassian's attendance tonight was purely selfish. He had arrived at the party fully expecting to be bored; bored was his baseline, occasionally punctuated by rage, regret, and remorse. But he'd been curious to know how Elle Gates had managed to find details about the murders that had managed to elude every Ripper researcher and aficionado to date. Before he could fully engage her and steer the conversation around to it, he felt the light, curious, and totally unexpected push at his mind. And now he found the answer gazing up at him with worried gray eyes; Elle Gates had used a psychic research assistant. Bingo! Oh, this woman was psychic all right, but she also recognized *his* ability and was trying to block him, and that was even more unexpected. What people said and what they thought were two entirely different things, and he found the latter to be far more useful. He suddenly found his boredom dissipating; this evening might turn out to be much more interesting than he had anticipated.

People falling all over him got really old, really fast. This Katrina Shephard was a decided improvement. Of average height, her head fell a few inches below his chin even in heels. She was slim, but with generous curves and gorgeous legs. Her wide gray eyes were heavily fringed, her lips lush and sexy. Thick, champagne-colored hair swept away from her face and piled in an intricate knot, emphasizing her long graceful neck and classic bone structure. Her attire was simple, yet elegant. Unlike her friend, she apparently didn't dress to call attention to herself, but it did nothing to disguise her allure. Certain he hadn't met her before, he couldn't shake the feeling there was something oddly familiar about her.

"Mr. McAllister," she continued quietly, "please get out of Elle's head. Just because you *can* do something, doesn't necessarily mean you should."

"You don't beat around the bush, do you?" he murmured. "It might surprise you to know that some people find me a little…intimidating. And they generally don't tell me what I can and can't do." He was satisfied to see she had the grace to flush.

"But, you're right…and I wasn't intruding on her privacy, only sending her away for a few minutes so that we could talk." He frowned. Now where the hell had that come from? Since when had he bothered to explain himself? It had been a long time since he cared about what anyone thought.

He grabbed a glass from a passing tray and quirked an enquiring brow. She shook her head, smiling a little to take the bite out of her refusal. He wondered if she was worried about keeping her wits intact without the added distraction of alcohol. It wasn't a problem he ever needed to consider.

"I'm sorry…I don't know what you could possibly want to talk to me about that wouldn't include Elle? After all, it's her book…oh, fudge, the advance," she muttered under her breath as though a thought suddenly occurred to her. Kassian touched her mind and had no difficulty discerning exactly what was running through it. She'd requested advance payment on a design project she'd been working on for McAllister Publishing which wasn't what she'd agreed to in her contract. The young clerk in accounting had not been at all happy about it, but he had a thing for Elle Gates, who had turned on exactly enough charm to get him to agree by making a few vague promises, none of which she intended to keep. It had obviously played on Kat Shephard's conscience, but Kassian could hardly get worked up about a figure that didn't even cover his pocket change.

"I'm sorry, Mr. McAllister, the opportunity to go to London with Elle came up so suddenly and I'd had some unexpected expenses at home. I know it's out of the ordinary, but I did make arrangements to get all of the work completed before I left…I see now that it might have been presumptuous of me…I take full responsibility; Elle had nothing to do…"

He held up a hand in mock defense. Damn, she was a hyper little thing.

"Whoa! First of all, I have people to handle that sort of thing…so unless you embezzled enormous amounts of company money or attempted to plant a bomb in the ladies' powder room, I doubt I would hear about it. Secondly, Miss Gates tells me your help was invaluable to her research. I've read the book. If it cost McAllister a few dollars to send you along, I would say it was money well spent. If anyone gives you grief, let me know and I'll take care of it."

"Let you know and you'll take care of it?" Kat echoed faintly. "Just out of curiosity, how exactly would I go about that? Letting you know, I mean. To be honest, I've done freelance work for McAllister for almost three years and was pretty much convinced you were a figment of someone's overactive imagination; you know, like unicorns and leprechauns. Accessibility isn't exactly your middle name."

Suddenly he smiled, really smiled, causing more than one female heart in the room to stutter and trip. He didn't genuinely smile very often, at least not in a way that reached his eyes as he knew it did now. He found little reason to do so. He was completely disinterested in the fact that the sight of it was nearly lethal to the fairer sex.

"Touché, Miss Shephard. I guess I should have seen that coming."

"Well, hello, you're standing there reading my mind!"

At that, Kassian laughed right out loud, resulting in even more heads swiveling in their direction, further decreasing the chances that their encounter would go unobserved.

"And let's be clear," she continued in a low voice

tinged with indignation. "My trip did not cost McAllister anything. I completed the work I contracted for. I earned the money. I only asked for it up front so I could confirm my travel plans, which in retrospect, I guess was a little unorthodox."

"Look, I'll make a deal with you." He knew they were attracting more attention than he'd intended, but Kassian found it inordinately refreshing to have a woman up in his face instead of falling at his feet. "You stop trying to get into my head and I'll stop trying to get into yours and we'll just agree to have a nice, normal conversation."

"Why?" She regarded him with narrowed eyes.

"Why? What do you mean, why?" Had she looked in a mirror recently? Why would she think he was any different than the next poor schmuck? Not to mention the telepathy thing and the fact that she'd actually tried to read him; that would have guaranteed his interest even if she looked like Janet Reno. She was obviously uncomfortable with her abilities. He found himself not only moderately entertained, but unwillingly curious.

"I mean, why would you want to have a nice, normal conversation with me? There are plenty of people here tripping all over themselves to get your attention. You don't even know me. I'm sorry if I'm being rude, but honestly, I was getting ready to leave when you came over. Did you want something?"

His eyes did a quick once-over, missing nothing. Hell, yeah, he wanted something, but he knew instinctively that she wasn't the anonymous-quickie-in-a-bathroom-stall type. He could have any woman in the room. That wasn't conceit talking, it was just a fact, a fact about as impressive to him as dry toast. And the only woman in the room he found remotely interesting was wishing she was anywhere but here with him. She wasn't flirting or making any effort to impress him. He suspected she would be more relieved than disappointed if he walked away right now. It was a completely new experience for him. And given his extensive experience that was saying something. She rubbed her forehead as though she was in pain. He wondered if trying to hold her shields securely while engaging in verbal repartee with him in a crowd was causing her discomfort. Maybe he should tell her to relax? She really wasn't blocking him very well anyway.

"Why were you leaving? Do you have to be somewhere?"

He surreptitiously glanced at her left hand. Katrina Shephard had piqued more than his physical interest, although she certainly was no slouch in that area. He couldn't remember the last time a woman had done that. He wasn't quite ready to relinquish her company to whoever might be waiting for her at home. After all, they were simply conversing in a public place; it should be harmless enough.

"No," she replied levelly, "and please don't take it personally, I don't really care for crowds. I only came for Elle's sake, and only planned to stay for a short time."

Kat rubbed her forehead again. He hadn't intended to make her uncomfortable; well, not physically at any rate. He was about to withdraw when he hesitated. Her mind suddenly descended into turmoil, her thoughts becoming increasingly scattered and disjointed. He realized it was more than trading banter with him, more than the crowd. Something was wrong.

****

Kat's unease increased in waves. Her eyes darted nervously around the room for the source of her discomfort, momentarily forgetting Kassian McAllister's presence completely. Everyone else in the room appeared oblivious to the threat; they were busy enjoying themselves, drinking, talking, and laughing. No one else seemed to notice how the air had thickened. A cold draft seemed to snake along the floor and creep around her limbs, bringing with it the unmistakable taint of evil. She felt sweat beading on her forehead and trickling down the valley between her breasts. Her stomach tightened in revulsion and her whole body suddenly seemed to rebel. The air around her felt heavy, suffocating, and her breath came in short, labored gasps. Her eyes widened in fear and she blindly grasped at McAllister's lapel, barely aware she had done so. Kat felt herself drowning in the overwhelming presence of a dark malevolence unlike anything she could ever have imagined. It crawled over her skin and crept through her body like a living thing. Her walls crumbled against the intensity of the assault and terror invaded her thoughts, mocking and insistent.

She felt McAllister's arms close around her as her mind spiraled out of control and her knees started to buckle. She was so cold and physically felt the color leave her face in a rush. She sensed McAllister probing deeper into her mind, trying to make sense of her sudden fear and horror. Her lips moved soundlessly as she tried to explain. Suddenly his eyes opened wide and he stared at her; right before her eyes rolled back and she doubled over, one hand clutching at her throat and the other wrapped around her middle with a silent scream of agony. His face was the last thing she saw; darkness overcame her as her mind succumbed to a sharp command which sent her into a deep sleep.

****

Kassian hooked an arm beneath her knees and swept her up, cradling her face against his broad chest. His driver lingered near the exit and he nodded once to indicate that he should bring the car. Elle elbowed a frantic path across the room to Kat's side.

"What did you do?" she demanded. Elle's lips trembled and her eyes were wide with alarm. Kassian sighed. He tried to be offended that she thought it was his fault. He really was used to a great deal more deference than he had gotten tonight from either of these women. "What is it? What happened?"

Kassian leaned in close so he wouldn't be overheard. "She's an empath, isn't she?"

"How did you…."she began, then bit her lip at his expression and nodded quickly. "Yes, among other things. It's why she has such a difficult time in crowds. This is my fault, she didn't want to come tonight…she did it for me." He didn't have time to deal with her self-recrimination at the moment. He nodded shortly and began to move toward the door.

"Wait…where are you going? Are you taking her to the hospital? Shouldn't we call 911?"

"I've got this," he replied quietly. "She'll be okay…I think she picked up on something she shouldn't have. Trust me."

Elle looked as if she wanted to say more, much more. Something in his eyes must have convinced her that he was sincere. Before the crowd around them became impassable, Elle quickly dug through her sequined clutch and stuffed her card in his pocket. She pulled the lapel of Kassian's jacket forward to shield Kat's pale face from the photographers who were already sighting down their lenses in her direction and coming in for the kill.

"Promise you'll have her call me?"

"I promise…now, can you handle things here? Say whatever you're comfortable with that makes sense and won't cause her any embarrassment. Convince everyone this is not a big deal. Can you handle it?"

"Yes, yes, of course…" she replied in a shaky voice. Her eyes never left Katrina who remained still and pale. Elle was obviously distraught, and Kassian hoped his cool composure would provide her with some degree of reassurance. There would be fewer questions that way. She pushed ahead of him, clearing a path through the crowd to the rear exit.

"Did Miss Shephard come with you tonight?" Kassian asked.

"What? Oh, no, I took a cab… Kat drove in from her place, why?"

"She did? Why?" Friday night city traffic was hell, and parking was worse. No one in their right mind drove in it if they didn't have to.

"Kat doesn't live in the city, she was crashing at my place tonight," Elle replied moving closer to McAllister, further thwarting the more rabid photographers from getting a shot.

"I'd like you to wait for my driver …I'll send Jerry back to take you home." She opened her mouth as though she would protest, but he cut her off with a tight smile. "I insist. I'm afraid I'll have to ask you to trust me again."

"I don't understand…"

"I know you don't, and I can't explain right now…but promise me you will wait for Jerry."

She nodded up at him, her blue eyes swimming. He turned away. He wasn't the comforting-tearful-women-type and at the moment he was focused on getting the Shephard woman out. Hell, this hadn't been on his agenda for the evening. He didn't know what was going on, but he had a pretty good suspicion. If he had an ounce of common sense, he would leave right this minute and call in his men to check it out. He felt the responsibility like the weight of the woman in his arms; but until he could confirm it one way or the other, he wasn't taking chances. Kat Shephard had detected the taint of evil before he'd felt even the faintest hint of prickling shocks creeping up and down his spine, and that was worrisome. He'd have to figure that out later. She was obviously very sensitive; right now he needed to distance her from the area as soon as possible.

Jerry held the car door as Kassian ducked into the back seat settling Kat on his lap. The door slammed behind him as soon as he pulled his legs in, and the tinted windows shielded them from the trailing photographers and curious onlookers. He pulled a blanket from under the seat and tucked it around her as he realized he hadn't thought to see if she had a coat and the November evening was chilly. The atmosphere still felt heavy and oppressive with something dark, though it was less pronounced now. He tucked the blanket more closely around the motionless woman in his arms. In sleep, she looked like a child, young and defenseless, her fisted hand resting quietly on his chest, her thick lashes forming dark crescents against her pale skin. Her intricate hairstyle had come loose and wisps of spun silk tickled his neck as Jerry cranked the heat and opened the rear vents. He absently stroked the softness of her cheek, his long fingers brushing a wayward strand of hair behind her ear and she curled into him like a lost kitten. He felt something heavy settle in his chest, a temptation in the air that had nothing to do with evil, but everything to do with sin. Damn, this was so not on his agenda.

Chapter 2

"What in the hell were you thinking?" The question was quietly spoken with no hint of the underlying concern it contained.

Kassian stared unseeing out of the smoked glass floor to ceiling windows, his expression tight. A slight lift of his chin was the only indication he'd heard. His tall, broad form blocked a good deal of the weak, early morning sunlight as he surveyed the orderly grid of the city spread out below. This morning he felt every damn one of his six hundred years. Over the last century, most of his emotions had become microcosmic. Emotions were a weakness; a vulnerability. Emotions got you, or those you cared about, killed. Empty detachment allowed him to survive. Now his resolve was shaken. The silver eyed woman had touched him, in a matter of minutes, somewhere deep and forgotten. Hell, he should have walked away. Instead, he brought her home. To his bed. With the press on their heels. He hadn't intended it, couldn't defend it. He sure as hell wasn't looking for a woman; he'd gotten quite used to being alone with his culpability for companionship. On the rare occasions he slept at all, he slept alone. He found little pleasure in anything. Living for revenge had eaten at his soul until it was nearly consumed and he firmly believed revenge was the only thing that could restore it. He felt the quiet censure of the visitor enveloped in the comfortable embrace of Corinthian leather on the other side of the immense mahogany desk. It had been so long since anyone had been able to touch him. No, he hadn't been thinking, he'd been feeling; and what the hell was up with that?

The expensive leather whooshed like satin on silk as Luca Fiorelli shifted his position in the chair. He endured the lack of response without complaint, exuding arbitrary elegance, each feature perfect and timeless. Long and lean, his black wool slacks were perfectly tailored, topped with an ivory, cashmere pullover stretched across the expanse of his wide shoulders. Not a single strand of the silver blonde hair, waving back from his high, smooth forehead and curling over the top of his collar, was out of place. His cool gray eyes were wide and placid as he regarded his friend across the polished expanse of aged wood.

Luca watched quietly as Kassian began to pace, striding about the confines of the large room like a sleek, caged panther. At over six and a half feet, his size alone was daunting enough, but the anger and frustration radiating from him in waves was almost palpable.

"Well, she's here now, so we'll deal with it. You need to get a grip, my brother," Luca said in an even voice. "You have to find a way to distance yourself, make it less personal."

"Less personal?" Kassian choked out tightly. "How the hell do you suggest I do that? It doesn't get any more personal. Shit, Luca, you know that as well as anyone. I need to finish this."

He straightened to his full height and looked down his long straight nose at the seated man, his dark eyes narrowed and spitting fire. Luca continued to regard him with an expectant expression, long legs casually crossed, looking as unruffled and relaxed as if he'd stopped by for brunch. Kassian envied him his cool composure. He returned to the window and fixed his gaze on the first stirrings of Saturday morning traffic. From his vantage point, high above the streets in his sanctuary of thick carpeting and soundproof glass, it was like watching a television with the volume set on mute. He concentrated on the easy, regular sound of his own breathing as the long minutes ticked by, fighting to maintain a relaxed stance. Kassian's formidable anger had simmered below the surface for over a hundred years. Oh yeah, this was personal; damn personal.

"He knows exactly how to push your buttons, Mac…he always has. You need to get a handle on this. You wanted to tease him out of hiding, right? And now you have, but if you go out there half-cocked with both barrels blazing, you're going to get yourself killed. You've waited this long, doing some recon first is the only sensible thing to do."

Before last night, Kassian wouldn't have thought getting killed was the worst thing that could happen, once Callista was avenged and Rapier was dead, of course. Before last night, he might have welcomed death. Death would be a release from the emptiness that had come to pass for his existence and the ever-present awareness of his mother's grief and his own shortcomings. But last night, Katrina Shephard had awakened something he'd thought lost forever. He hadn't yet decided how he felt about it.

"It was him?" Kassian inquired in a low voice, but he already knew the answer. There was no question about who they were dealing with. It had taken over a hundred years, but his patience had finally paid off; the bastard had re-surfaced at last. The mutilated body found last night in the Dumpster near Finley's certainly bore the signs of Rapier's proclivities. It was Whitechapel 1888 all over again. He and Luca had both seen it before. Brother warriors, they were part of the elite *Defensori* guard appointed to fight the *Fallen* and their *animorti*, a threat to both the mortal and supernatural order. Scotland Yard had never had a prayer all those years ago; Jack the Ripper wasn't even human.

"The dead girl's last known address was the House of Angels," Luca shrugged casually, but the grimness in his tone was unmistakable.

Kassian had established the women's shelter a few years ago, ostensibly in memory of his sister. His motives weren't purely altruistic, however, no matter what anyone thought. He'd secretly hoped that the familiar reference, when associated with the McAllister name, would pique Jacques's interest enough to draw him out after he'd remained hidden and stubbornly elusive for the last hundred or so years. Apparently the gamble had finally paid off. Unfortunately, Kassian's single-mindedness failed to take into account that someone might pay for his bluff with her life, nor had he anticipated that an innocent like Katrina Shephard would get caught in the crossfire. The oversight was a testament to how obsessed he had let himself become with Rapier. Others were paying for his fixation. Hell, he'd been carrying the burden of blame all of these years, what were a few more rocks on the growing mountain of his guilt?

The *Defensori* had noticed the increased numbers of *animorti* in the city over the last several weeks and suspected that something might be imminent. *Animorti* were little more than animated corpses recruited by the *Fallen* from the dregs of humanity; sycophants and slime pumped up on rage and lacking insight, lowlifes easily persuaded by the promise of power. The only entry fee into their society was a soul; most didn't have much of one left anyway. By the time they realized the price they would pay for the empty promises of their *Fallen* masters, they were nothing more than expendable sponges for the evil of their makers, puppets nearly incapable of independent thought.

"Well, I'm sure he knows he's gotten our attention," Kassian said at last. "We should have guessed the coward wouldn't come at us directly and would revert to hiding behind a helpless woman. He never changes his M.O. Get in touch with everyone and bring them up to speed."

Kassian paused to pull his black tee off over his head and toss it across one shoulder. After depositing Kat in the middle of his king-sized bed last night, and barely resisting the urge to crawl in beside her, he'd spent the remainder of the dark hours walking the floors and waiting for Luca to return his call. The thick muscles in his back rippled as he stretched and flexed the stiffness from his tired body. An intricately tattooed claymore rippled along the length of his spine. The pommel started just below his hairline, the grip covering the back of his neck, and the perpendicular guard extending out along the bulky muscles of his shoulders. The double edged blade ran straight and true, ending in a sharp point above his tailbone. It was a handy way to carry a weapon. But like Luca, he preferred the quickness and convenience of daggers, and both warriors wore one embedded in the complicated tattoos on the inner aspect of each forearm from elbow to wrist.

"Oh, and assign someone to watch Elle Gates for the next few days. I was seen with her last night, too; he might perceive her as a connection to me. I don't want to take any chances." After spending the last century, and in fact the better part of his long life in the *Defensori*, avoiding relationships that could be used against him, there was no way he was giving his enemy any access to Kat or her friend at this stage of the game.

"Mac, you know as well as I do that we have a limited number of men available at the moment, we can't afford to be a man down to babysit the Gates woman. We need to be at full strength if we are going to bring Rapier down this time."

Kassian frowned. "Maybe you're right…well, then let's put some *sigil*s up around her place; at least that way she'll be safe at home, and we can have someone check on her periodically. Jerry took her home; he can give you the address."

"Consider it done." Luca stood and stretched, as well. The two warriors moved out of the office, through the bright, open living space, and into the galley style kitchen where recessed lighting gleamed on chrome, black granite, and stainless steel efficiency. Kassian poured two steaming mugs of coffee, while Luca peered into a white bakery box on the counter. He made a selection, propped a hip against the counter and munched contentedly on a crunchy, chocolate filled *cornetto*.

"God, these are good….do you remember that little *pasticceria* in the *Borgo*? Ah, Giovanna…now there was a delicacy I could sink my teeth into."

He flashed a wolfish grin. Kassian swallowed a large gulp of coffee and shook his head.

"Luca, you are such a freakin' hound."

"You know my motto," Luca grinned. "Love isn't only blind, it's also deaf and dumb and should be avoided like the plague. I, for one, know when to cut and run. Love softens and distracts a man, or as in my father's case, destroys him. Better to avoid it altogether. There's no room for divided loyalty in battle." He pointed the remainder of his pastry at Kassian. "You should keep that in mind."

Kassian rolled his eyes. He'd heard it all before. But simply because Luca didn't believe in getting emotionally involved didn't mean he didn't believe in enjoying himself. Often. And there was never a shortage of willing partners.

"I don't think you need to worry about the Gates woman, she's basically an employee of sorts, one of many authors your company publishes," Luca continued in a thoughtful tone." No one would consider it abnormal or suspicious that you'd conversed with her at a party in her honor. But, this one…" He nodded toward the closed bedroom door. "What do you plan to do about her?"

"After I take a shower, I plan to wake her up, ply her with coffee, and send her home. We'll put *sigil*s on her place, as well. She's done some freelance graphic work for the company so basically she could be seen as an employee of sorts too, and one not even connected to McAllister, really."

"An employee of sorts who spent the night in your bed, Mac. Let's not forget *that* little complication." Luca's narrowed eyes spoke volumes. "And there were plenty of people, reporters included, who witnessed your less than stealthy exit. Have you seen the papers? You two looked quite cozy as you departed the party last night."

"Alone, Luca...see if you can pull your mind out of the gutter for five minutes. She spent the night in my bed, alone."

The blonde warrior shrugged.

"My mind is only down there keeping everyone else's company, my brother. How many people who saw you carry her out of there last night or read about it this morning will believe she spent the night in your bed alone? You know that, and I know that... correction, you know that...I just got here," Luca chuckled ducking the swat aimed at his head. "The bottom line is Rapier doesn't know that. You've got to assume he's keeping tabs. The press will have done their homework; by now they'll know who she is, where she lives, and that she didn't go home last night. Sorry, brother." He chucked Kassian under the chin. "By keeping her here last night, you painted a big red bull's-eye right on her pretty little backside."

Kassian's jaw tightened as he prepared to disagree. Unfortunately, he didn't have a valid argument available; Luca was right. He had made one hell of a mess even bigger. Katrina Shephard was a complication on more levels than he cared to contemplate at the moment.

"So, what do you suggest? She didn't ask for this...she just got caught in the psychic crossfire." He should have followed his initial instincts and stayed the hell home last night. He could have assigned one of his assistants to look into the information the Gates woman had uncovered. Of course, there was no telling what would have happened to Kat Shephard had he not been there to shut her down and get her out. But, then he'd never have met her and it wouldn't be his problem. Yeah, right! Dragging a hand through his hair, he struggled to explain his uncharacteristic impulsivity to his friend, as well as to himself. "I'm telling you, Luca, I've never seen a mortal with her degree of empathic sensitivity. It was like she was physically experiencing the murder. I really thought she might not survive it…I had no choice but to put her out. Then what? Drop her off at home, pat her on the head, and leave her there alone and unprotected? Is that what you would have done?"

"Probably." Luca popped the last bite into his mouth and chewed rapidly, appearing fascinated by the pattern on his coffee mug.

"Bull! You would have done exactly the same thing and you know it. Sometimes, I think you forget who you're talking to."

"Well, maybe I would have," Luca grinned in acknowledgment. "But you can bet your ass she wouldn't have spent the night in that bed alone." This time Luca wasn't quick enough and the backhand caught the side of his head.

"Finish your coffee and get out of here," Kassian growled. He fished in his pocket and tossed the other man a set of keys. "Do me a favor and find her car…it should be somewhere in the vicinity of the pub. The registration in her bag says it's an '89 Ford." He grimaced and saw that Luca did the same. "Drop it back here and then send someone to put the *sigil*s around Elle Gates' place." He'd planned to send Jerry for Kat's car, but by the time he'd taken Elle home, it was late and Kassian figured the poor guy deserved a break. This morning was soon enough to retrieve her car... it wasn't like she'd need it anytime soon. At that moment he realized he'd already made his decision. His whole plan, or rather, lack of one, had seemed a hell of a lot simpler last night.

"Have I mentioned you're a really cranky bastard in the morning?" Luca gulped the last of his coffee and rinsed the mug in the sink. "What are you going to do about sleeping beauty?" He hitched a thumb in the general direction of the master suite.

"She stays with me." Kassian wearily pinched the bridge of his nose between his thumb and forefinger. He had no idea how he would get her to agree. Didn't really matter. She needed protection, and that was his middle name. She was staying whether she saw it his way or not, but it would be nice to be less of a bastard for a change. He had a strong suspicion that Kat was not going to be a happy camper. He ran a hand through his loose, shoulder length hair in frustration.

"What are you planning to tell her?"

"Oh hell, I don't know," he muttered darkly.

"Well, hey...that sounds like a *fabulous* plan. Let me know how it works out for you," Luca smirked. "We could always go with putting *sigil*s on her, too, you know."

Rapier had finally surfaced and the situation was bound to get ugly. Not only had Kassian managed to put an unsuspecting woman in danger, the woman was the one person on Earth who had managed to somehow touch his emotions, something he hadn't experienced in years. He sure as hell hadn't been looking, and he wasn't sure how he felt about it. One thing he was sure of, there was no way he was going to let anything happen to her.

"No, she stays with me. If for no other reason, it will make Rapier think I have something to lose and that may keep him from disappearing before we can get to him."

"You're suggesting we use her for bait?"

"Not exactly." But wasn't it exactly what he was doing? Still, he'd already put her in danger, as Luca so thoughtfully pointed out, so keeping her with him was really the best course of action. The pulse pounding attraction he felt for her had absolutely nothing to do with it. Nope, nothing at all.

"But…" Luca began, but Kassian held up a hand to stop him.

"Not now, Luca…I just… not now. Now get out of here and get Elle Gates protected and get everyone up to speed." His tone suggested that Luca drop the subject of Kat Shephard for the time being, and wisely, he did.

"Yeah…I'm going, I'm going." Before the door closed behind him he was punching a code into his cell and barking orders.

Kassian crossed to the bedroom, quietly cracked open the door, and stuck his head inside. Kat remained deeply asleep, burrowed into the linens so that only the wild tumble of her fair hair spread out like a golden curtain against the dark sheets was visible. He was irritated to realize the he liked seeing her curled up in his bed. She looked like she belonged there. He swore softly. He would always put her in danger. Kassian did not want to be that man. It was simply better for everyone concerned if he steered clear of this. His lifestyle wasn't fair to any woman. Fighting the strong draw he felt toward her was already a problem. And regarding anything supernatural, he would bet she was as completely in the dark as the majority of the human population. Figuring she would sleep for a while yet, he grabbed a clean pair of jeans and headed for the bathroom. A hot shower might ease his tight muscles, but a cold one was probably the better bet to ease the unwelcome tightness he felt elsewhere.

****

Kat struggled awake through the dark layers of dreamless sleep. She felt a curious lethargy and vaguely registered the muted sound of running water. With eyes still closed, the caress of satin sheets instead of serviceable flannel against her skin told her immediately that she was not in her own bed. Swallowing her alarm, she struggled to recall the events of the previous evening. Her head throbbed as she remembered the evil crippling her, and then there'd been nothing except dark oblivion. Logically, she knew she must have passed out from the pain. But where was she and how had she gotten here? She groaned silently into the pillow. Way to hover in the background, Kat.

Cautiously, she opened one eye and surveyed her surroundings. She was lying in the middle of an enormous bed that was expensively dressed in black satin. The room itself was huge, furnished in sleek, modern furniture, the far wall comprised entirely of closets shuttered in black, lacquered doors. The sound of running water from behind the closed door to her right had stopped. She assumed it was a bathroom. But whose? The only things in the room that looked at all familiar to her were her black cocktail dress hanging on a closet door, her clutch on the dresser, and a gray jacket carelessly thrown over a chair, a jacket she recognized as the one Kassian McAllister had been wearing the previous evening. Oh, God! What had she done? A quick glance under the sheet told her that at least she was still wearing her black lace slip. Surely she would remember if they…? But he had been able to influence Elle's actions with his mind last evening…no, NO, there was no way…she would remember if anything had happened between them. Wouldn't she?

She struggled to a sitting position, clutching the slippery sheet to her breasts with one hand while pushing the heavy mass of tangled blonde out of her face with the other. She had only a moment to notice there was no indentation in the other pillow to indicate that anyone had slept beside her. Then, the bathroom door opened. Kassian McAllister filled the doorway surrounded by a halo of billowing steam like a denim clad god rising from the mist. His chest and feet were bare, and his unbuttoned jeans rode low on his slim hips, exposing the taut, defined muscles of his flat belly. His dark hair tumbled around his shoulders in damp disarray. He looked impossibly appealing, a monument to masculinity in faded jeans and a shadow of stubble. The butterfly parade in her stomach started all over again and her throat felt too dry to swallow.

"Um, hi," she offered cautiously, biting her lip. What exactly was the appropriate small talk for waking up half dressed in the bed of a psychically powerful, extremely hot mystery man you'd hardly met, with no recollection of how you got there or what might have happened once you did? Sure, the only Emily Post column on etiquette that she'd missed. Figures.

"I…um, guess you were taking a shower." She closed her eyes and stifled a groan. Good one, Captain Obvious.

****

Kassian was momentarily stunned senseless at the sight of her, warm and sleep tousled, watching him with wide, worried eyes from the middle of his bed. It wasn't as though he'd never seen a woman there before, though his usual preference in bedmates ran to experienced, jaded women with their own agendas. The choice was deliberate. They were nothing more than temporary distractions. And he never invited them to stay the night. Kat Shephard was in a league all her own. She had an unconscious innocence completely lacking in the others; simply looking at her jumpstarted every protective and erotic instinct he had. He'd hoped that maybe he was mistaken, but his lust hadn't cooled in the grim light of day. He noticed her white knuckling the sheet, and realized she wasn't quite as indifferent as she was trying to appear.

"Hi," he replied, moving forward slowly to balance cautiously on the edge of the bed, not wanting to make her any more nervous and uncomfortable than she already was. "I didn't think you'd be awake yet. How do you feel?"

"A little confused," she admitted slowly. "I remember the party …and then this overwhelming sense of evil…" She shook her head thoughtfully. "I've never felt anything quite like it." She was still too pale and trembled noticeably as she recalled the evening.

"There was so much pain…and then, nothing. It was like everything just went black. I guess I must have passed out?"

She raised her wide gray eyes to his, and he saw the questions and the faint shadows that still lingered. He couldn't resist that innocent need for reassurance. He reached out, intending to place an encouraging hand on her shoulder, but instead found himself burrowing a hand into the softness of her hair and cupping the side of her neck. He'd only intended to comfort her, but the feel of her demanded something more. His thumb lazily stroked along the curve of her jaw then rubbed across her full bottom lip. Her pulse raced against his palm and he heard her breath stop, and then stutter. He leaned closer until he was only a breath away, eyes roving her face with a predatory awareness as he shifted on the bed to relieve the discomfort of the heavy fullness suddenly straining his jeans. Her eyes widened in alarm, but she didn't pull away. He had to taste her, if only once.

Kat's lids fluttered down as he moved closer. He nearly groaned aloud when he felt her mouth against his, warm, soft, seeking. The moment their lips met, the tight, iron shackle binding Kassian's heart shattered in a million pieces. His hand slid around to her nape as he pulled her closer and deepened the kiss, his tongue stroking the crease in her lips until she opened for him. He felt her tentatively lay one soft hand on the smooth, hard expanse of his chest, and his muscles jumped in involuntary response. She raised the other to his unshaven cheek, the stubble rasping against her fingertips as she lightly stroked his face. His breath hitched at her touch and he shifted again. True to its nature, the satin top sheet began to slide. In a heartbeat he was off the edge of the bed, landing hard on his backside. He sat back and regarded her incredulously. She burst out laughing, her smile wide and genuine, eyes dancing with silver stars.

"Did you hurt anything?"

"Only my pride," he acknowledged ruefully. He rocked to his feet and stepped back. He needed to get some distance. He could get lost in this woman; hell, he knew he might already be halfway gone. He was in trouble, or maybe she was. He might be worn out and jaded, but her kiss packed a wallop and if he spent too much time in her arms, she could make him forget all of the reasons he shouldn't.

"Listen, if you want to take a shower, I'm sure I can find something for you to throw on for the time being." He walked to the far wall and pulled open a closet, his back to her, and began rifling through hangers and digging through drawers like his life depended on it.

****

His spicy, masculine, scent teased her nostrils even after he stepped away. She felt so drawn to him that it never entered her mind to resist the kiss even though he was essentially a stranger. When his lips closed over hers, Kat had been afraid she might drown in the sheer physical sensation of a kiss unaccompanied by incoming commentary in her head. Nothing says buzz-kill faster than knowing the person you're kissing thinks you're too fat, too thin, too smart, too dumb, or worse, is thinking of something or someone else altogether. Yeah, psychic dating was a challenge; she'd chosen to avoid it for the most part aside from a few ill-conceived college romances. But this, she thought touching her fingertips to her still tingling lips, this must be how other people felt, the bone melting rush, the tingle of electric sparks skipping along her skin, the sensation of waiting, wanting, needing. His shields were impenetrable; she hadn't been able to read a thing. Desire without distraction. She finally had an inkling of what all the fuss was about. It was almost like being normal.

She regarded his back and frowned. She didn't have much experience with men, but she would have sworn he was enjoying that kiss as much as she was. Now it was as though he'd flipped a switch. Oh, well. Rejection wasn't a novelty to her. What would a man like Kassian McAllister see in someone like her, anyway? He was a well-known, wealthy pseudo-celebrity and she was a solitary house mouse. She wasn't his type at all. She still had no idea how she'd ended up in his bed, but his sudden about-face made it clear that however it had come about, he had no desire to share it with her. Which was fine with her; she functioned much better in solitude anyway. The silence stretched uncomfortably as he continued to slide hangers and slam drawers keeping his back to her.

Still staring at his back, she couldn't help but notice the tattoo. Though he was all the way across the room she could see that it was incredible work. The sword was so well done that it looked almost real, at least what she could see of it; the top of the ornate hilt was hidden by his hair. The daggers on his forearms were equally detailed. She had never been a huge ink fan, but McAllister certainly wore it well. Actually, to her surprise, on him she found it kind of sexy. She would never have suspected he sported all of that art under his custom tailored Italian suits. Then again, he'd been full of surprises from the moment he walked in the door last night.

"Nice tats," she observed with studied casualness. "The sword is incredible. Where did you have them done?"

He visibly stiffened. "Italy," he responded in an odd voice turning his head to stare hard at her before returning to his search. He pulled a pair of gray sweatpants and a plain gray tee from a drawer and tossed them behind him on the bed.

"These should work temporarily. Can't do much about shoes, I'm afraid."

She continued to watch as he pulled another tee from the drawer, this one black, and drew it over his head and down his torso where it clung like a second skin. He tucked it in, but he didn't button his jeans.

He hadn't turned around and she began to feel incredibly vulnerable, lost in the middle of the endless bed staring at his rigid back. Her lame attempt at starting a conversation had gotten her nothing but a one word answer and an icy stare.

"You know what?" she announced with sudden firmness, throwing back the sheet. "I think maybe I'll wash up a bit, throw my own clothes back on, and get a shower when I get home. Would you mind running me back to Finley's for my car? Or I can grab a cab…whatever." He hadn't offered any explanation as to how she'd gotten here, but she wasn't about to stick around to find out. Maybe Elle could fill her in later on what had happened at the party after she'd passed out.

She stepped past him determinedly and reached for her dress. Kassian flinched away. It never occurred to her that her soft curves undulating beneath the silk and lace were inadvertently alluring as she lifted her arms to the hanger, hiking up the hem of her slip and revealing a tantalizing glimpse of firm, rounded buttocks. He reached over her head, snagged the dress, and stuffed it in the closet, slamming the door forcefully. Kassian cleared his throat and she regarded him with and enquiring look.

"Listen, Kat, your car is downstairs, or it will be soon, so you don't need to worry about it. Take a shower and put those on...you'll feel better. There are clean towels in the cabinet and an extra toothbrush under the sink. You aren't going home."

"What do you mean I'm not going home?" Her gray eyes narrowed suspiciously. "Of course I'm going home. In case you wondered, I don't exactly make a habit of waking up in strange men's beds with no memory of how I got there. I don't know what happened, or what you did, or why you think you are entitled to make decisions for me, but I. Am. Leaving."

She spun on her heel and pushed past him, grabbing at the clothes on the bed. She could ill afford to lose that dress, but she wasn't strong enough to fight him for it either. His sweats would have to do. She couldn't very well drive through the city in November in her underwear. She hoped he couldn't see how her hands were shaking. Who in the hell did he think he was anyway? They were virtually strangers. Well, the rest of the world might jump to do the bidding of the great and powerful Kassian McAllister, but then she'd never really fit in with the rest of the world, had she? She felt Kassian step up behind her, and she gasped as he spun her to face him with a hand on either shoulder.

She lifted her chin defiantly, eyes flashing.

"Get your hands off of me."

Her voice was thick with anger, confusion, and unshed tears, but she met his gaze squarely. Her fingertips tingled and they both felt the jolt of electricity as she pushed at him ineffectually, sparks arcing between them. Kat winced, and shook out her wrists. He grasped her hand and held it in a firm grip, examining her palms and fingertips curiously.

"Does that happen often?"

"Haven't you ever heard of static electricity? Go rub a balloon on your head and see what happens..." She huffed and showed him her back.

Kassian heaved a heavy sigh behind her. Kat knew a man in his position was used to giving orders and getting his own way; she doubted he was accustomed to using persuasion. She figured it probably wasn't a good idea to point out that, so far, she didn't really think he was very good at it.

"Kat," he began in what she was sure he thought was a soothing tone. "Last night...I had to break the empathic connection you were experiencing. Elle, I'm sure, made a brilliant cover, and I brought you here and put you to bed...alone. Does that make you feel better? Should I have let you suffer when I could prevent it?"

She wasn't any happier, but still she turned back to face him.

"How? How did you break the connection?" She had never heard of anything like that and it didn't exactly make her feel better to think he had that kind of power, especially considering she was in his bedroom wearing nothing but her lingerie. In fact, it was more than a little frightening wondering exactly what else he could do. She was honest enough with herself to admit that he hadn't been influencing her reaction to his kiss. There was nothing wrong with her hormones, only her ability to function in close proximity to others.

"It's just something I can do…the way you can feel emotions. Now, be a good girl, go take a nice, hot shower, and then come on out and have some coffee and we'll talk."

"Be a good girl?" she muttered. "Would you like to pat me on the head next?"

"C'mon, Kat, I'm not your enemy. Oh, and you might want to call Elle. She probably has the National Guard out looking for you."

That got a ghost of a smile. He was right about Elle. Kat wouldn't be surprised to see her face on the milk carton. She drew a shaky breath and straightened her spine. He wasn't some depraved serial killer. She didn't want to trust him, had no reason to trust him, but on some level, inexplicably, she did. In theory. She could use a cup of coffee, anyway; the caffeine would help to dissipate the faint, lingering headache. And then, she was leaving.

"Fine. I'll listen, but after that, I'm out of here."

He shot her a smirk and headed for the door. She sensed his amusement. Did he think he'd won?

Well, she was amused, too. She found it extraordinarily humorous that he thought "fine" meant she agreed with him when it really meant anything from "you're an idiot" to "sleep with one eye open, sucker." So, fine. She would take a shower and get dressed. At least with clothes on she would feel less vulnerable. He could talk until he was blue in the face while she drank her coffee. Then she would get in her car and go home.

Chapter 3

So this was how the other half lived! The glass-encased, black marble monstrosity that passed for Kassian McAllister's shower was as big as her entire bathroom. Water pulsed and sprayed from every conceivable direction and she felt positively decadent using thirty minutes and a half bottle of herbal body wash to lather, rinse, and repeat. She didn't even allow herself a twinge of guilt knowing he could well afford to replace it. Besides, she had been perfectly willing to shower at home; he was the one who insisted she stay. The gloriously hot water left her skin pink and steaming as she stepped out and wrapped herself in a thick, soft bath sheet that hung to the floor. It was strangely intimate standing naked except for a towel in a room still humid with the steam and scent of McAllister. She dried her hair and brushed it up into a high ponytail securing it with an elastic band she found in a wicker basket in the cabinet along with some leather slides similar to the one he'd worn last evening. She hoped he wouldn't mind but decided it was too bad if he did. The clothes were enormous on her slight frame, the elastic waist of the sweats hanging low, catching on the full swell of her hips. She rolled the legs up into cuffs above her ankles, and twisted the hem of the tee, tying a knot at her waist that left a tantalizing strip of her flat midriff bare and emphasized her narrow waist. Regarding herself in the mirror, she decided she wouldn't win any beauty contests, but at least she was clean and comfortable...and reasonably well covered.

Barefoot, she padded back into the bedroom and saw that the door was closed. Determined that she would wither away and turn to dust right here in this room before she would give him the satisfaction of looking for him, she spent some time straightening the bed, then looked around searching for some clue to the man. It was a beautiful space, a decorator's dream, but as cold and impersonal as it was sleek and elegant. Not a photo or personal item of any kind marred the perfect balance of streamlined style. It was lovely, but it was cold, empty.

She plopped herself aimlessly into a gray microfiber club chair near the window and absently examined the small stack of books on the table beside it. A wide grin split her face as she noticed a slim volume of poetry; *Sing to the Moon* by K.L. Brookes. It fell open readily, the spine well worn, indicating it had been read often. Well, well, well. She usually avoided reading her own work once it had gone to print. She invariably saw room for improvement. Typical author; her own worst critic. This book was her first and had been a limited run by a small independent press. She wondered how McAlister came to have a copy. She settled back into the comfortable chair and began to read the words she knew by heart.

The night is death's domain and latched windows and bolted doors cannot keep its stealthy invasion at bay...

For months after her mother's death, Kat's nightmares alternated with the darkness that was her waking reality. Night after night, every time she closed her eyes and drifted off she relived the accident. She'd feel the warm summer wind blowing through the wide open windows, tossing and tangling her mother's golden hair while she sang along to some silly song on the radio. They'd been happy, basking in the simple joy of being together. Until the truck came out of nowhere, the driver's gaze blank and staring, followed by the squeal of tires, the screeching grind of metal, her mother's screams, and the hot, blinding flash of blue-white fire that should have burned, but didn't, blotting out the world.

In what seemed like an instant, she'd opened her eyes at the side of the road surrounded by sirens, lights, and people, all of whom were trying to shield her from the mangled inferno that had been her mother's car. Everyone believed it was a miracle Kat had been thrown clear without a scratch. Kat found herself incapable of believing in any miracle that reduced her remarkable, singular mother to a handful of dust in a pretty marquetry box.

In the weeks and months that followed, dreading sleep, Kat began to write. She passed the long, dark hours pouring out her heart on page after page, grief, loss, the conviction that it was impossible for anyone to ever really love her as unconditionally as her mother had. Kat's only remaining relative was an older cousin of her mother's. Miranda unenthusiastically stayed long enough to settle Kat's mother's affairs and make arrangements for the payment of the insurance. It wasn't a fortune, but it was enough to allow Kat the security of keeping the house. It also stretched to cover Kat's college tuition. Miranda and Kat's mother had never been close, and Kat's self-imposed solitude didn't invite intimacy. The old busybody had insisted they go through all of her mother's things, but Kat hadn't been ready to face the prospect yet. The day Kat came home and found Miranda rummaging through her mother's room and packing things into boxes, she'd asked her to leave. Bristling with offended self-importance, Miranda returned to her antiques business in her New England cottage filled with herbs and cats, nose in the air and secure in her martyrdom, having done all that she could to fulfill her unwanted responsibilities. Though they didn't see one another often, Miranda had made it a point to keep in touch and never failed to call or send a card when the occasion demanded. In actual fact, she made far more effort to maintain the relationship than Kat did. She'd never been able to read Miranda, and something about the older woman always rubbed her the wrong way.

It was Kat's college English professor who suggested she consider submitting her work for publication after reading some of the poems that she submitted for a class assignment. He had contacted a friend in publishing who'd been happy to take a look, and the rest, as they say, was history. She would never be wealthy, but she didn't require much and with a degree in graphic design, her freelance work helped make ends meet.

Lost in thought, Kat didn't notice the soft click of the door. She sat cross legged in the chair, bare feet tucked underneath her knees, with the small book open in her lap, and took a deep breath. The work spoke to a place of dark desolation. It was not a comfortable read. It had not been comfortable to write. But remembering was easier than it used to be. Eyes closed, her graceful fingers moved over the page as she softly recited from memory...*And in my dreams, my lost one sings, sad story songs that linger on, but never see the light of day...*

****

In solitude, her defenses were down. In that brief, unguarded moment, Kassian saw the place inside that she hid from everyone else, the place where she believed she was destined to be alone, so different that no one could ever really love her. The icy cage around his heart was melting fast. Stopping himself from wanting her was like trying to contain an atom bomb in a paper bag. He, who had focused on a singular purpose for as long as he could remember, found himself distracted. His thoughts wandered, and since first laying eyes on her last night, he felt like he was in a constant state of arousal. She was smart and sweet and even lost in the folds of his old sweats, she was trip-over-your-own-feet-and-fall-on-your-ass sexy. And she didn't take his crap. He had no right to want her, and less right to keep her. Hell, who was he kidding? If she knew the truth she would run as far and fast as she could, anyway. The biggest favor he could do for her was to ensure her safety as soon as possible and let her get back to her life. Maybe he should just seduce her and get her out of his system so that he could concentrate on his revenge.

"One of my favorites. You have good taste." He said quietly.

Kat's eyes flew open and she jumped to her feet, snapping the book closed, along with her mind. She awkwardly replaced the book on the table.

"Um, thanks. Not the most cheerful work, however." She smiled ruefully.

"Karma is arbitrary." He shrugged casually, but his eyes were shadowed. "Grief, loss…they're universal. No one gets by unscathed."

"Speaking from experience?"

"Everyone loses someone, sometime." His lips twisted wryly. If you lived long enough, you lost nearly everyone who mattered.

"I'm sorry," she said softly. "I wouldn't wish the emptiness embodied in that book on my worst enemy. Those are the words of a lost soul, a soul crying for comfort, for acceptance, for love."

"*Sometimes love hurts in places you didn't know you had,*" he quoted the final line. He wondered if she would think him any less of a bastard if she knew how closely he personally identified with the work. There was no humor in his quick smile.

"Sometimes it does," she agreed. "But I think that when something speaks to you on such a visceral level and makes you realize that the emotion and experience isn't uniquely yours, it's somehow comforting."

"I couldn't agree more," he said, surprised that she'd verbalized his exact feelings. "Well, before we both feel compelled to throw ourselves from the terrace, how about some coffee? I seem to remember promising you some. Apparently you know your Brookes," he added and she bit her lip.

"Um, yeah. Yeah, coffee would be great. Then I really do need to go. I have tons of things to do."

He didn't argue, he simply pushed the door wide, indicating with a wave of his hand that she should follow. She trailed behind him through the beautiful, open living room decorated in the same style as the bedroom. He led her into the equally sterile kitchen. Every room was so sleek, so shiny, so beautiful. So cold. He'd hired one of the most sought after decorators in the city and had been more than pleased with the result. He just hadn't realized how empty and uncongenial it was until he saw it as her eyes might be seeing it now.

"How do you take it?" He poured the dark, steaming brew into two heavy earthenware mugs. "Hungry?" He indicated a white pastry box on the counter

"Black is fine...and no, thanks."

He handed her a mug and shortened his long strides to allow her to keep up as she padded behind him in bare feet back through the living room and then through a set of double doors on the opposite side of the apartment. He thought she appeared more at home in here, this room where he spent most of his time. The office was lush and comfortable, all dark wood, warm earthy colors, and thick carpeting. The walls were lined with book-filled shelves, though even here he was careful to avoid any display of photographs and personal mementos. The room was neat and well organized, except for the top of the desk which was cluttered with CDs and papers, an open laptop pushed off to the side. He waved her into one of the plush leather chairs and moved around the vast expanse of the desk to sit across from her, choosing the furthest point in the room from where she sat. He figured he was safer that way. He leaned back in the chair and sipped his coffee thoughtfully, in no hurry to speak.

After a few minutes of uncomfortable silence had

passed, Kat apparently decided she'd been as patient as it was possible to be.

"Look, Mr. McAllister, I appreciate that you got me out of there last night. I don't know what happened, but whatever happened, it wasn't pleasant. I don't mean to appear ungrateful, but you implied earlier that I can't go home. That isn't acceptable to me, so maybe an explanation of why you feel that's even an option would be a great place to start."

He blew lightly on the surface of the hot liquid, took another sip, and let out a long breath before meeting her dove gray gaze with his own dark one. With her hair pulled back, her face free of make-up, and a bare foot tucked beneath her, she reminded him of a high school cheerleader. It did nothing to quench his lust.

"How old are you?" he asked curiously. She appeared incredibly young, but then again he didn't look so bad for his age either. *Earthbound*s weren't immortal, but they did live an incredibly long time by human standards, unless someone managed to strike a lucky blow with a blade forged in either Heaven or Hell. After reaching the age of thirty-five or so, they aged so slowly that it was barely perceptible over a human lifetime. It was one of the reasons many were forced to move to a new place every few decades.

"Twenty-five, why? What does that have to do with anything?"

"Nothing, I was just curious." He couldn't even remember who he'd been at twenty-five. He plunked the mug on the desk and sat forward in the chair. "You really have been patient. I wouldn't have been half as pleasant under the circumstances." Actually, someone would probably have ended up dead by now. He took a deep breath. "A woman was murdered near Finley's last night. Her body was found in a Dumpster early this morning. You're an empath..." He raised a brow when she opened her mouth and started to shake her head. "Why would you deny it?"

"Why? Let's see, maybe because you already knew enough about me to scare most people silly? I don't see the need to parade any more little freak show talents in front of you. Look, Mr. McAllister, I don't exactly go around flaunting my abilities. They tend to...well; let's just say they can be a bit off-putting to some people. As you have a few talents of your own, I'd think you'd understand that better than anyone. I wasn't intending to be dishonest, it's simply become second nature to hide what I can do."

"I'm sorry," he said quietly. It was clear she'd had to struggle with her abilities. Furthermore, it was becoming more apparent to him with every passing moment that she also had no idea that she wasn't human. Well, not completely human at any rate. She'd been able to see his blade hidden in the intricate ink of his tattoo, a blade that wasn't visible to the human eye.

"Why?" She shrugged. "It isn't your fault."

"No," he agreed. "But it sounds like you haven't had an easy time."

She didn't answer and simply shrugged. She continued to regard him levelly across the desk. When he realized he was enjoying the sensation of losing himself in her wide gray eyes way more than he should be, he shifted uncomfortably in his chair and continued.

"Anyway, about this murder...I think what happened last night was that you intercepted and absorbed the energy. It seems to be the most sensible conclusion. I've known one or two empaths in my day and sometimes it's next to impossible to block very strong emotion. What emotion could be stronger than someone being attacked and murdered?"

He watched as the color drained from her face. Damn, he hoped she wasn't going to be sick on his Savonnerie; the carpet had been a gift from a rather memorable French aristocrat and he'd had it for over three hundred years.

"Oh, my God, as bad as it was for me, how much worse must it have been for her?" Kat's eyes filled with tears.

"She wasn't the first, and the killer is still out there." And he's all mine, he thought grimly. "So, you see why you can't go home yet…it isn't safe." There, it was out. Now, surely she would see the logic in his reasoning.

Kat stared at him incredulously.

"No offense, but I see no logic in your reasoning, whatsoever! Other than getting dropkicked by some rogue energy, I have no connection to the victim or the situation. Honestly, Mr. McAllister, it's a sad commentary on society, but no one is safe these days and I can hardly see why I would be any more at risk than anyone else. I have no idea what you think the problem is, but I am leaving and if you're so worried about my safety, hire a bodyguard…God knows you can afford it." She started to get up. "You obviously have some warped and overdeveloped sense of responsibility. Admirable, I suppose, but hardly my problem."

"Sit. Down." His voice was as cold as death. She

froze; and the look she gave him said she wondered if he might be the one she should be afraid of.

"Sit down, Kat," he said more gently, and then waited until she hesitantly complied. He slid a folder across the desk. Kassian knew that showing her the photographs made him about as subtle as a sawed off shotgun, but she needed to understand the seriousness of the situation. "Open it."

Kat flipped open the folder and gasped. She clapped a hand to her mouth while her throat worked convulsively. She flipped through the photos, one by one, each image more depraved and disturbing than the last before she closed the folder. The eyes she raised to his were filled with grief and they tore at his conscience.

"I...this is unspeakable...there are no words...," she croaked. She swiped at her eyes and pushed the folder carefully across the desk. She took several deep breaths and cleared her throat. "I see what you mean, it's horrible, but I still don't understand what it has to do with me."

"That girl's death was a message, Kat...a message meant for me. She wasn't the first. This animal and I have been enemies for a long time. He knows you left that party with me and he also knows you spent the night. The press is still downstairs," he said by way of an explanation. She closed her eyes and groaned. "The point is, right or wrong, you are now someone of interest he'll think he can use to hurt me. He's done it before. It's my fault that you're in danger. You may not like it any better than I do, but, it's now my job to keep you safe."

She was quiet, frighteningly so. He wished he

knew what she was thinking, but, except for the one unguarded moment when he'd entered the bedroom, her shields were firmly in place this morning; even her expression wasn't giving her away. She was staying, one way or the other, but it would be easier if she didn't fight him. Maybe he should have kept the photos to himself; they'd obviously scared the hell out of her. Then again, fear would keep her on her toes; of course that was irrelevant as he had no intention of letting her out of his sight.

"Well." He heard the tremor in her voice, but she looked him straight in the eyes. "First of all, I don't know if I buy the theory that my spending the night makes me a target. What if something *had* happened between us? Hasn't this guy ever heard of a one-night stand? Not a whole lot of emotional attachment going on there as a rule. Secondly, you apparently know who you're dealing with, right? Why can't you simply go to the police and let them handle it?"

"It's…complicated. The police can't help."

Christ, he was lame. She'd known him less than twenty-four hours and already he'd knocked her out, kissed her senseless, locked her up, threatened her with being murdered, then informed her the police couldn't help. Oh yeah, she should trust him, all right. He was about as smooth as sandpaper on gravel.

"Complicated?" Her brows drew together. "I mean, I get it that someone in your position is bound to have enemies, but a killer who would murder women to get your attention? That's one extremely sick ticket if you don't mind my saying so. Is it…well, like organized crime or something?"

"Or something…" The explanation worked as well

as anything for the time being, and it was a comparison that she could relate to. The truth would make him look crazier than he suspected she might already think he was.

He made his way around the desk and leaned back against the edge towering over her. Staring down from his great height, he realized that he'd automatically assumed a position of dominance in an unconscious attempt to intimidate her into going along with his wishes. The technique had served him well in business. She craned her neck and stared back. Funny, she looked more annoyed and inconvenienced than intimidated.

"You aren't involved in anything illegal, are you?"

"No." Of course, he operated by a completely different set of laws, but she didn't need to know that.

"You would physically prevent me from leaving?"

"I would rather not have to, but yes. Kat, you are staying until I can resolve this. You don't have to understand it, and you don't have to like it. The bottom line is, I'm not asking you, I'm telling you. You are staying."

She squinted up at him. He sighed deeply. She was angry and she was suspicious. Hell, he couldn't blame her. He was trying to be gentle and accommodating, but he wasn't sure he remembered how. He squatted in front of her and barely restrained himself from taking her hand. Considering he already wanted her like a drunk wants whiskey he hoped he was able to maintain his objectivity. He needed to remember that Rapier was his focus; it was only coincidence that he needed to protect this woman in the process.

"I'm trying to protect you, Kat. I don't hold women hostage."

****

Kat concentrated intently, looking into his eyes and assessing the reassurances he offered. She wished she could read him, but his shields were firmly in place and she had to rely on what little her empathy was able to pick up. Though she still sensed a certain darkness around him, she felt no sense of evil or deceit. Whatever she'd landed in the middle of, it wasn't good and he sincerely believed she needed protection. His hair was still damp and loose around his shoulders and she fought a sudden urge to reach out and stroke it back from his face as he waited quietly for her reaction.

"I don't see why I can't just go home with a bodyguard or something, but strangely enough I believe you mean it when you say you're trying to keep me safe."

"Not trying, Kat. I will keep you safe."

She thought of the weekend ahead. Did she really have so much to look forward to? She'd spent a lifetime isolating herself because of her abilities. With Kassian McAllister, at least she didn't have to pretend. He was the first true psychic she had encountered since her mother died and even her limited experience told her that he was incredibly powerful in a way her mother had never been. Maybe, just maybe, she could learn a few things.

"Just so we're clear, I am not happy about this, but I guess you aren't some crazy axe murderer. I'm going to call Elle, though, so someone knows where I am and what's going on."

"That's fine. I'm not particularly happy about it either. But it is what it is. We'll discuss your call to Elle later."

"Discuss my call?" her eyes narrowed. "Why would we need to discuss my call?"

"I really am trying here, Katrina but I'm much better at giving orders than at explaining myself," he replied in an exasperated tone. "Think about it. Do you want to put her in danger, too?"

"Oh…well, no, of course not." Her eyes widened thoughtfully. It wasn't as though she had so many friends that she could afford to lose one.

Kat took a deep breath and let it out slowly. "Okay, I guess I could give you the benefit of the doubt for the weekend, but I have something to ask in return. You already know I have certain…abilities. I have a pretty good handle on the telepathy most of the time, but my empathy is really difficult to block effectively for any length of time. I couldn't help noticing that I can't read you at all; you're like white noise when I try. Obviously you're really good at holding your shields. Maybe you could help me learn to improve mine?"

"Maybe," he replied in a wary voice.

"Well, I guess what I'm asking is, would you? I mean, if I'm going to be stuck here for a few days anyway?"

"Well, I'm not an empath, so I'm not sure how much I can help, but sure, why not? You deserve better than to be forced into self-imposed solitude to survive, and maybe there are some exercises and techniques that could work. I'll ask around."

"Really?" The possibility made her head spin and she couldn't suppress a wide smile. McAllister obviously functioned perfectly well in public and all kinds of social situations, almost like it was second nature. She could control her gifts for short periods, but it always cost her. He'd answered so casually; she wondered if he realized he'd given her the first glimmer of hope she'd ever had for living something approaching a normal life. Almost anything was worth that.

"I mean, think about it. If you'd been able to block your empathy effectively last night, none of this would have happened."

Kat stiffened. "Oh, so now this is all *my* fault?"

"Damn, that didn't come out right. No, of course I didn't mean any of this was your fault. I only meant that if you'd been able to block effectively, you could have been spared everything you had to go through last night," he finished in a rush.

"I see." Though she wasn't completely convinced that was really what he meant. "I guess that's true. Okay, then you can have the guest room," she offered magnanimously. "It hasn't been used in a few years, so you'll have to give me some time to freshen it up, but it's really quite comfortable."

"The guest room?" His eyes widened.

"Well, yes," she answered slowly. Surely he didn't think she was giving up her own room in her own house?

"Woman, I don't know what you thought, but I won't be staying in anyone's guest room. We are staying right here where I can control the situation."

"The *situation*?" she returned, the heat rising in her voice. "Is that some cute billionaire euphemism to refer to me?"

"Don't be childish, Kat," he replied, clearly annoyed. "I need to be in the city to take care of this. All of my resources are here, and Elle already told me that you don't live in town. Besides, there's no telling how many innocent people could get caught in the crossfire if the killer decided to follow us to some family friendly neighborhood in the suburbs. Do you want that on your conscience?"

"No, of course not! It's just, well I need my own things," Kat argued. "I can't keep wearing your clothes and the only shoes I have here are heels. And then there's my cat."

"I don't know," Kassian smirked. "I kind of like what you're wearing at the moment, and I've always had a weakness for a woman in heels. I really don't see the problem."

"Now you're making fun of me. You think I don't know I look ridiculous? Couldn't we at least go to my place and pick up enough of my things for a few days and then come back?"

"Yeah, I guess we can do that," he replied after a moment's hesitation.

Kat took a deep breath. She must be crazy. Solitude had kept her sane. She barely knew Kassian McAllister and here she was handing herself into his keeping. But there was something almost approaching peace in the fact that he didn't give her abilities a second thought, and she couldn't read him at will. She'd never been able to enjoy such complete silence in her head in the company of another person. Well, whatever was going on would probably be resolved quickly. Kassian McAllister didn't strike her as a man who waited around to get things done. It was only one weekend. It might be nice to have someone around without having her senses bombarded. In any event, it would be different. And if he could help her tame her empathy…well, that would be the most unexpected gift! And she had to admit, there was something about him that drew her, and it was more than the fact that he was anything but hard on the eyes. He was still in front of her, waiting, his dark eyes intense, but unreadable, his thoughts inaccessible. She smiled and jumped to her feet… knocking him on his ass for the second time that day.

Chapter 4

Once he convinced Kat to stay and agreed to take her for her things, Kassian's next challenge was to figure out a way to avoid the press. He'd been dealing with them for years and knew that the more tenacious members of the corps would still be camped outside his building hoping for the big money photo. He wasn't about to put either himself or Kat through that circus. It occurred to him they would be looking for his car, not hers. No one in their right mind would be looking for Kassian McAllister in a beat-up twenty-year-old Ford. It would have been simpler to send his secretary shopping for whatever she needed, but he instinctively knew Kat would be more comfortable with her own things. He was annoyed to find himself wanting to make her happy. He was supposed to protect her, not entertain her. And he wasn't thrilled about letting her go out in public until he neutralized the threat. In his penthouse, she was safe. The entire place was protected by *sigil*s, ancient angelic symbols woven into a web of impenetrable protection. No one could fade in or out, so there was never any danger of an unannounced attack. He grinned to himself; all *Defensori* used protection at their home base, all except Luca. Hard-ass was always spoiling for a fight, despite his blasé demeanor. In fact, if they were going to Kat's place, it might be a good idea to have Luca meet them there, just in case. Hell, he hoped she had a cat sitter, he hated the damn things.

Feeling like an undercover agent, Kassian discovered his assumption that the press wouldn't be paying much attention to Kat's car was right on the money. Kat hunkered down in the passenger seat wrapped in one of his fleece-lined sweatshirts with the hood pulled up over her bright hair, casting her face into shadow. Even if the paparazzi managed to get a shot, it would be difficult for anyone to identify her. Kassian wore another fleece with his hair hanging loose around his face and a Yankees cap pulled low on his forehead. They exited the parking garage, cruising right past the small knot of reporters gathered near the lobby entrance drinking coffee and smoking cigarettes. No one gave them so much as a passing glance. Kassian could understand why as he fought the urge to drive right to the recycling center and pay them to take her car off of his hands. Assuming the piece of crap would make it that far. The seat was adjusted for someone Kat's size, and as luck would have it, the mechanism was jammed. His knees hovered practically around his ears and he banged his shin under the dash every time he released the clutch.

"Do you want me to drive?"

"No, and we are so getting you a new car."

"We are so not. Do you make a habit of thinking you can take over a person's life? What's wrong with my car? I know it doesn't quite measure up to your standards, but it suits me fine. And it's paid for."

"It's a deathtrap. It's older than you. Do it a favor, Kat, and put it out of its misery."

"McAllister, I am not buying a new car and you are sure as hell not buying me one. I may have agreed to stay with you for a few days for my own safety, but the bottom line is that I barely know you!"

"Think of it as a favor to me. I'll sleep better at night knowing you aren't risking life and limb zipping down the highway in this piece of shit." Actually, he was pretty sure it couldn't really zip anywhere. He held his breath and prayed it would do the speed limit once they were on the interstate. "Why do you live all the way out there, anyway? Wouldn't it make more sense to move into the city?"

"Maybe, but I can do most of my work from home and I like it all the way out there."

"Why? It would make more sense to sell the house and move into the city. You wouldn't even need a car. Think how much you'd save on gas. The commute has to be at least an hour each way."

"I don't mind the drive." Kat smiled. "It's incredibly peaceful. Actually, you might be surprised at the number of people who prefer a more suburban lifestyle and drive in daily from the mountains for work."

"Then there must be car pools… and buses must run a regular schedule back and forth during the week. Why don't you take a bus instead of driving this rat trap?"

"Tried that once. An hour in an enclosed vehicle trying to avoid the emotions of thirty frustrated and unhappy people? I felt like I'd already put in a full day by the time we pulled into the terminal." Kat laughed. "Besides, it's my mom's house. You'll probably think it's silly, but it's the one place I can still feel her around me."

"No, I don't think it's silly," Kassian replied

quietly. He suddenly pulled off of the next exit and veered into the parking lot of a combination gas station and convenience store. It was already early afternoon and it occurred to him that she hadn't eaten anything yet today. Some protector he was turning out to be. He'd keep her safe from Rapier; in the meantime she would starve to death. He jiggled the gearshift into neutral, banged his knee yet again, closed his eyes and prayed for patience, then reached for the keys.

"Don't turn it... off," Kat began, but he'd already clicked off the ignition and pocketed the keys. She sighed.

"What's wrong?"

"Well, sometimes it's a little temperamental." She muttered, color creeping into her cheeks.

"Brilliant!" he snapped. "So you are telling me we are now stranded here in the middle of nowhere?"

"Actually, we aren't in the middle of nowhere, we're on the outskirts of somewhere, and don't worry... I can get it started; it just might take a little effort. Run along and get your goodies, McAllister, you're the one who couldn't wait until we got to the house."

"C'mon, you aren't staying out here by yourself."

"For the love of Pete, do you honestly think someone is hiding over there in the bushes waiting to jump out and grab me as soon as I'm alone? You really are a little paranoid, you know that?

"Out."

Kassian opened her door and stood back impatiently while Kat took her own sweet time climbing out of the passenger seat. He steered her toward the door with a hand at the small of her back, surveying the area carefully for anything out of the ordinary. Once they were in the store he directed Kat to grab two bottles of water from the cooler while he gathered together some pre-packaged sandwiches and threw a couple of granola bars on the counter.

"Do you want anything else?"

"M&M's…peanut, please," she smiled. "Breakfast of champions."

He glanced at his watch. "Lunch of champions, maybe," he frowned. "You haven't eaten anything since last night. You should eat something besides candy."

"Aw, thanks, Dad," she snarked, tearing open the bag "but I'm good."

Kassian paid the cashier, a pimply face boy with braces and a plastic name tag that said Jared. Jared looked Kat up and down with a suggestive grin. The grin faded immediately as Kassian glared at him over her head. Kassian grabbed the bag, and hustled Kat back to the car. He stayed so close that she tripped over him once or twice. When she was safely back in her seat with the door closed, he crammed himself behind the wheel and turned the key. Click. Click. Click. He heaved a heavy sigh of annoyance.

"Told you not to turn it off," she mumbled through a mouthful of crunchy, chocolate candies. "Hang on…pop the trunk, would you?"

She jerked open the door before he could stop her and ran around to the back of the car. He heard her rummaging around in the trunk, then watched as she tottered on her heels back to the front and lifted the hood. He tried to get out, but the door handle jammed. He settled for rolling the window down, but before it was halfway the crank came off in his hand. He swore eloquently in several languages and fiddled it back in place.

"What in the hell are you doing?"

Her head was under the hood and he heard her jiggling something metallic and murmuring to the engine in a coaxing tone. Did she think she could sweet talk the damn thing into starting?

"Okay, hold in the clutch and try it now."

To his astonishment, the engine turned right over. She slammed the hood and hopped back into the passenger side, tossing a long screwdriver into the backseat. She smiled sweetly before popping another handful of candy in her mouth.

"We're good. Let's go."

He continued to stare. Wasn't he supposed to be the one doing the rescuing? Of course, it really wasn't his fault; he was a knight in shining armor that usually drove a better horse.

"What?" she blinked innocently. "Bad solenoid, okay? I haven't had a chance to get it fixed. You just have to remember to carry a screwdriver, stick it in there between the positive pole and the relay to complete the circuit, and presto, back on the road. No big deal."

"No big deal? How long have you been having this problem?" He felt his temper begin to flare. She'd been driving over a hundred miles round trip every time she came into the city. A slideshow of every horrible thing that could have happened to her stranded alone on some isolated stretch of highway shuffled through his mind. "How long?"

"A while," she admitted, looking out the window and away from his eyes. "Look, McAllister, I know you think I am this helpless little piece of fluff, but I've been taking care of myself for a very long time."

"You are so getting a new car."

"This conversation is over."

"You're right, it is."

And Monday morning this hunk of junk would be chopped up for tin cans, paper clips, and bottle caps whether she liked it or not. It seemed kind of pointless to take her under his protection only to have her drive off in a death trap at the first opportunity.

"What's your favorite color?"

She completely ignored him and continued to stare out the side window where the winter bare trees marched by like silent sentinels. He reached across and waved a bottle of water in her averted face, which she took without speaking, chugging half of it down before replacing the cap and shoving it between the seat and the console.

"I thought women liked gifts," he said in a puzzled tone. "I've never had a problem with anyone accepting one before." In fact, more often than not they were happy to provide him with a wish list.

"I'll just bet you haven't," she muttered under her breath.

"Did you say something?"

"McAllister, a box of candy is a gift, a bottle of wine is a gift, a car is, well, I don't know what it is, but it isn't a gift. The car you drive is probably worth more than my house."

"It's a gift if I say it's a gift. It's only money, Kat." Living for hundreds of years provided unlimited opportunities to accumulate wealth. Kassian enjoyed his comforts, but ultimately, money meant nothing more to him than a means to an end.

"Spoken by someone who is truly rolling in it," she laughed. "Look, Elvis, no car, okay? I can pay my own way in the world. Can we just drop it?"

"Elvis?"

"Yeah, you know Elvis? He went around buying new cars for total strangers…oh, never mind! Take the next exit and hang a left at the stop sign."

****

Her cat was sitting in the bay window watching for her as the car crunched into the drive. The house, as always, seemed timeless; wooden rockers on the front porch, the porch swing off to the side, comfortably attired in peeling paint and rusted chains, swaying and creaking in the slight breeze. It had been her grandmother's house and later, her mother's, a house safe for dreaming. Kat's mother, Lilly, had acquired the house shortly before Kat's birth, along with a stepfather for Kat who hadn't lasted long enough to leave more than a fuzzy memory and his name. It was the only home Kat had ever known. Inconvenience aside, the main reason Kat had never moved into the city was because wherever she went, she was only partly there; a piece of her was always here.

Kassian followed her up the walk. His eyes widened as she reached for the loose board on the second step. She lifted it and smiled, triumphantly showing him the front door key. Kassian closed his eyes and counted aloud to ten.

"That is not where you leave your key when you go out."

"Don't be silly. I usually don't lock the door at all unless I'm going in to the city overnight."

"You're serious, aren't you?" He winced. "How have you survived this long?"

"Interestingly, I've never really had a problem with dangerous situations until I met you, McAllister." She smiled as she said it. She'd meant it as a joke, but by the look on his face she could see he took it far more seriously than she'd intended. Wisely, she let it drop.

She unlocked the door and reached inside to flick on the hall light. One of the bulbs was burned out and she made a mental note to replace it. Sid had seen her coming up the walk and was waiting inside the door to weave acrobatic figure eights around her legs.

"Hi, baby…miss me?" She scooped up the purring calico and rubbed her face into his fur. She turned to Kassian to make the introductions but stopped when he took a quick step back. He was obviously not a cat person.

"What's wrong?" she crooned, scratching Sid under the chin. "Is the big strong tycoon afraid of the itty bitty kitty?"

"You aren't planning to take that beast back with us, are you?" He grimaced.

"Well, I was considering it." She laughed out loud at the look of horror on his face. "Relax, McAllister. My neighbor, Mrs. Norton, will take care of him for a few days. I just have to let her know I'll be away."

Kat bent to deposit the animal back on the floor and headed into the kitchen.

****

Kassian was relieved when he heard her calling the neighbor to make arrangements for the cat. He wouldn't have refused her if she insisted on bringing it along as she was obviously attached to the creature, but he would not have been happy about it either. The damn thing probably slept with her. While she chatted briefly with the neighbor, Kassian scanned the place with a practiced eye. Her house was about as secure as a pup tent. Now that he'd had a chance to look it over, there was no way she was staying here, even if he'd been almost willing to consider slumming it in her guest room if it would make her more comfortable with the whole situation. He heard Kat moving around in the kitchen and the click of the answering machine followed by the sound of Elle Gates' voice. He couldn't make out the words, but could guess the content by the increasingly frantic tone following each succeeding beep.

"You'd better call Miss Gates," he called from the living room. "I forgot to tell you that I promised her you would."

"Yeah, thanks…that would explain the eight messages bordering on hysteria." She reproached ruefully.

She dug her cell phone out of her bag as she passed back through the living room.

"I'm going to send Elle a quick text to let her know I'm okay and will call her later. If I call her back now, I'll never get off the phone and I'm guessing you're anxious to get back to the city?" He nodded, but she didn't pick up her head long enough to notice.

"Make yourself comfortable," she called as she breezed through the hall and headed for the stairs. "There's juice in the fridge, or beer if you'd rather, although then I'll be driving back so you might want to take that into consideration before you decide."

Alcohol didn't affect him in the least unless he

ingested massive quantities, and there was no way she was driving him anywhere. The car itself was enough of a risk. He noticed the damn cat stuck to her like glue, and Kassian sadly realized he might have to investigate aversion therapy. But there was no way it was ever sleeping on his bed. He glanced at his watch; Luca should have been here by now.

He listened to the faint sounds of Kat moving around upstairs and stretched, wincing as his spine cracked in several places from the long, cramped ride in her car. He clamped a hand to the back of his neck, rubbing out the kinks as he wandered around the downstairs rooms. The front door opened into a cozy hallway leading straight back to a spacious farmhouse style kitchen. To the left of the hallway was the living room and behind that, a formal dining room with a large, heavy table which looked like it dated to the twenties. All of the furniture was old and mismatched with no distinctive style. It was well used and in need of replacement, but the overall feeling was warm and welcoming. Unlike his penthouse, the place felt lived in, loved; it felt like a home. It had been a long time since he'd lived in a place that actually did. It was a surprise to discover that somewhere deep down, he missed the feeling.

He turned back toward the hall when he heard her thumping down the stairs. She'd changed into a faded pair of jeans that hugged her curves in all the right places, a pair of tennis shoes, and a soft, yellow V-neck sweater that flashed a tantalizing glimpse of lace and cleavage when she moved exactly the right way. She carried a brown quilted vest with a faux fur collar over her arm. She'd brushed out her hair and it cascaded down her back and around her shoulders in a soft, silvery cloud. Kassian took a firm grip on the gut wrenching lust that rose to bubble and hiss at the sight of her. She was struggling with a duffle bag. He moved forward and plucked it from her like it weighed nothing and set it near the door.

Kassian felt the first faint shocks racing up his spine as Kat opened her mouth to say something. The words never came as he saw the blast of sensation affect her first before hitting him mere moments later. It was far less toxic than last night, but it was definitely evil. Sid yowled in alarm and ran for the kitchen. Kat's eyes widened and locked on Kassian. In one long stride, he reached her side and shoved her behind him, her back against the wall. There was a loud crack like a light bulb exploding and Luca appeared in a bright flash, crouched in the middle of the living room, a dagger already gripped in either hand.

"Incoming," he called, just as the air near the fireplace began to shimmer. Kassian reached behind him and slid a long, deadly looking blade from the neck of his shirt, moving toward the disruption, but Luca was quicker. As soon as the figure had fully materialized, the dagger in his left hand whistled through the air, straight and true, burying itself in the dark figure's throat just as it became solid. The thing immediately collapsed into an oily looking puddle with a gurgle and a hiss. Luca casually strode across the room and fished his dagger out of the slime, holding it between his thumb and forefinger with a moue of distaste. He glanced around and grabbed a couple of Kleenex from a box on the table and wiped it clean. He laid it against his forearm, where it dissolved back into his tattoo, did the same with the second dagger, then tugged the sleeves of his sweater back down. "Sorry I'm late."

Kassian slid the sword back into his shirt where it also dissolved into the tattoo Kat had admired earlier in the day.

"Shit, Luca!" Kassian roared striding across the room.

"Sorry about the mess," Luca said quietly, rubbing his palms together briskly as an eerie blue glow began to emanate from them. He looked beyond Kassian and nodded in Kat's direction. "I'll take care of this. You might want to take care of that."

Kassian spun to where he'd left Kat and his heart contracted painfully. She'd slid to the floor and huddled against the wall, curled into herself, frozen and wide eyed. Her gaze was fixed on Luca who'd turned his palms toward the oily remains of the intruder, vaporizing them almost instantly.

"Ah, damn." Kassian reached for her and she flinched away. He picked her up anyway and carried her to the sofa where he held her carefully on his lap.

"Breathe, Kat," he coaxed gently. "It's okay, just breathe."

Kat remained silent, sitting stiffly in the circle of Kassian's arms, her eyes darting between Luca and the spot where the puddle had been. Kassian looked helplessly over her head at Luca, who offered nothing more than a raised brow and a shrug in the way of assistance.

"Mac, maybe we should get out of here. I think I lost the rest of them, but…" He shrugged again. "Looks like Rapier already knows where she lives." He eyed Kassian meaningfully.

Kat's head turned slowly in Luca's direction.

"The rest?" she croaked hoarsely. "There are more of those...whatever they are...coming here?"

"It's possible," Kassian replied carefully, "but once we leave they have no reason to bother. C'mon, let's get Sid some food and water and then we'll go." He set her on her feet as he got up, but kept an arm around her waist, just in case.

****

Kat stifled a completely inappropriate urge to laugh hysterically. She'd been worried about what he might think of her freaky baggage? He could apparently pull a sword out of his body and had friends who just popped in; really popped in. Oh, and those friends could also make themselves glow in the dark. In comparison, she was the all American girl! As for his friend, she couldn't even allow her mind to go there at the moment. She decided to pull a Scarlett O'Hara and think about it tomorrow, or the next day, or whenever she was able to wrap her head around it. If ever. At any rate, she was pretty sure that whatever was going on had nothing to do with organized crime, or anything else even remotely connected with her sphere of reality. She didn't know how Kassian could have even begun to explain what she'd just witnessed, so maybe she shouldn't hold it against him that he hadn't. Oh, yeah, she was scared nearly witless at the moment, not to mention confused as hell, but implausibly, she still trusted him to keep her safe. And how twisted was that since at the moment she rather doubted either he or his friend was even human? And if that was the case, what did it make her? Kat couldn't stop staring at Luca and knew the look in her eyes was murderous.

"Kat, look at me," Kassian gave her a little shake. "C'mon, we need to leave now. I'll explain later, but we need to go now."

****

Kassian stood and tucked her in beneath his arm and held the length of her body close against his side to ensure she would stay on her feet. To his surprise, she wrapped her arms around his waist and held on for dear life. He doubted she was even aware of it, but right at the moment he figured that he was her life preserver in a rapidly rising sea of confusion.

"Grab that, will you?" he said to Luca, nodding toward her duffle.

Kat stayed pressed against him, following his lead like a mindless marionette. Outside, Kassian took the key from her numb fingers and relocked the door, replacing it under the loose board for the neighbor. He all but dragged her down the sidewalk to the car, and threw open the door. It apparently took her that long to regain any semblance of composure or coherent thought. She roused suddenly and pushed him away. Placing her hands on her thighs, she bent forward, dropping her head between her arms and taking several deep breaths. She straightened at last and searched his face, her eyes begging for answers.

"What in the hell was that?"

He reached out to stroke her hair, gently tucking a stray strand behind her ear. "We'll talk about it later. C'mon, we need to get going."

Kat took a deep breath. "No, we'll talk about it now. If I'm in the middle of this, I need to know what it is. You said you got me into this…in that case, don't you think you at least owe me the truth?"

He glanced over her head at Luca who shrugged helpfully yet again. Kassian took a deep breath and let it out slowly before answering.

"It was an *animorti*…it was a, well, a kind of ghoul is the best comparison I can think of at the moment."

Kat appeared to digest that for a moment. "A ghoul. Of course, I should have known that right away. Who wouldn't? I mean, it was obvious, right? Riiiiight."

Kassian knew they had to move, but he wanted to give her a minute. Hell, after what she'd just been through she deserved an hour.

"A ghoul," she repeated mechanically. "I see."

She began edging carefully out of the space between him and the car and held up a forefinger. "Hold that thought for a minute, okay?"

She started back toward the house, walking quickly, picking up speed as she went. He didn't know why she was running; after what she'd just seen, she had to know there was nowhere she could go that he couldn't follow. Her fingers were closing around the key when Kassian's arms snaked around her and pulled her back against his chest. He briefly buried his face in her hair. God, she smelled good.

"What do you think you're doing?" he asked mildly. Okay, her breathing was a little erratic and he felt her heart pounding against his forearm where it rested below her breasts, but she wasn't hysterical…yet. He hoped it was a good sign.

"I, um, thought I'd better check to see if the fairies and gnomes needed anything before we left," she choked out.

Kassian laughed loudly, giving her a quick squeeze

and dropping a kiss on the top of her head. Even with *animorti* on their tail and Rapier on the prowl, he hadn't felt this good in centuries. "Gnomes are nasty little creatures and fairies are pretty self-sufficient…I think we're good."

He swung her up in his arms before she could protest and carried her back to the car. He set her down in the drive and waited for her to climb in. So far, he was doing a bang up job of keeping her safe; he'd almost allowed them to get to her in her own home. He found it a little hard to breathe when he thought of how close that had been. In a matter of hours, she'd invaded his soul and given him something that made it nearly unthinkable for him to go back to what he had been— nothing, an empty shell whose only company was bitterness and regret. He swallowed the little bubble of hope that had begun to percolate somewhere in the region of his heart by telling himself he still had unfinished business and couldn't afford to be deterred, not when vengeance was so close at hand. But, now that he'd found her, could he really let her go and spend the rest of his life thinking of her with someone else?

"Listen, McAllister, I'm sure you two have some important ghoulie business or something to take care of, so maybe you should just snap, crackle, and pop your way back to your place. I'm sure it's much quicker." She glanced furtively at Luca. "I think maybe I'll…um…catch up with you later, okay?" She sounded so hopeful. He hated to disappoint her, and hated even more to push her, but they really needed to get out of here before more *animorti* arrived.

"I understand you're upset and confused, but you can't stay here alone. You understand that, right?" If

Luca hadn't materialized already prepared to fight, Kassian knew he might have been a split second too late to protect Kat and that had scared the hell out of him. It was an unfamiliar feeling, and one he wasn't at all comfortable with.

****

Kat motioned Kassian down to her level, put her lips to his ear, and whispered, "Then can *he* snap, crackle, and pop his way back?" Whatever they were, whatever was going on, at least she felt relatively sure that McAllister felt some kind of responsibility to protect her. As for Luca, he was a wild card and she didn't trust him as far as she could throw him. No doubt he had a genetic predisposition to indifference.

Kassian gave her a puzzled look. "What's up? Luca's no threat...hell, I've known him forever."

"Not quite that long, but close enough." Luca frowned across the roof. "Wait a minute, does she think we're the bad guys?"

Kat's brows drew together in confusion as she looked from one to the other. She hadn't really thought about it one way or the other. In fact, she hadn't really had time to give it much thought, at all.

Luca's face split in a wide grin that went from ear to ear. "No worries, sweetness... we're the good guys!"

Chapter 5

"Head back but stay close. I'll feel better knowing you've got my back if we run into trouble."

"No problem." Luca shrugged. *"Hey, about before...I did plan to knock. I couldn't very well materialize outside with him right behind me not knowing if there were witnesses around."*

"No worries, my brother, I get it. I just really hadn't planned on telling her...at least not yet, and certainly not like this."

"So, what are you going to do?"

"No idea." And he didn't like feeling so indecisive. It was another emotion he wasn't comfortable with, but one that certainly seemed to be afflicting him more since he'd first laid eyes on Katrina Shephard.

"Well, maybe you could start by not talking about me as if I'm not here," Kat snapped.

"Well, damn!" Luca gasped looking hard at Kassian.

If the situation were less serious, Kassian would have laughed out loud at the comical expression on Luca's usually unreadable face. He was certain he wore a similar expression on his own, as they turned in unison to gape at her. Kat had unknowingly intercepted a telepathic conversation they were having on a mental pathway used exclusively by *Earthbounds*.

"What?" She crossed her arms over her chest and glared at them both. "You knew I was telepathic, McAllister. You can't blame a girl for eavesdropping under the circumstances."

No, he couldn't. But only another *Earthbound* should have been able to hear the exchange. He'd suspected this morning that she wasn't completely human; this all but confirmed it. He threw Luca a warning glance.

"It's fine, Kat. Luca, we'll see you back at my place. Feel free to pick up some Chinese on the way. I'm starving and I'm sure Kat will be, too." Luca chose another mental pathway that was specific to him and McAllister, as opposed to the general one that they had been using.

"How?"

"No idea, but apparently she isn't completely human."

"Stop it!"

"You heard that, too?" Luca's eyes widened incredulously and he actually looked alarmed. It was the most expression he'd exhibited since he appeared in the living room. Kassian reflected it might be the most expression he'd seen Luca exhibit in years.

"No, but I'm not a moron, despite the fact that I might have appeared to be a blubbering idiot when you literally popped into my house. I'd apologize for my reaction, but my guests normally enter through the front door, not the Twilight Zone." She protested, slouching down in the car seat.

"She seems to be recovering nicely. I think I might be falling in love." Luca's voice filled Kassian's head with laughter.

"Back off, Luca..."

"Ah, so that's how it is. You planning to keep her?"

"Get bent, my brother."

"Okay, children," Luca said out loud. "Let's get a move on. Are you sure this rat trap will make it back? I had a helluva time starting it this morning. Did you know it has a bad solenoid? Katrina, you really should think about getting a new car." Kassian smirked and climbed in beside her while Kat rolled her eyes. With a quick glance around and a subdued snap, Luca disappeared.

Kat closed her eyes as though bracing for it, but she jumped anyway.

"You okay?" Kassian ground the car into reverse and backed out of the drive. Thankfully the car started right up without any intervention from Kat and her screwdriver.

"Define okay. But if you mean that..." she gestured toward the spot where Luca had been standing. "Well, whatever you call it...sorry, it takes a little getting used to. And in case you were wondering, yes, I am a master of understatement." She was silent for so long that Kassian felt as though his nerves would snap. She was blocking like a trooper and he had no idea what she was thinking. But whatever it was, he was pretty sure it couldn't be good.

"Kat, are you afraid of me?" he asked at last as they pulled onto the interstate. Oddly, he realized it mattered to him.

****

Oddly, she wasn't. Common sense told her she should be, but she was more afraid of her attraction to

84

him. Over the years, she'd gotten a reputation for being well…frigid, among the men of her acquaintance. It was impossible to maintain a mental block during foreplay, and reading your partners' thoughts could be a very effective libido suppressant. That sure as hell wasn't a problem with McAllister. And on top of everything else, she struggled to contain the escalating fear of the truths she might be about to find out about herself.

"What are you, McAllister?" It slipped out before she could stop it. Well, that sounded fabulous. She risked a glance, relieved to see that he didn't appear offended. In fact, he smiled slightly as he mulled over his answer; as if he'd been expecting just that question.

"Well, I guess it would depend on who you ask, but basically I guess the best way to explain it is, technically…we're angels."

"Angels?" she echoed faintly. Okay, that hadn't even made her Top Ten list of possibilities. Demons, aliens, day-walking vampires, Big Foot's prettier cousins maybe, but angels? "Let me get this straight; you want me to believe that the two of you are card-carrying, wing-flapping, harp-playing, halo-wearing angels?" Her brows drew together skeptically. And for the record, there was no way she could picture either of them in flowing white robes lounging on a cloud somewhere, either. He reached over and drew her hand onto his thigh, covering it with his own.

"Just in case you decide to take a dive onto the interstate rather than stay in the car with me," he explained with a faint smile. His voice was teasing, but she suspected he might actually be worried. Since she didn't have the slightest idea what to expect next, she had to admit his concern might be warranted. Still, her empathy had yet to detect anything threatening about the man and he *had* stepped in front of her when that creature appeared. She didn't pull away.

"Hmm, well, I'm an *Earthbound*, so no wings. I've been told I'm tone deaf, so I doubt I'd be much good at the harp. Halo? Yeah, well if I had one it would be more than a little bent and tarnished. In fact, I probably would have misplaced it somewhere by now," he laughed.

"So, then, are you a...fallen angel?" That was probably a bad thing, right? She'd read about fallen angels. Of course, she'd never actually thought the stories were true. Wasn't Satan reputed to be a fallen angel? Well, McAllister definitely was as hot as the devil, but she'd never sensed evil around him.

"You've obviously heard of the *Fallen*, at least the commonly accepted legends, but no, we're not *Fallen*. Okay, not, exactly...well, at least not anymore. We do share a common history...up to a point. If you've heard of the *Fallen*, then you probably know they were cast out of the heavens and damned for sedition and disobedience?"

Kat nodded cautiously. When he didn't continue right away, she tugged on his hand to urge him to continue. He flashed a quick smile and squeezed her fingers before continuing.

"After the fall, some of the rebels realized they'd mistakenly backed the wrong horse. There was a lot of political maneuvering going on back then and it turned out that things weren't the way they'd been made to appear. Forgiveness wasn't exactly easy to come by, but finally, Michael the Archangel brokered a deal. In exchange for an agreement to give up their wings and spend their lives on earth, fighting the *Fallen* and thwarting their evil for the rest of eternity, he was authorized to restore their souls and create a new order...*Earthbound*s. No wings, no harps, no halos, although we do have a couple of special powers. We're born and spend our lives on Earth, as you do, and our primary purpose is to protect humanity."

"From...?"

"Itself, mostly." He glanced over with a frown. "Female *Earthbound*s generally involve themselves in humanitarian causes and charities, guiding and influencing humanity to do the right thing by example. The *Defensori* that Luca and I belong to are a group of specialized combat warriors, but all *Earthbound* males are warriors in a sense, businessmen, politicians, scientists. *Earthbound*s battle in many arenas to thwart the *Fallen* and their puppets."

"Hmm."

"Hmm? That's it? You seem to be taking all of this pretty calmly."

Kat leaned back against the seat, absorbed in thought. Despite the unruffled exterior she struggled to present to McAllister, she felt profoundly shaken. She had always known there were things in the world that went beyond the obvious, some hazy impression, a vague awareness that she was not really alone in her isolation or so different in her differences. Today's events had thrown open a door of knowledge that let in the light of understanding through cracked and discolored glass. She had been paralyzed by the sense of instant recognition when Luca appeared. Had her mother known the truth? She must have, of course. And yet she had never said a word; and right at this moment, that hurt more than she cared to admit. Kat had spent a lifetime wishing for a place to really belong; now she wondered if she should have been a little more specific. Her life had just been rewritten and she had no choice but to weigh who and what she'd always believed about herself against whom and what she actually might be.

She turned her head and regarded McAllister, an angel, a warrior, so dark and classically beautiful. Her initial terror had faded, but the sense of unreality remained. He kept his eyes on the road, but she felt the sidelong glances of concern from time to time. He brought her hand to his lips, pressing a slow kiss in the hollow of her palm that somehow felt more intimate to her than the kiss they'd shared in his bedroom that morning. She knew he intended it as some kind of comforting gesture, but she felt it on a far more visceral level; her bones felt as though they were melting. She also didn't need empathy to feel his regret; he hadn't intended to involve her in any of this. Now, after seeing Luca and being slapped in the head with a healthy dose of reality, she wondered if maybe it had been fate, after all.

"What are you thinking?" he asked, at last. His thumb was stroking her wrist in the most distracting way. She wondered if he even realized he was doing it.

"Do you always assume the guilt for everything that happens around you? I was unlucky enough to be in the wrong place at the wrong time, Kassian. You had no control over it, you aren't responsible for it."

The set of his jaw told her everything. He wasn't going to allow himself to be exonerated.

****

No matter what she said, he *was* responsible. Sure, he couldn't have controlled her attendance at the party, but he sure as hell could have walked away and kept her out of it. He thought about why he'd brought her home instead of letting Elle take over after he'd broken her connection to the murdered woman. It didn't improve his opinion of himself to realize that the truth was he'd seen something he unconsciously craved and had taken it, though even then he realized on some level it put her in an impossible situation. He wasn't thinking, he was feeling, something he rarely allowed himself these days. He was a selfish bastard, all right. He was touched by her attempt to assuage his guilt, but she was wrong; this was totally on him. There was no way she could get it. He'd failed so many people in his life; he didn't want to add her to that list.

He glanced at her face. On the surface, she appeared completely calm. He couldn't believe how well she was taking all this. In fact, since she'd followed that brief initial instinct to run, she'd been remarkably composed. Maybe she was in shock or something? Most people simply rejected the supernatural out of hand or considered it something to be investigated, disproven, or taken out for entertainment value and cheap thrills. Most didn't calmly and thoughtfully accept it as truth the way Kat appeared to be doing. Today she'd gotten whacked right upside the head with a whole dump-truck load of truth that would send most people off the deep end and her response was "hmm"? Was that even normal? Oh, wait, look who was talking about normal. Right, like he would know.

"Kat, I…"

The sudden blare of Kat's cell phone interrupted whatever he had been about to say. Idina Menzel was singing about Defying Gravity as Kat dug in her bag with one hand and checked the display. She bit her lip.

"It's Elle."

He reluctantly disengaged her fingers, releasing her hand.

"Maybe you should take it. She must be worried sick by now."

****

Kat knew he was right; although she wasn't exactly sure what she was going to say. So much had happened that she hadn't fully wrapped her own head around it yet. She took a deep breath and clicked accept.

"Hey," she breathed in a cheerful voice.

"Kat, thank God! I've been going crazy! Where are you?"

"Coming through the tunnel, what's up?"

"What's up? You have to be kidding! Are you okay? What happened last night? Where have you been? Are you on your way here? Did you hear about that poor girl they found in the Dumpster?"

"Did you want me to answer in any particular order?" Kat laughed fondly. Typical Elle; so many thoughts, so little time. It felt good to know there was still one person in the world that actually worried about her. She remembered McAllister's comment this morning about limiting the information she shared with Elle to keep her safe. "I'm fine, yes, I heard about it, and no, I'm not on my way there."

"You aren't?" Elle responded blankly. "Well, where are you going?"

"I, uh…to McAllister's actually. He seems to think

I might be in danger because of what happened last night and has appointed himself my own personal bodyguard. Aren't I lucky?" She glanced at Kassian, who rolled his eyes.

"Oh my God, Kat, please tell me you are not buying that pathetic crock! Did he offer to show you his etchings and sell you some swamp land in Queens, too?"

"Not yet." Kat bit back a smile. "But the night is young."

"Katrina Shephard!" Elle gasped in mock horror. "I am your best friend! How could I not know you were such a tramp? Seriously, honey...he's...well, it's McAllister. Are you sure you aren't in over your head?"

"I think I should be insulted...on so many levels," Kat laughed wryly. "Don't worry about me. I'll be in fine. I love you. I'll be in touch."

"You bet your ass you will! And I'll expect the details, all of them. I, uh...I'm researching my next book...The Wallflower and the Billionaire. And please take note that I'm seriously envious and might actually hate you right now. Love you more, doll. Call me," she warned before terminating the connection.

Kat clicked off and dropped the phone back in her bag.

"Now, where were we? Oh yeah, this guilt on steroids thing you have going on." She smiled. He didn't.

"Elle is a good friend?" Kat immediately recognized his attempt to divert her attention to a new subject. Clearly he didn't want to talk about it anymore, so she let it go. For now.

"Yeah, she is. She's the sister I never had." They'd

met in college shortly after Kat's mother died and Elle later moved into Kat's place to escape a bad situation at home. She was Kat's most loyal supporter, fiercest defender, and closest companion.

"Fudge!" she exclaimed suddenly. "I forgot my laptop."

Kassian shrugged. "No big deal, you can use mine."

"Thanks, but I had some files on there that I can't access on yours." She supposed she could get caught up on Monday, but she was a little OCD about deadlines; she was a lot more comfortable getting things done three weeks early. You never knew when all hell would break loose and put you behind schedule. Today was nothing if not proof of that!

"Just tell me what you need and where it is and Luca will go back for it later."

"No!" Kat cried sharply. The last person she wanted snooping around her house unsupervised right now was Luca. She hadn't quite decided how she was going to handle him yet, so for now, the less anyone else knew, the better. "I mean, um, thanks, but it can wait."

****

Kassian pulled into the parking garage beneath his building and turned off the motor. He'd noticed a few diehards from the press still hanging around outside the lobby, but most had given up and gone home. He was puzzled at her reaction. What was her problem with Luca anyway? Well, okay, so maybe he had exploded into her living room and vaporized an *animorti* right in front of her, but still, now that she knew the truth, she had to realize Luca was no threat to her.

"Kat, about Luca…" he began, but she cut him off.

"Did I hear you mention Chinese food? I'm starving." She was talking too fast and started toward the elevator without waiting as he grabbed her duffle from the back seat. He caught up with her in a few long strides and grabbed her hand to keep her close. He tugged her back, bringing her to a halt.

"Tell me." He gazed at her steadily without blinking and she looked away.

"Don't you dare try your hocus-pocus mind control crap on me, McAllister. You remind me of Bella Lugosi when you do that. I told you, I'm hungry. A girl can't live by M&M's alone." Something was bothering her, he was sure of it. And it had something to do with Luca, which made no sense to him at all.

"Is the food here yet?" she asked. Kassian sought Luca on the common path. He was already parked in front of Kassian's big screen, having a beer, and watching the Yankees kick Boston's ass.

"You better hurry; the lo mein is almost gone."

"Not a fan of lo mein anyway," Kat remarked. "But tell him he'd better keep his paws off the sweet and sour. If that's gone when we get up there, angel or not, I won't be responsible for what happens to him."

Chapter 6

"Rivera is, hands down, the greatest closer to ever play the game." Luca tugged down the brim of his Yankees cap and settled back, locking his hands behind his head with a satisfied sigh. Mariano had just thrown a sizzling strike, dead center over the plate, to end the game and ensure the Yankee victory.

The chrome and glass coffee table was strewn with half-empty cardboard cartons, chopsticks, and bottles of warming beer. Luca sprawled in the armchair and Kassian occupied one corner of the deep leather sofa with his feet propped up on the coffee table while Kat sat slumped in the other struggling to keep her heavy lids from closing. It wasn't very late, but the emotional rollercoaster she'd had a free pass for all day was catching up with her. She crawled stiffly off of the couch, stifling a yawn and began to gather up the bottles and greasy food containers, an automatic habit of living alone and taking care of herself. Kassian and Luca both jumped to their feet.

"Kat, you're beat... go to bed. Luca and I will clear this up."

"I guess I am kind of tired," she sighed with a faint smile. All three of them had studiously stuck to small talk all evening, as if nothing unusual had happened earlier in the afternoon. She'd felt Kassian's thoughtful gaze on her more than once, and it caused a slow heat to curl in her stomach every time. Luca remained politely indifferent and stuck to commentary on the game. Always a fan, she now knew more about the Yankees than she'd ever thought possible. Kat sank back into the couch while Kassian and Luca made short work of the leftovers. All three turned at the unexpected knock on the door.

"Dimitri," Luca said grimly, obviously having scanned for the newcomer. He moved to open the door after the two men exchanged a look. Kat gasped at the sight of the imposing figure who stomped in. Bigger than either Kassian or Luca, he reminded her of a biker who'd gotten on the wrong side of a bar fight. He was dressed in black leather from head to toe and a wicked scar ran along the right side of his face from his temple to the corner of his mouth. Hanging in a thick braid halfway down his broad back, his thick, dark hair was held away from his face by a black bandana tied around his forehead. His clothes were spattered with a dark, oily substance that looked suspiciously like the puddle in Kat's living room when Luca had killed the *animorti*. There were jagged slashes in both his jacket and the snug, leather pants clinging to his massive thighs. Instinctively she moved closer to Kassian, who tucked her into his side and partially behind him without speaking or taking his eyes from Dimitri.

"You can see why I am having such a problem buying this whole angel thing," she whispered under her breath. "That guy isn't any sane person's idea of an angel." Kassian simply squeezed her to silence in reply.

"Talk," said Luca in a low, clipped voice. Kat couldn't help staring. The change in Luca was astounding. Gone was the laid-back baseball fan. Tall and broad, he stood at tense attention. His smile was grim and cruel with no hint of warmth or welcome. Dimitri eyed Kat suspiciously, and waited until Kassian's imperceptible nod let him know it was safe to speak.

"We posted a couple of our people around the House of Angels as you asked. About half an hour ago, a girl tried to get in at the back entrance. It was after curfew, so the doors were locked. The *animorti* started moving in almost as soon as she got there, and they came in from every direction…a lot of them…Rapier must be recruiting heavily." He shook his head like a massive lion tossing his mane. "We managed to drive them back, away from her. We took out most of them, but a couple got away and have no doubt run back to report to their maker."

"The girl?"

"She was pretty shaken up, but she wasn't hurt. Galen wiped her memory and she's at the shelter now with Estelle. She'll be fine."

"Casualties?"

"Nothing serious…Alec got the worst of it, but as usual, they were using mortal weapons and he's a fast healer." He glanced nervously at Kassian and then quickly away.

****

"Alec?" Kassian said quietly at first, but his voice quickly rose. "Alec! What in the hell was Alec doing there and why didn't I know about it?" He finished slightly short of a roar glaring at Luca. Luca, in typical fashion, arched a brow and simply shrugged. Kassian's eyes narrowed, sending Luca a message without words to let him know the discussion was not over, not by a long shot.

"Have Galen bring Alec here," Kassian directed in a clipped tone. "Put him in the guest room." He'd deal with his brother later. He hoped Dimitri was right and Alec was a quick healer because as soon as he was recovered, Kassian planned to pound the living hell out of him. "What about…the other location?" The other location was Elle Gates' apartment, but Kat didn't need to know that.

"Quiet."

Well, at least something was going according to plan. Dimitri nodded and turned to leave, presumably to contact Galen and have Alec delivered to his brother. Luca followed him out without a word to either Kassian or Kat.

"Make it snappy!" Kassian called after him.

When the door closed behind him, Kassian moved Kat around to stand in front of him with a hand on either shoulder. Her earlier fatigue had all but vanished, replaced by adrenaline and alarm. He saw it in her eyes and rubbed his hands briskly up and down her arms.

"I need to go out for a while."

"Uh huh. House of Angels?"

So, she hadn't missed the reference. Of course she hadn't. She was a bright girl.

"Yeah…"

"That's so funny, McAllister," her voice was deceptively mild. "There was a shelter in the East End of London in 1888 with the same name; all of Jack the Ripper's victims were affiliated with that shelter in some way." She looked at him steadily and swallowed hard. He could almost hear her mind working though her shields were up, her research with Elle Gates, the girl in the dumpster, the photographs. He knew the moment all of the ugly pieces began to fall into place. The color left her face in a rush and she swayed slightly.

"But of course, you already know that, right?" She cleared her throat repeatedly and swallowed hard again. "Exactly how old are you, McAllister?"

"Old enough to know better and young enough to get away with it?" he quipped with a quick grin. She didn't return his smile.

"Jack the Ripper…he wasn't human, was he? That's why he was never caught."

"No, he isn't human." He knew the fact that he'd said "isn't" and not "wasn't" didn't escape her, either.

There wasn't much time, but he was determined to let her work it out for herself. He would answer her questions as honestly as he could; but he wasn't offering anything, either. God knew she'd already had more dumped on her today than most women would have ever been able to cope with. She gripped his wrists so hard that her knuckles turned white and her nails drew blood. He doubted she was even aware of it.

"He's here, isn't he? The murdered woman, the evil I felt, the energy I intercepted at the party…it's him. *He's* who you think is after me?" Her voice rose dangerously and he gave her a little shake to get her attention.

"Kat, you're safe here, this place is protected. No one can get in except through the door until I get back, and there will be a guard there. No snap, crackle, popping allowed, okay? Haven't you noticed even Luca comes and goes in a civilized manner? Not that he likes it." He flashed a tense smile. She let go of his wrists and wrapped her arms around herself.

"I know I'll be safe, but what about you? Why don't you send that Dimitri guy? He looks like he could take down a rhino," she mumbled. She didn't look at him when she made the suggestion.

Kassian froze. When was the last time anyone had been concerned about his safety? He really needed to teach her to have a little more faith in his abilities. Maybe it was only that she was afraid of what might happen to her if he didn't come back. Either way, he didn't want her sitting here worrying about it all night. And he couldn't afford to be distracted by thinking about her worrying.

"I'll be fine, Kat. I doubt he'll even show his face tonight. He prefers to send his peons to do his dirty work, and his little entourage is down by quite a few at the moment according to Dimitri. It'll take some time for him to regroup. Luca and I are going out to have a look around, that's all. It'll be fine."

****

Luca chose that moment to strut back in, obviously having popped home to change. He was clad in black leather from head to toe. Gone was the blasé GQ model in cashmere and khakis. In his place was a cold, calculating killing machine. The sleeves of the jacket had snaps from wrist to elbow to allow easy access to his daggers. Kat simply stared. His cold indifference was gone; he looked positively lethal.

"C'mon, Mac…get moving before we miss all the fun."

McAllister eased Kat away from him, pushed her down into the chair, and strode into the bedroom. Luca paced restlessly while Kat simply watched. Finally,

Luca stopped and spun to face her.

"What exactly is your problem with me, Kat?" he demanded.

"What makes you think I have a problem?" Her chin came up.

"Maybe because you seem completely pissed off at me for no reason?" Luca glared at her for half a minute, and then shook his head and forced his features into his trademark look of disinterest. It was obvious she wasn't about to talk. So he'd showed up unannounced and killed an *animorti* in her living room. Granted, there were better ways to make a first impression, but otherwise he thought he'd been perfectly charming. And he'd even taken care to clean up after himself. Women! But he'd have to be blind to have missed the change in Mac, and that was something to consider. Mac had been like the walking dead ever since Callista was taken. Luca reckoned he could put up with a hell of a lot from anyone who might have the ability to help Mac get over himself.

"Just because you don't *know* the reason, doesn't mean I don't *have* one," Kat countered.

The conversation ended when Kassian marched back into the room dressed almost identically to Luca with the exception of his coat, which was a long leather duster. There was a sharp rap on the door and Luca opened it to find Dimitri filling the doorway with another man slung limply over his shoulder.

"Galen should be right behind me," he told Luca. "He'll stay out here and keep an eye on..." His eyes flicked to Kat. "...things until you get back."

****

"In here." Kassian opened a door off of the

lacquered wall of the living room. The door was almost invisibly flush and led to a second bedroom Kat hadn't realized was there. Dimitri shouldered past him and laid his burden on top of the king-sized bed with more gentleness than one would expect from such a large, rough-looking man. But it wasn't gently enough to stop the groan that rose from the man on the bed. He bore a strong resemblance to Kassian, though the younger man had a thick head of dark curls where Kassian's was longer and nearly straight. His face was white and tense with pain. As Dimitri stepped back, the reason became obvious. The entire right side of his black tee was soaked with blood. Kat gasped, and Alec opened one startling blue eye and focused it on her.

"Only a flesh wound, honey." He tried to smile, but Kassian chose that moment to roll him over to check his back, and it turned into more of a grimace. Kat frowned as Kassian rolled him back again and lifted the tee to reveal a long, wicked-looking gash that started near his armpit and extended almost to the waistband of his leather pants. Alec opened the same eye again and regarded his brother calmly.

"How bad is it?"

"Only a flesh wound, honey." Kassian mocked with a tense grin. "Hell, Alec, you could be dead and you'd still find a way to flirt. I guess there's comfort in seeing that some things never change.

"But you can damn well find someone else to flirt with, brother."

Alec's eye widened and he stared at his brother.

"McAllister, that needs stitches." Kat gnawed on her lower lip.

"He's fine, Kat… it isn't as bad as it looks."

Luca came out of the en suite with a first aid kit along with a couple of towels. Kassian used a pair of scissors to cut off the tee and then the leather jacket, the latter over loud protests from the patient, complaining that he'd finally gotten it broken in to his liking. He deftly made quick work of cleaning the wound, and after rubbing his palms together briskly and giving the wound a dose of the blue light special, he pressed a heavy layer of bandages in place, taping them tightly. His hands worked with a competency and confidence of someone who'd done this many times before. He pulled off Alec's boots and lifted him in his arms motioning to Kat, who moved forward quickly and turned down the bed, then stepped back out of the way. Kassian placed his brother gently in the center and pulled the sheet up to his chest.

"Alec, what in the hell…" Kassian began hotly.

"Kass, how 'bout sleep now, lecture later, huh?" Alec interrupted through stiff lips. There were white lines at the corners of his mouth and a deep furrow between his brows. It was evident that he was in more pain than he was letting on. Kassian swallowed whatever he had been about to say and motioned for everyone to precede him from the room. Kat paused and waited in the doorway as he leaned down and tenderly stroked the curls away from his brother's forehead then laid the back of his hand against Alec's cheek. He straightened to leave and Alec's lips moved again.

"Kass?"

"Yeah?"

"It's good to see you, brother." He smiled without opening his eyes. Kassian swallowed hard and his voice sounded hoarse when he replied.

"It's good to see you, too. Get some rest and we'll talk later. Kat will be here if you need anything."

Kat stepped back to let him pass and closed the door quietly behind her. She ignored Luca and Dimitri who were waiting and watching, and surprised everyone by stepping up and laying her palms against McAllister's solid chest. He was as hard as stone, but even stone could crumble. She knew he wasn't the heartless tough guy he presented to the world, even if he didn't. She felt his hesitation and then his arms came around her, pulling her close. She tilted back her head and stared directly into his eyes. Was it the novelty of a man she didn't have to hide her abilities from combined with his overwhelming sensuality, or could she really have come to care about this man so quickly? She'd never felt such an instant attraction to anyone in her life. He was gorgeous, he was funny, he was strong and unyielding when he wanted his own way, and yet she'd also seen him be gentle and tender and take on the responsibility for everyone around him. She guessed maybe he really was an angel…sometimes. She knew he was some ancient warrior and had probably fought thousands of battles, but she didn't want him to go out there tonight. She was afraid that either he or Luca would be hurt. And a selfish little part of her that she wasn't especially proud of at the moment cared more about keeping them with her than sending them off to fight the monster, though she knew it was the right thing to do. It was who they were. She might not know very much about them yet, but she already knew that much.

****

Kassian saw the worry shimmering in the depths of her deep gray eyes and prepared himself for an argument. This was who he was and she had to accept it. And if she couldn't? As long as Jacques lived, people were in danger, she was in danger, whether she stayed with him or not. It would be hard to watch her walk away, but it would be much harder to watch her die.

"Be careful, McAllister."

Kassian drew back in amazement. He looked quickly at Luca and Dimitri. Neither of them gave any indication that they'd heard. She'd found her own mental pathway to communicate with him privately. What the hell? Truthfully, she was beginning to freak him right the hell out. He had no idea what she might come off with next.

"Kat, I don't know how you did that. You shouldn't have been able to hear us earlier either. Is there any chance either of your parents were Earthbound?"

"I have a theory about that. We can talk about it later. Right now I want you to promise me that you will be careful and come home in one piece."

"You got it."

For the first time in as long as he could remember, he felt reluctant to go out hunting and that was something he couldn't allow. Rapier had to be stopped at all costs; he couldn't allow anything to become more important than that. He owed it to his sister, his mother, and every other woman whom Rapier had destroyed. Reluctantly he put Kat away from him and turned toward the door.

"McAllister?" He turned back and regarded her expectantly.

"Bring Luca home in one piece, too." She closed

her eyes and grimaced as though the request had been painful. He smiled broadly looking from her to Luca and back again.

"It's good of you to worry about him."

"I'm not worried about him; I'm worried about you. It would upset you to lose him."

Kassian burst out laughing. Luca's brows lowered ominously.

"She's doing it again, isn't she?"

Kassian only laughed harder and shoved Luca in the direction of the door. "Let's go. Kat...try to get some rest. There's aspirin in the bathroom if Alec needs it when he wakes up. I'll see you later."

"McAllister?"

"Yeah?"

"I'm going to be really pissed if you let something happen to you."

****

His warm laughter wrapped around her like a security blanket as the door closed behind him. She caught a glimpse of a bald giant with gauges in his ears and tattoos that looked suspiciously like shurikens all over his skull, standing right outside the door. He was looking at McAllister with an odd expression; as though he'd never heard him laugh before. This, she assumed, was Galen. Yeah, she could not see this dude in a long, white robe singing the "Hallelujah Chorus" either, no matter how good her imagination was.

She glanced at her watch; it was a little before eleven. She wandered into the bedroom where Kassian had deposited her bag earlier and dug through it until she found her pink, flannel sleep pants and a white cotton tank. She changed into them, washed her face, brushed her teeth, and stuck her head in to check on Alec. He seemed to be sleeping comfortably, but she left the door open a crack, just in case, so that she could hear him if he called out.

Uneasy and at loose ends, she curled up on the sofa, pulled a chenille throw around her shoulders, and pointed the remote at the TV. She thought of calling Elle now that she was alone and had some time to talk, but it was already late. And really, what would she say? Kassian was right; it was better to keep Elle as far out of this loop as possible until it was resolved. After clicking through what seemed like a hundred channels, Kat decided that there wasn't a single thing on that could capture her interest long enough to distract her from wondering what was happening beyond the safe, protected walls of the penthouse. She hated that she was suddenly uneasy being alone. She spent most of her time that way, by choice, and had never minded it before. At least not that she would admit to herself. So why did she feel like something was missing now? She threw back the blanket and wandered into Kassian's office thinking maybe she could find something to read.

She clicked on the lamp and a soft glow lit the room. She wandered over to the bookshelves which seemed to hold an endless supply of books, some looking as though they had gone undisturbed for years. Many were antiques and first editions. She smiled faintly when she noticed three more slim volumes by K.L. Brookes. On another shelf, in a row of dusty yellowed texts in foreign languages, she found something that appeared to be an old photo album. Feeling like a thief, she slid it from the shelf and began to carefully turn the brittle pages. The photos seemed to be from the nineteenth century, but Kat didn't know enough about fashion to approximate the year. There were several of Kassian and Alec, looking much the same as they did today, but there was a mischievous lightheartedness to Kassian in the photos, despite the typically somber expressions of the period, that was absent now. She still had trouble wrapping her head around the fact that he had to be several hundred years old, at minimum. Another photo showed a handsome couple that Kat guessed might be his parents, and then she saw a portrait of an extremely delicate and beautiful young woman. Her stare was frank and direct; a Mona Lisa smile hovered on her lips, hinting at secrets she wouldn't share.

"My sister, Callista." Kat hadn't heard Alec come up behind her. She jumped guiltily and snapped the album closed.

"Sorry," he smiled. "I didn't mean to startle you."

"No, it's fine. I didn't hear you. I was being nosy, I guess. I came in to look for a book and found the album. She's beautiful." Why hadn't Kassian mentioned that he had a sister?

"Yeah, she was."

"What are you doing out of bed, anyway? I would really hate to have to explain to your brother when he comes home and finds you in a heap on the floor. You should have called me if you needed something." Shouldn't he be pale and weak looking? He actually looked remarkably recovered and...virile. Her eyes darted to the bandages on his side. There was no evidence of blood seeping through. Before she had time to think or protest, he tore them off and tossed them in the wastebasket. Where the horrible gash had been, only an angry-looking pink line remained.

"I guess Tall, Dark, and Ugly wasn't kidding when he said you were a quick healer."

"Dimitri? Don't let him hear you say that; he thinks he's quite a ladies' man."

"Well, I guess it depends on your definition of a lady."

"You don't seem very surprised to see me up and about."

"After the day I've had, I'm not sure much of anything could surprise me." She smiled ruefully. "But maybe you should go back to bed; it looked like you lost a lot of blood. I could get you something to eat if you're hungry? There's some leftover Chinese. I'd be happy to heat it up."

Alec shook his head and lowered himself stiffly into one of the leather chairs and patted the seat of the other, inviting her to do the same. She perched on the edge, eyeing him cautiously. Alec McAllister was a truly beautiful man. Tall, broad, and well-muscled like his brother, he had a mass of thick, dark curls, piercing blue eyes, and deep dimples when he smiled as he was doing now. Curiously, while she could admire his prettiness, she didn't feel the least bit physically attracted.

"I'm good for now...maybe in a while. So what's the story with you and my brother?"

"Well, that's kind of a personal question to ask someone you just met," she replied cautiously. "Why do you ask?"

"Couple of reasons. One, I wanted to know if you were available." He laughed when she blushed uncomfortably. "But mostly, because you make him laugh. I haven't heard him laugh in a very long time. It's nice to see him happy."

Kat hesitated, unsure how to answer. What *was* the story with her and Kassian McAllister? He didn't think she was a freak. That alone was enough to win him some points. Being with Kassian gave her a peace she'd hardly ever known in her life. She didn't feel different with him, she felt...at home. She felt an almost unnatural attraction toward him. One look from him could turn her bones to butter. But she was only here because he felt responsible for her and though he seemed to like her well enough, he hadn't given her any indication that he felt any real attraction to her since that first kiss when she'd awakened in his bed.

"I'm not sure." She answered honestly, at last. "We've only just met, actually."

"Fair enough."

"So, I...um, gather that your brother wasn't expecting you?"

"You picked up on that, huh? Smart girl. I heard Jacques was back skulking around; I wasn't about to sit on my hands this time and do nothing no matter what my brother said. It was more...expedient not to let him know about it ahead of time." He flashed those deadly dimples again.

"I gather Jacques isn't a very popular guy?"

"That doesn't even begin to cover it, sweetness." Alec flashed his teeth, but the smile had no humor in it.

"But why? I mean aside from the obvious fact that he's a conscienceless serial killer," she added quickly. "Your brother...you all... seem to have some personal stake in this. He told me the murder last night was a message for him."

Alec took a deep breath and rubbed a hand wearily over his face. It was obviously not a topic he was comfortable with. "I guess in human terms, Rapier might be considered a sociopath," he began slowly. "Back then, it was known as moral insanity. *Fallen* are evil by nature, but usually with some self-serving purpose…Rapier has a complete lack of regard for any moral or legal standards…not society's, not even those of the *Fallen*, such as they are. He was someone that probably tortured small animals as a kid for no other reason than because he could. No sympathy, no remorse, an overdeveloped sense of entitlement and invincibility…completely oblivious to the devastation he causes, unwilling to accept blame…well, you get the picture."

Kat nodded, and gripped the arms of the chair, bracing herself. She tried to read him but he had his blocks firmly in place. Curious, she followed the pattern. It was different from Kassian's and unlike anything she had tried herself and she made note of it. Still, her empathy felt the anger and grief coming off of him in waves. Between that and the look in Alec's eyes, she knew whatever was coming wouldn't be pretty.

"Rapier had a twin brother, Jean-Marc. If there was anyone on the planet Jacques cared for, anyone who was able to control Jacques at all, it was him. He knew what Jacques was capable of, but he thought he could keep him on a tight enough leash, keep him out of trouble. But, Jacques was clever and managed to get away from him and that was when the Whitechapel killings began. The Rapier brothers were hundreds of years older than any of us, so I'm sure it wasn't the first time Jacques went on a killing spree; but it was the first time he'd crossed paths with Kassian."

Alec stood and began pacing the confines of the office restlessly. Kat sat quietly, waiting patiently for him to continue. She'd figured out earlier that this wasn't Kassian's first run-in with Rapier, but a knot of dread had begun to settle in her stomach as Alec talked. Whatever had happened back then was much more personal to Kassian than she had imagined.

"Anyway," Alec continued, stopping with his back to her and looking out the windows into the darkness. "We all knew that he needed to be stopped. Callista was distraught because all of the women he killed had frequented her shelter, House of Angels, at one time or another and she felt responsible, which was ridiculous, but that was our Calli." His short laugh was bitter. "She was a lot like Kass in that way. Jean-Marc was desperate to find Jacques and get him back under lock and key before the *Defensori* found him, or someone among the *Fallen* decided to take him out on their own. He wasn't exactly keeping a low profile and it called attention to those who would have preferred to fly under the radar. Jean-Marc found his brother at Miller's Court about the same time the *Defensori* did. In the ensuing battle, Jean-Marc was killed; at the end of Kassian's sword. Jacques went wild. I guess he cared for Jean-Marc as much as it was possible for him to care about anyone, and he swore vengeance. Callista, stubborn female that she was, made it easier than it ever should have been. Kass had ordered her to stay home, behind locked doors, protected by guards and *sigil*s, but as soon as he left, she found a way to sneak out and tried to make her way to the shelter. At least, we think that's where she was headed. I guess she thought she could help, but honestly, I don't know what she was thinking going off on her own like that. She never was cut out to be the properly obedient Victorian lady." Alec sighed sadly. "She should have trusted that Kass and Luca knew what they were doing. When they got back she was gone. No one had seen her. She never made it to the shelter. Kass knew how stubborn and determined Calli could be and he's blamed himself for what happened ever since."

"Oh my God, Rapier killed her," Kat whispered in horror. Her chest ached with Alec's grief.

Kat held her breath waiting for the answer. They both knew the cruelty Rapier was capable of; and it had been over a hundred years. Alec turned back to Kat with a look of despair etched deeply in his beautiful face.

"God, I hope so."

Chapter 7

Jacques Rapier was a creature of the dark. He lived for it, breathed it, and embraced it. Tonight, once again he'd been a faceless prowler of the night lounging against the cold stone of the art deco building, indistinguishable from the shadows that concealed him. He was hungry for the thrill and hoped the whore would be leaving soon; he had been patient for so long, and patience was not an attribute that came easily to him. As if she heard his silent command, there was an increased volume of slurred shouts and laughter across the way heralding the opening of the door of the after-hours bar across the street. His red eyes narrowed to speculative slits. Finally! It wasn't the one he'd been waiting for; he preferred brunettes, but it was getting late. The blonde would have to do. He pushed all other thoughts aside, growled in satisfaction and anticipation...and melted into the shadows in her wake.

Jacques relished the sound of the rasping breath in the darkness as the woman realized that she was being followed and quickened her pace. He smiled delightedly as he scented the sickly tang of terror. Those arrogant *Defensori* thought they knew him; thought they understood him. It amused him to no end that McAllister thought he wouldn't be able to resist making an appearance when the modern day House of Angels was dedicated. It was such an obvious in-your-face ploy that Jacques had been more entertained than tempted. The publicity blitz put on by McAllister Publishing for that silly woman's book was yet another poorly concealed attempt to bait him. He'd been such a good boy for so long. It was time to show McAllister that the *Defensori* were no closer to catching him now than they had been a century ago. He was smarter than all of them and he would always elude them. Killing McAllister would be too easy; no, he wanted him to suffer. He had planned to tweak McAllister's rage and then resume a low profile to emphasize the fact that he could. But it was turning out to be so much more of a rush than he remembered, and now it looked like McAllister might have even more to lose. He couldn't wait to get his hands on the Shephard woman. After he had his fun with her, he would conveniently disappear again, leaving McAllister to marinate in his misery and his failure.

He turned to the young blonde who now shivered in terror against the packing crates. The disturbance above was getting closer. He lived for the anticipation, but it was time to begin if he didn't want the evening to be a complete waste of his time. Jacques loved the delicious thrill of death. A slice to the throat to silence the voice, slick and clean and only deep enough to postpone the inevitable while watching the fear growing in the eyes as life slowly ebbed through the garish necklace he so lovingly bestowed. A few stabs, not too deep at first, but sufficient to cause pain and heighten the terror. The adrenaline rush was without equal. The best ones were the ones who died slowly, pain and terror mounting as he savored the catch of cold steel segmenting cartilage and bone, carving through the skin. The worst ones ruined his fun in minutes, bleeding out too quickly or taken by the terror before he had a chance to enjoy himself. His eyes took on a demonic, red glow as he reached for the terrified girl, his blade winking wickedly in the dim light. It was important to him that McAllister know that he had been oh, so close, but too late once again. He was a little annoyed that he would have to hurry with this one, but her death was really little more than another turn of the screw and he knew it was only a matter of time until he could satisfy his hunger again.

****

Kassian and Luca materialized almost simultaneously behind the House of Angels, regaining solid form under a cold drizzle that was valiantly trying to turn to snow. The shelter was quiet, with only the faint glow of a nightlight burning in the hallway on the second floor. The building itself was well protected with *sigil*s, so the sleeping inhabitants were safe for the evening. Dimitri was already waiting. He and Galen had taken the liberty of vaporizing the *animorti* that had been killed earlier before returning to Kassian's with Alec; all that remained was a tell-tale trail of inky slime left involuntarily by the few that had gotten away. The alley was dark, cast into the deep shadows of the surrounding buildings and ripe with the odors of alcohol, urine, and cheap, stale sex. An icy breeze came out of nowhere, ruffling orphaned newspaper pages and empty plastic wrappers and dispelling the odors for a few brief moments.

Dimitri took the lead as they set off in the direction the escaping *animorti* had taken. Though large, the *Defensori* were used to secrecy and concealment. They

115

moved with stealth, their black-leather-clad bodies blending into the dark, using the shadows for cover, and becoming part of them. No one paid attention. People of the night weren't exactly the upstanding law-abiding sort who wanted to call any more attention to themselves than necessary. These were the miscreants and malcontents, the seedy looking for the seedier, a subculture of society who were greedy for sin and ready to roll. They were happy to remain anonymous and generally looked the other way regarding anything that didn't directly involve them.

The warriors followed the faint trail through the alley until they felt the pin pricks racing along their nerves, a sure sign they were getting close to something unsavory. Shrinking back against the rough caress of the brick building, Kassian eased forward to peer around the corner. Two *Fallen* stood facing in his general direction, heavy boots planted on top of the rusted metal doors of a backstreet freight elevator. Well, what have we here? They'd been expecting *animorti*. Killing a few soulless sponges was exactly what Kassian needed to take the edge off. The opportunity to take out a few *Fallen* was a bonus he hadn't dreamed of.

Kassian felt a black aura of barely suppressed rage surrounding him and his lips stretched taut in a lethal smile. He was more than ready for the fight. These two were connected to Rapier; they had to be. It was too much of a coincidence that they were here at the end of the *animorti*'s trail. He withdrew the long deadly blade from his back and silently opened his sleeves as he discerned Luca with a dagger already in his hand and an expression on his face that could freeze molten lava.

The muscles in Kassian's arms twitched in anticipation. Dimitri had circled around the building to come in from the other direction and do some recon. They didn't want any unexpected surprises.

Dimitri sent the message that he was in position and they began to move in, nothing more than deep shadows in denser darkness, yet the two guards had become visibly edgy as if sensing they were no longer alone. Luca and Kassian stepped into the dim light of the bare bulb hanging over the doorway behind the *Fallen* at the same time, their heavy boots callously shattering the glistening panes of fresh, thin ice skimming the tops of shallow puddles. The *Fallen* froze for a heartbeat before palming their weapons and falling into a crouch. Luca tossed his dagger carelessly from one hand to the other, wearing a come-and-get-me sneer, his eyes deepening to the dark gray of tempered steel. A low growl issued from the *Fallen* on the right as he and his companion moved forward with slow, plodding steps. Luca and Kassian moved to their right, forcing the *Fallen* out into the alley and away from the relative protection of the building at their backs. They had been fighting side by side for years and each knew the other's next move like partners in a well-rehearsed dance.

"Well, well, well …the dynamic duo, predictable as ever, I see," taunted the larger of the *Fallen*.

"Hell, Degnan, you didn't think we'd miss a chance to catch up on old times now, did you? Things must be pretty rough for you if you're desperate enough to throw in with a lowlife like Rapier," Kassian countered in a bored voice, his eyes never leaving the other man's. *Fallen* didn't answer to one another as a rule; arrogant and autocratic, they despised any authority but their own. Of course, Rapier would have no pangs of conscience about using and sacrificing some of his own kind. "Too bad you picked the wrong circus to join...I doubt either you or your misguided friend here really believes the sick bastard is worth dying for...but hey, your call, man."

"Rapier's money is as good as anyone else's," Degnan growled, confirming Kassian's suspicions that they were affiliated with Jacques. "As for dying, didn't your mama ever teach you not to count your chickens before they're hatched, McAllister?"

Kassian's eyes never wavered from his opponent. He was so going to enjoy this. He saw the precise instant the attack would come and steel met steel with a resounding clash, sparks lighting the darkness like a kid's sparkler on the Fourth of July and reflecting on the wet pavement of the alley with every impact.

"You really should choose your friends more carefully, Degnan," Kassian grunted as he parried and spun away from the *Fallen*'s lunging blade yet again. The force of the last thrust had put Degnan off balance and Kassian planted his feet as he came out of the spin and brought his sword up and across the other man in midstride, slashing a deep gash that looked like a wide, macabre cummerbund across his torso from side to side. Degnan went down with a breathless grunt, first to his knees and then flat on his face, his steel clattering away into the darkness as he kissed the cold pavement. Kassian was barely winded. He glanced to his right and saw that Luca had his opponent well in hand. They were nowhere near evenly matched and Luca was amusing himself more than anything. Dimitri leaned against the building near where the *Fallen* had stood, arms crossed and looking bored, ready to step in if either of his brothers needed assistance.

Kassian rolled Degnan onto his back with the heel of his steel-toed boot. The *Fallen* had a glazed expression of disbelief in his eyes as he stared straight up, the wet snow melting on his face as it landed. Better enjoy it now, sucker, there won't be any snow where you're going, Kassian thought grimly. Not unless hell actually does freeze over. The *Fallen*'s great, black wings were half unfurled, bent and crumpled beneath his dying body. He'd waited a heartbeat too long to attempt an escape.

"Now, what was that about counting chickens, asshole?"

Degnan remained stubbornly silent except for the heaving gurgle of his labored breathing.

"Where is he?" Kassian roughly grasped the neck of the *Fallen*'s jacket and heaved his upper body from the pavement, leaning forward until they were almost nose to nose. He knew the bastard was bleeding out fast; he didn't have much time.

"I *said,* where is he?"

Degnan spat a mouthful of blood in the general direction of Kassian's face, but he didn't have the strength left to do more than produce a fine spray while the rest dribbled from the side of his mouth. His voice was weak and reedy, but no less malicious as he hissed something unintelligible through the blood bubbling up to choke him.

"What did you say to me?"

Degnan began to cough and choke, fighting for air as he drew in a harsh, wet breath.

"You won't save her..."

Something in Kassian snapped and he became a rabid animal. Using his fist like a battering ram he pounded Degnan's face over and over. He first felt the nose and eye sockets give way, and then the wicked satisfaction of the cheekbones crumbling beneath the assault. With the crack of every impact, the *Fallen*'s blood spewed from the pulp of his face. The gore from the gut wound continued to pool around Kassian's boots and at some point he knew he was battering a corpse. He didn't care. With every strike, he felt the blood soaking him and still he wanted more. His hands were raw and swollen when Luca finally put an end to the gory rampage by grabbing and pinning Kassian's arms from behind. The body that he dropped back to the wet and bloody pavement was unrecognizable.

Kassian's breathing was the heavy snort of a charging bull as he regarded the mess he'd made and struggled to regain his control. His gut clenched and shook in anger and frustration. Luca simply held him, arms locked around his friend's chest, and waited until the breathing became less ragged.

"You good?"

"Yeah, I'm good," he lied. The tragedy was that he didn't feel any better and was no closer to an answer. Luca tugged on his sleeve and nodded toward the freight elevator.

"C'mon, let's see what's down there."

Dimitri yanked on the handle of the elevator door. The steel slab gave way with a rusty scream that echoed through the alley and the chamber below as they peered cautiously into the yawning black pit. There was no urgent sense of danger, no pin pricks racing along their nerves. Whatever or whoever the *Fallen* had been guarding was long gone, probably alerted by the sounds of the battle. Dimitri was about to release the door and let it fall back into place when the sweet metallic tang of fresh blood caught their attention and brought Luca's head up.

"Wait."

Kassian quickly rubbed his palms together and directed a blue glow into the darkness below. In the far corner, a body slumped against a pile of unpacked freight. Her throat was slit nearly to the spine, her lifeblood pooled beneath a mop of matted blonde hair, soaking into the cardboard cartons against which her small frame rested. Kassian guessed their arrival had interrupted Jacques' work and he'd decided to go for a quick kill and retreat. He tried to take comfort in the fact that though they hadn't saved her, at least her death had been relatively quick compared to other victims they'd seen. They all knew the degeneracy that Jacques was capable of descending to. She couldn't have been any older than Kat. Dimitri fished an untraceable pay-as-you-go cell from inside his jacket and called the body's location in to the police. He pulled the bandana from his head, carefully wiped down the phone for prints, and shoved it haphazardly in a nearby Dumpster under some rotting cabbage and the used coffee grounds that had spilled from a plastic bag. Then he buffed his palms together until they glowed and vaporized the bodies of the *Fallen*.

"I think we're done here for tonight," Luca said, clapping Dimitri on the back. "Thanks for your help, brother."

"We'll get the bastard, bro." Dimitri punched

Kassian's shoulder affectionately and faded out.

"Let's go home, my brother...you could use a shower. All that *Fallen* blood...you smell like rotten eggs." Luca tugged Kassian away from the pit.

"Yeah," Kassian agreed wearily, "I am so rocking this Eau de Sulfur. What time is it, anyway?"

Luca squinted at his gold Movado. "A little after three, why?"

"Alec should be up by now...I don't think I have the energy to kick his ass tonight, though."

"Don't be too hard on him...he lost her too, you know. He wants to help."

"I know that, but I won't lose him, too. Callista was my responsibility and I'm the one who failed her. I'll take the risks and I'll be the one to take the bastard out." Luca was silent for a minute, regarding McAllister through narrowed eyes.

"Okay, you know what? I've kept my mouth shut for years and I have to say something whether it pisses you off or not. You'll get over it. Probably." Luca shrugged. "Look, Mac, we've been friends a long time and I'm going to speak frankly. You may not like what I have to say, but someone needs to say it and more importantly, you need to hear it. I loved Calli, too. I will stand beside you in any battle, do whatever it takes to get Rapier...you know that." Kassian kept his expression guarded, but he nodded shortly as Luca continued. "I've watched you beat the hell out of yourself for over a century because you think you failed your sister, because you think you didn't protect her. That's bullshit, Mac. Callista wasn't a child and she wasn't stupid. She was an intelligent, headstrong, fully grown woman who made her own choices. She was going to do what she wanted no matter what you said. She felt a responsibility to protect those women exactly like you felt a responsibility to protect her. That was Callista. Do you blame me for her death? I knew what she was like as well as you did. No? Then why are you any more responsible than you think I am? What happened isn't on you, Mac…and you're the only one who believes it is."

"I could have stopped her," Kassian argued.

"You couldn't…because she never intended you to. She always did exactly what she wanted, and your father, in his own misguided way, encouraged it. She didn't take his orders, and she didn't take yours. It still sucks, but what happened is on her, not you. And somewhere deep down, you know it."

"I know this isn't your fight, Luca," Kassian acknowledged stiffly. His jaw was clenched so tightly with emotion that it ached. Luca was as close as any blood brother. He had always stood beside Kassian, even through this last century of his all-consuming need for vengeance; all of the *Defensori* had. It was understandable if they were tired of putting aside their own lives in pursuit of his objective. "I understand if you've had enough. No worries, no hard feelings."

"Don't be an ass, Mac," Luca frowned, replacing his dagger against his forearm with an angry slap. "And don't deliberately misunderstand me, either. The bastard will pay no matter how long it takes, for Callista, and for all of the others who didn't have anyone to avenge them, and I'll be right there with you… that's not what I'm talking about and you know it. You need to step back, you know? Get over yourself. This thing has eaten you alive to the point where I feel like I spend my time with a walking corpse." He jabbed a finger in Kassian's chest near the region of his heart. "There's nothing in there anymore, Mac. Today was the first glimpse I've had of the real you in years. Maybe you should think about *that*. Letting go of the guilt and letting yourself in on some happiness doesn't mean you give up the goal. Give yourself a break, my brother...it's time."

Was it time? Could he shed the mantle of responsibility he'd worn all these years and place it squarely where Luca thought it belonged, on Callista? Did it mean he loved her less? Or did it mean that he saw her clearly for the first time? All these years he thought if he could avenge his sister he could... what? Forgive himself? He didn't know what to think anymore. But Luca was right about one thing; he'd only been half alive for a long time. It hadn't seemed to matter so much until he'd found Kat.

"I'll give it some thought, okay?" he conceded wearily. "Let's go home."

"You look like hell...Kat sees you like that you are going to have some 'splaining to do," Luca pronounced in his best Cuban bandleader voice.

Kassian sent his mind out into the night. His place was only a few blocks south, close enough to touch Alec's mind.

"She's asleep. Alec is waiting up, though."

"Okay, let's go." Luca started to fade.

"Luca..." Luca solidified and stood waiting with one brow raised quizzically. "Um...thanks, brother."

Luca offered his characteristic shrug, but he couldn't hide the faint smile curving his lips as he faded out.

Chapter 8

Kat awoke to the sound of subdued voices beyond the bedroom door. She squinted at the digital clock glowing four thirty-two in eerie, neon green. The last thing she remembered was watching something on the Sci-Fi channel with Alec, which struck her as ironic, really, considering she felt as though she was starring in her own little drama of good and evil, murder and magic, a supernatural world whose existence she could never have imagined. Alec had been less than forthcoming after his initial confidences, perhaps fearing he'd already said too much. She'd nuked the remaining Chinese, and he'd spent the rest of the evening pretending to be completely absorbed in the poorly done B movie after he chowed down every scrap of the leftovers. She guessed she'd dozed off and he carried her into the bedroom. She sure didn't remember navigating here on her own. She sat up slowly, disoriented in the dark, and fumbled around on the bedside table for the lamp switch. Was McAllister back yet? She literally slipped from the bed and padded barefoot to the door. Before she could reach for the knob, the door flew open. The sight that met her eyes stopped her in her tracks and sent her heart leaping into her throat. Oh my God, so much blood! She began to shake so hard her teeth chattered. She felt the color drain from her face and her knees buckled, pain shooting up her spine as her butt hit the floor, hard, fully waking her as nothing else could have. She recovered quickly, scrambled to her feet, and took charge, tugging at Kassian's sleeves to get the blood soaked clothes off of him and pushing him toward the bed so that she could assess the damage.

"How bad is it? Damn you, McAllister, you promised! Get those clothes off and get in that bed…where the hell is Luca?"

She realized he must be blocking his feelings exceedingly well; she couldn't detect even a whisper of pain or distress coming from him.

"Alec! Get in here and help me…" Her hands trembled and her teeth locked into her lower lip hard enough to draw blood to keep from bursting into tears, but it didn't impede her determination. The leather was stiff and sticky, and refused to cooperate with her desperate attempts to remove it. She had to find the source of the bleeding and stop it; she didn't care what he was, angel or demon, no one could lose this much blood and live. She prayed the quick healing thing ran in the family. If something happened to him…sonofabitch! How dare he barrel-ass his way into her life and then go out and get himself killed?

****

"Kat…" Kassian had expected to find Kat sleeping and so was totally unprepared to deal with her reaction. She shrank back a bit and it was then he realized that not only was he a gory mess, he stank to high hell. No wonder she looked sick. He reached for her and realized that given the condition of his knuckles, maybe that wasn't such a hot idea either.

He grabbed her hands and tried to hold her still.

"Kat, listen to me…" as she continued her fight with his duster. "It's not my blood."

It was a few seconds before his words seemed to penetrate her galloping fear and her breathing gradually slowed and became more regular.

"It's not?" Her breath left her in a great rush.

"No, it's not." He released her hands and ran his palms soothingly up and down her arms. "We ran into…a little trouble. You should see the other guy." She didn't look amused by his lame joke, and he realized that it was probably much better if she didn't see the other guy. In fact, she probably didn't ever need to know he was even capable of such brutality. His first instinct was to kiss away the worried pucker between her eyes, but he could see by the way she'd wrinkled her nose and started to frown that the smell had finally penetrated her panic.

"God, you are *foul*!" She held a hand to her nose and waved the other one in front of her to disperse the odor. "Where's your trusty sidekick, by the way?"

"Yeah, *Fallen* blood…a little dab'll do ya!" he smiled in relief. She didn't seem nearly as upset by the gallons of blood now that she knew it wasn't his. "Luca is fine…he's gone back to his place, and Alec went to bed. Let me get out of these things and hop in the shower. Is there any of that Chinese left?"

"Whew! I think you'll have to burn those clothes. And no, your brother polished it off earlier."

"Figures…"

"I could throw together an omelet or something if you're hungry?"

"You can cook?"

"Well, you don't have to sound so surprised! I'm

no domestic goddess, but I think I can manage to keep you from starving."

"Oh, I'm sure you can," he grinned in a way that let her know he wasn't talking about food. He gave her arms a squeeze and stepped back. He peeled the long duster off and tossed it in the corner, then followed it with the black tee.

****

Kat's mouth went dry at the sight of him, broad, smooth, and shirtless, his tight, leather pants hugging him like a second skin and leaving very little to her rapidly overheating imagination. He pulled the slide from his hair and shook the dark mass loose around his shoulders.

"Cut the crap, McAllister…you scared the hell out of me. Don't think a little come-hither look is going to make me forget that!" She knew she was staring, but she couldn't seem to tear her gaze away, and her legs felt too rubbery to move. The smoldering look he flashed her from beneath half-closed lids told her he was well aware of the effect he was having and enjoying every minute of it. When he undid his belt and reached for the button at his waistband, she was galvanized into action.

"I'll…uh…get started on that omelet while you get cleaned up." She darted past him pulling the bedroom door closed behind her. His low chuckle echoed in her head as she flew to the kitchen and began to rummage around in the fridge.

"Kat? No onions."

The response she sent back was more a growl than any comprehensible words. She felt his laughter wrap around her again and couldn't suppress an exasperated smile.

By the time Kat found everything she needed in the unfamiliar kitchen and put together the tomato, mushroom, and cheese omelet, no onions, with toast on the side, it was almost time for breakfast anyway. She slid the fluffy creation onto a plate, grabbed two steaming mugs of coffee by the handles, and carried everything into the living room. Kassian had apparently finished his shower and turned on the gas fireplace before stretching out on the vast leather sofa in nothing but his jeans. He looked so relaxed and appealing in sleep with one arm across his taut abdomen and the other thrown casually above his head, she felt her heart skip a beat. Kat carefully set the loaded plate and the mugs on the coffee table and reached to gently brush an errant lock of dark hair away from his face. Her fingertips had barely touched him when his hand shot out to lock painfully around her wrist and his eyes flew open.

"Ouch! Jeez, McAllister, overreact much? Your omelet is done." As soon as he realized it was her, his eyes softened and he pressed his lips to the tender skin over her pulse, causing it to quicken, before he released her. She rubbed it absently enjoying the lingering sensation of his lips and thinking his fingers were probably going to leave a mark. She'd always bruised easily.

"Sorry, force of habit." He rubbed a hand over his face, stretched and rolled his massive shoulders, and swung his legs over the side to sit up. "That smells great, thanks."

She handed him the plate, sank down in the chair next to the sofa and sipped her coffee in silence while he all but inhaled the omelet. Despite the shower and the cat nap, he still looked tired.

"So, what happened?" she asked as he swallowed the last bite. "Did you find him?"

Kassian briefly recounted the events of the evening, omitting the details surrounding his uncharacteristic loss of control. He told her he planned to go to the House of Angels later in the day to ascertain whether the girl in the pit had any connections to the shelter, or whether she was simply randomly unfortunate. She could feel his frustration at the fact that Rapier seemed to always be able to stay one step ahead of them because they never knew where he was likely to strike next.

"Can I go with you?" Kat asked quietly. She'd always thought she might like to volunteer at such a place, but worried she would be overwhelmed by the emotions. If she went with McAllister, at least she could find out. She knew that he could shut her down and get her out as he had at the party if she became overwhelmed. She saw the shutter slam down on his expression as soon as she asked.

"Absolutely not," he replied in a voice that didn't invite discussion. "You will stay right here where you're safe."

Kat sighed patiently.

"McAllister," she argued reasonably, "I get that I'm safe here, but it's kind of like being a present in a pretty box. How long do you think this can continue?"

"As long as it takes."

"He's been out there for over a hundred years, Kassian...what if you don't find him? Will you keep me here indefinitely, all tied up with a shiny bow? It may be safe, but it's no way to live. Surely you see that?"

She watched the emotions play over his face and felt the indecision rolling off of him in waves. She was challenging every protective instinct he possessed. Sometimes she could read him so easily, using nothing more than her empathy. Trying to mentally follow the blocks that Kassian and the other *Earthbound*s used had helped her change and improve her own, exactly as she'd hoped, but when she opened herself she could feel his emotions swirling dangerously. He continued to wallow in guilt and it broke her heart. But surely he couldn't fault her logic; if they never got Rapier, she had to leave the apartment sometime.

"We'll see." He deferred diplomatically. She knew he didn't like admitting she had a point. But he couldn't realistically expect her to stay cooped up in the apartment forever. He leaned back against the sofa and closed his eyes with a jaw cracking yawn.

He looked so damn tired. Kat found herself wanting to comfort him, but she had no idea how to begin. He had been trying and failing to avenge his sister for over a hundred years. She loved his strength and his humor, and even his ridiculously overdeveloped sense of responsibility. Dear Lord, she was falling in love with him! Probably not a good idea, even if she had the ability to control it. She barely knew him and though he might care about her, she was nothing more than an obligation that he felt responsible for at the moment. She could almost hear her mother's voice; *if you don't go after what you want, how do you ever expect to get it?* So, maybe she should take what she could get for as long as she had it. What did she have to lose besides her heart? She suspected it was already lost, anyway. She slid from the chair to sit at his feet, stacking her hands on his solid thigh and resting her chin on them. If he was surprised by her action, he hid it well and simply placed one large hand on her head and stroked her hair absently.

"Kassian?"

"Mmmm?" His head had fallen back and his eyes were closed again. He began winding long tendrils of her hair around his fingers.

"Why didn't you tell me about Callista?"

He picked his head up, brows drawn together. "Who told you...never mind, I'll be having a talk with my brother later," he said tightly as he answered his own question before he finished it.

"Why didn't you tell me yourself?"

"I don't know..." He sighed and put his head back again, closing his eyes as if it hurt to look at her. "Maybe I needed you to believe I could protect you...maybe *I* needed to believe it. I sure as hell didn't protect *her*." Kat's heart ached at the raw honesty in his voice. Part of her wished she had his sister in front of her right now; she would have liked to, well, slap her. Hard. Callista had known Kassian as well as anyone. Had she spared one thought for what her actions might cost the people who loved her? Why hadn't she waited? She understood the risk and she went anyway. Kat quickly suppressed her reaction. She knew in her heart Callista had paid a higher price than anyone for her foolishness.

"McAllister, I know you'll never admit that maybe I can take care of myself, though I might surprise you, but that aside, I *do* believe you can protect me. And I also believe that you protected your sister...inasmuch as she allowed it. She was a big girl who made her own decisions...you could protect her from a lot of things but no one could have protected her from herself. By all means, kill Rapier if you have to...but do it because it needs to be done, not because you have to make up for any failure on your part."

He didn't open his eyes, but the corners of his mouth tugged up slightly. "It seems everyone's trying to let me off the hook tonight."

"What?"

"Nothing." He opened his eyes and pulled her up to lie beside him, tucking her under his shoulder. "Luca said something like that earlier."

"Did he?" she responded thoughtfully laying her head cautiously on the pillow of his chest right over his heart and draping an arm across his flat middle. "Maybe he has more sense than I gave him credit for." Her tank top had ridden up and his hand rested in the curve of her waist, his thumb stroking absently below her ribcage. His other hand tipped her chin up allowing him to reach her lips. His mouth was soft as he slowly rubbed his lips on hers, nipping at her lower lip with his teeth and flicking his tongue along the crease of her lips. She felt a slow coil of heat unfurl in her stomach and begin to spread lower. She extended the tip of her tongue to tentatively sweep along his full lower lip. His stomach muscles tightened under her hand in reaction and he pulled her closer, hitching her up by the waist to give him better access. His tongue swept inside, seeking, stroking, plundering, as if he couldn't get enough of the kiss, enough of her. His hands moved restlessly, possessively over whatever bit of her skin he could find and left a path of fire in their wake. He skimmed his hand along her back, down her spine, to knead her smooth, firm buttocks through her flannel pants. Desire exploded through her body, and Kat moved restlessly, against him, wanting more. Her hand swept across his taut stomach, and splayed across his wide, smooth chest. As her nails lightly grazed his small, hard nipple, she heard him suck in a breath. Her fingers caressed a path that traced the well-defined muscles of his stomach and took her perilously close to the waistband of his jeans. As her seeking fingers, of their own accord, began moving lower, he snatched her hand with a painful groan and brought it to his chest where he held it trapped beneath his, and dropped his own hand back to her waist. She felt the force of his heart hammering frantically against her palm. She raised her eyes to his with passion and confusion clouding her vision. Her breathing was as harsh and ragged as his. He sighed, but it sounded more like a growl vibrating in his chest.

Kat had been so caught up in the unfamiliar sensations, she hadn't been aware of a thing; she only knew that once again, Kassian had been the one to pull away. Her cheeks burned as she realized she'd practically thrown herself at him. Then she became aware of the sounds coming from behind the guestroom door. She had completely forgotten Alec was there! She started to pull away, but Kassian hauled her back against him.

"Just stay here and let me hold you while I sleep. Okay?"

He dropped a kiss on her mouth, tugged her tank down, and then tucked her head under his chin. He yanked the throw from the back of the couch and tossed it over both of them, effectively concealing the obvious bulge tenting his jeans.

Kat smiled into his chest. While he was kissing her, she'd gotten a brief glimpse into his mind. She hadn't had time to read him too closely, but she thought maybe his feelings for her went beyond mere duty. It was a revelation she held close to her heart.

"Kassian…"

"Hmmm?"

"Do you remember when you said you thought I must have some *Earthbound* in me?"

"Mmm hmmm." He didn't open his eyes and his thumb continued to stroke the indentation of her waist in a lazy, relaxed fashion.

"I think you're right. Does the name Lillian Brookes mean anything to you?" She wished that had sounded as casual and careless as she'd planned.

His hand at her waist stilled and his eyes flew open as though the question hit him like a slap. He didn't answer immediately, but his reaction was answer enough. He definitely knew the name. His hand came up to tangle in her hair and he tilted her head back to look at her. Her wide gray eyes met his steadily.

"Why?"

****

She continued looking at him, raised a brow, and shrugged. The truth hit him like a freight train. He sat up so quickly that only his arm about her waist kept her from tumbling to the floor. The vague familiarity he sensed from the moment he met her, her incredible psychic sensitivity, the "static electricity" when she was angry or upset…her inexplicable hostility toward Luca.

Everything suddenly made sense.

"She was my mother." She drew a deep, shaky breath. "And I think it's possible that Luca…"

"…is your brother." He finished for her. It wasn't a question. His voice was strangely flat.

Kassian only vaguely remembered Lilly Brookes, but he well remembered Nicola Fiorelli's obsession with the woman. When the relationship ended, Nicola had gone on a solitary killing spree that eliminated more *Fallen* in one year than the *Defensori* had managed to eradicate in the previous three decades. Then he'd gone into seclusion, cutting himself off from everyone, including his only son. Luca had been left alone years before his father finally died. Kat said she was twenty-five…the timeline certainly fit.

Kassian released her and got to his feet. The tender lover of moments ago had left the building; a cold stranger had taken his place in the space of a heartbeat. Facing the fireplace, he braced his hands against the mantel, the massive sword undulating over his taut and twitching back muscles.

"How long have you known?" The words were bitten out.

"I guess from the moment he appeared in my living room. I never knew my father. After my mother died… I found a photo of the two of them in a locket in her nightstand. I could see the resemblance and knew it must be my father…but I had no idea who he was or how to find him. Since he'd left before I was born and never attempted to contact me, I figured he wouldn't welcome me looking for him anyway. I tried to forget about it…until I saw Luca. He looked so much like the picture of my father, I knew it couldn't be a coincidence. All my differences suddenly began to make sense."

"And you expect me to believe you had no idea what we were...what you were...or that Luca existed? You expect me to believe that your mother never told you any of this?" Kassian began in a low, controlled voice, then stopped and cleared his throat as if the words were stuck.

"What? Of course, I didn't know!"

He didn't turn, he couldn't answer. Had she used him to get to Luca? His lungs suddenly felt too tight to draw in air. He knew he was throwing off waves and waves of emotion. He made no attempt to block it. Her empathy had to be sensing it and at the moment he didn't care. Her easy acceptance of everything was suddenly so clear.

"Well, Nicola is dead so you can forget about a big, happy reunion with him and Lillian Brookes is a big part of the reason. Don't expect Luca to welcome you with open arms," he said harshly.

"My father was dead to me my whole life, and I never knew Luca existed, so I guess I'm really not missing anything, am I? Believe what you will, McAllister," she murmured in a voice thick with hurt and disbelief. "I almost convinced myself that there was something for me here, that maybe I belonged in your world in a way I'd never belonged in mine. I thought you were different. I guess it was pretty naïve of me. At least in my world, I never got sucker punched; experience taught me to expect nothing; I always knew where I stood."

He didn't move. He didn't speak. Kassian was exuding a chill that was palpable. Even the heat from the fire could not dispel the sudden drop in temperature.

****

Kat felt a sick jolt, as though someone had kicked her in the gut wearing steel-toed boots. Clearly, if Kassian McAllister had any feelings for her at all, trust wasn't among them. And without trust there didn't seem to be much point in anything else. She felt his emotions swirling about him and filling the space between them like a thick, dark cloud. She knew he could block them, so obviously he meant for her to feel them. He'd been in her mind, yet he clearly didn't know her at all.

She wrapped every ounce of dignity she could muster around herself like a suit of armor and rose stiffly to her feet. She walked into the bedroom and closed the door behind her with a quiet click. Quickly pulling on jeans and a sweater, she pushed her bare feet into her tennis shoes and stuffed her few belongings into her duffle. Then she grabbed her car keys from the dresser where Kassian had tossed them, and shoved them in her pocket. She didn't fit in here any more than she did anywhere else; she'd been kidding herself. Well, at least she'd learned exactly where she stood before it had gone any further. She'd been alone before and she could be alone again. Solitude was better than a brother who didn't want her and a man who didn't trust her. Being alone wasn't so bad if you didn't know any other alternative. And now that she did? Well, the hell with Kassian McAllister and his whole messed up world. She'd given him the benefit of the doubt and trusted him at every turn; and some of those turns had been real hairpins. In return he'd taken her heart and handed it back to her sliced and diced on a silver platter. She'd been fooling herself to think that she'd ever been anything more to him than an inopportune burden. And she probably didn't love him anyway; she'd only allowed herself to believe she felt something because he'd been so accepting of her abilities. At the moment, she didn't even like him. She took a last look around to make sure she hadn't forgotten anything, and opened the door.

Kassian remained exactly as she'd left him, his shoulders bunched tensely, his hands white knuckling the mantel. He didn't acknowledge her presence and if he read her distress, he gave no indication. She couldn't speak beyond the painful ache lodged in her throat. It didn't matter; there was nothing left to say.

She reached for the knob and wrenched open the door.

"Don't even think about it."

"Go to hell."

****

He turned finally, and winced at the sight of her pain bright eyes, feeling like he'd kicked a puppy. He knew that his knee jerk reaction was three hundred and sixty degrees from the truth; too bad his insecurity hadn't kept its opinion to itself until his common sense kicked in. From the moment he brought her home it had been all about him. He'd arrogantly decided what was best for her and whether or not he would keep her and never bothered to consider how she felt about anything. He'd selfishly and arbitrarily brought her into his life and his world and expected her to accept it while he never thought to learn anything about hers. There was no way she could have known about Luca. No one had known that Kassian would be at the party so she could hardly have planned the meeting; that aside, all he had to do was remember her reaction to Luca's appearance in her living room. She had been shocked senseless. Not even a professional could act that well. He'd thought at the time that her reaction was all about the *animorti*, but in hindsight he realized that had only been part of it. Hell, she hadn't known about anything until after she'd met him; he could see that now. When had he become such a complete ass? He swore softly and would have moved toward her if the coffee table hadn't chosen that moment to slide across the room and slam into his shins right below his knees, painfully and effectively halting his progress.

"Did I forget to mention I was telekinetic, too?" She didn't even try to keep the bitterness from her voice. "My bad...I guess I'm so used to weaving my complicated webs of deception that I can't keep them straight, huh?"

"Kat, I didn't mean it. I ..." He didn't have to be able to read her mind to know what she was thinking; the truth was written all over her face. He'd asked for her trust and she'd given it without hesitation. But he hadn't trusted her in return. He wanted to kick himself...except at the moment his shins throbbed like hell from the hit they'd taken.

"Yeah," she interrupted firmly. "Well, don't worry about me, McAllister, I'm used to people's misconceptions, and I've been dealing with them my whole life. Despite your cave man mentality, I'm not helpless and I don't need some misguided champion looking to assuage his conscience by protecting me from the big, bad wolf. I've managed to take care of myself all this time, and I'll continue to do precisely that. Consider yourself absolved of any responsibility for me. Good-bye, McAllister." She walked out the door and pulled it closed behind her.

The soft click of the door was eclipsed by the crash of the coffee table smashing against the wall and the painful sound of breaking glass. Kassian stood with fists clenched, breathing heavily, surveying the results of the mess he'd made. Smoked glass and twisted metal was everywhere; and Kat was gone.

"Feel better?" Alec lounged in the doorway of the guestroom surveying the mess, arms crossed over his broad chest and a shoulder propped against the frame.

"Not now, Alec," Kassian growled in warning. He needed to think, he didn't want to be distracted trading barbs with his brother.

"Really, Kass? Then when?" Alec levered himself away from the doorway and came to stand in front of his brother. "That girl is the best thing that ever happened to you...whatever you did, you need to fix it."

She *was* the best thing that had ever happened to him. He'd been fighting the knowledge since the moment he laid eyes on her. Having her here in his home only reinforced it. She was hurt and angry right now; but she would calm down soon, right? She would realize he didn't mean it. And then he would fix it. He didn't think he could return to the emotionless void in which he'd existed before she came. He'd never realized how truly empty he was until she came along and reminded him of what was missing. He'd only been going through the motions. As empty as he'd been before she came, he knew that it was nothing compared to the hollow shell that would remain if she left him.

His feelings for her were something he'd never expected, something he'd never wanted. He was beginning to believe she really might be his salvation and his destiny. But at the moment, she was out there on her own. He could stop her and force her back, but that wouldn't exactly help his cause at the moment. He knew she needed some time. Still, his priority was her safety; he could not contemplate any harm coming to her. Alec slugged down his coffee and volunteered to play babysitter. After all, he smirked, she wasn't pissed at him. He disappeared into the bedroom to throw on some clothes while Kassian grabbed his cell from the table and punched in Luca's number. If there was one bright spot in this whole situation, it was anticipating the look on Luca's face when he told him the news.

Chapter 9

Kat soon discovered that copious tears were not conducive to safe driving. Speaking of safety, her current watchdog, Alec McAllister, was about as subtle as a two by four across the forehead. The third time Kat pulled over to mop at her eyes, she almost found herself grinning despite her misery; damned if he didn't pop up right on the hood of her car and wave cheekily before disappearing again. He was making no attempt to conceal the fact that he was tagging along to keep an eye on her, and she was sure it had everything to do with wanting her to know exactly who had put him up to it. She hadn't spared a thought for her physical safety when she left McAllister's apartment; she'd been more concerned with protecting her heart and what little pride she had left. Maybe she had subconsciously counted on his ridiculous sense of duty. He didn't have to give a damn about her personally to feel an obligation to protect her; it was simply the way he was made.

Her day continued its downward spiral when she pulled into her driveway nearly an hour later and spied Luca sprawled on the porch swing with Sid contentedly snoozing on his lap. Fabulous! It hadn't taken McAllister long to put out the news alert via the *Earthbound* party line. She refused to even glance in his direction as she dragged her feet up the walk and reached for the loose board where her key was hidden.

"Door's open."

"Of course it is," she sighed tiredly. She finally risked a glance. His eyes never left her, and his placid expression gave nothing away. "C'mon, Sid." The cat picked his head up and gave her the once-over, yawned widely, and snuggled back down into Luca's lap.

"Traitor," she mumbled sadly, shuffling on into the house, closing the door firmly behind her. Maybe she would throw herself a great big pity party, table for one. She tossed her keys on the hall table, and then nearly jumped out of her skin when a subdued pop sounded in the living room. Neither Luca nor Sid had changed position, but they were now reclining on her sagging sofa instead of the peeling porch swing.

"Oh, sorry…where are my manners? Won't you please come in?" Her voice dripped with a sarcasm she made no attempt to conceal. She couldn't deal with him right now, not when she already felt so raw and exposed. Of course, he didn't look like he had any intention of leaving. She hesitated, then decided she might as well get all of the wretchedness out of the way at once; then both Kassian and Luca could go away to fight the bad guys and leave her alone to wallow. She'd been perfectly content with the life she'd made before either of them gate crashed her concept of reality; she'd be absolutely fine when they conveyed themselves back to whatever little black cloud they'd hijacked to get here. She stalked across the hall and fell heavily into the armchair with a resigned sigh. He continued to watch her, absently stroking the cat as the silence stretched uncomfortably between them.

"Well?" she demanded finally, unable to bear it any longer. "You obviously didn't come here to make nice with the cat. Say what you have to say and let's get this over with. I've really about reached the end of my rope for one day."

"I didn't know," he said in an odd, flat voice.

"What?"

"About you...I didn't know. My...our...father didn't know, either. When he came back...well, he thought Lilly's new husband was your father. He would never have left if he'd known."

"He came back? When?" She sat up a little straighter.

Luca shooed Sid from his lap, brushed the stray hairs from his crisp charcoal slacks, and stood, only to begin pacing aimlessly. He stopped in front of the mantel, examining the framed and matted record of the childhood he had missed. He lingered, examining each one in detail, and then finally paused to pick up a shot of Lilly holding an infant Kat in the air, both of them laughing as though sharing a secret joke, completely unaware of the camera. When he turned back to her, his eyes shimmered suspiciously and he had to forcefully clear his throat more than once before the words would come.

"First of all, you need to know that he loved your mother...he...well, he lost it when she ended things. He came back a little over a year later to try once more to change her mind, but she was already married to someone else, she had you, she'd moved out of the city. He thought she'd moved on...he didn't begrudge her happiness, but it killed him. Literally. He locked himself away from the world, away from me. I guess it never occurred to him that I'd lost first my own mother and then Lilly, too. And then he died. He willed himself to death. I blamed her. Deep down, I think a part of me even hated her. I'm sorry, I know she was your mother, but he was the only family I had." He shrugged, but it didn't have his usual insouciance. "Once he lost her, I guess I wasn't enough reason to stick around."

Kat could hardly reconcile the detached, impassive Luca that she'd known until now with this emotional man standing before her with tears in his eyes and a face lined with grief. Her mother had ended it? It seemed that every time she thought she'd found an answer, it turned out she'd only managed to find another question.

"He didn't know," she repeated in wonder. "It wasn't me…all this time….I thought it was me."

"Hell, why would you ever think that?"

"I thought he didn't want me…I thought that was why he left and never tried to find me." And now her father was dead. She hadn't been consciously looking for him, but if she was honest with herself somewhere deep down she'd always held out a tiny little spark of hope that someday he would show up. But he hadn't even known about her. He was dead; he would never come; she would never know him. She shook her head, her words caught between hiccoughs and sobs as she tried to maintain some degree of composure, but it was all too much. When the tears came, it felt as though they would never stop. She cried for every missed bedtime story, birthday party, and dance recital…for every time she'd felt abandoned, unwanted, and defective, for every time she blamed herself for the father who wasn't there. She cried because she miraculously had a brother and in the end, he'd ended up feeling as inadequate as she had. She cried because she missed her mother and felt betrayed at having never been told the truth. She cried for more reasons than she could fathom, giving in to pain and emotion that had remained corked tight and bottled up for years.

****

She was too distraught to block him. Her mind was wide open and Luca relived it all right along with her. He felt helpless, floundering in unfamiliar territory, unsure of his role, unsure of his reception. Finally, when he feared the depth of her grief might consume her, Luca strode across the room and pulled her out of the chair and into his arms. His own throat was aching with tears. His sister. He had a family. They'd both gotten the short end of the stick through no fault of their own. He'd spent so many years blaming Lilly; he'd never acknowledged that maybe his father was partly to blame. Nicola chose to make his grief and disappointment more important than his son, more important than his life. Luca had no idea how to comfort Kat, so he simply held her while the sobs wracked her small frame, stroking her bright hair, and she clung to him like an island in a stormy sea. Maybe in this place, in this moment, his arms were exactly what she needed. When the flood finally subsided to subdued sniffles, he pulled back slightly and peered down into her puffy face.

"Sorry, that was a little embarrassing." She sniffed with a small smile, dragging her forearm across her eyes in a futile effort to dry her face.

"Kat, none of it was anyone's fault…least of all yours. It was never yours."

"Would you have come, when my mom died…if you'd known about me?"

"Katrina Lucia Brookes Fiorelli …my beautiful, miraculous girl…I would have come long before then, if I'd known."

She pulled back with a gasp and regarded him with wide eyes as he thumbed a tear from her cheek.

"How did you know? I've always used Roger's surname."

He gestured to the pile of books and papers on the table near her laptop. Her work was no longer in the neat pile in which she'd left it.

"I'm not comfortable being at a disadvantage and I can travel a little faster than you do in that scrap heap you call a car. We are so getting you a new car."

"My car again? What is it about men and cars? Sheesh! And you were snooping!" she accused, her laugh catching on a hiccough.

"I was." He agreed with his typical shrug and not an ounce of remorse.

"I guess I probably would have done the same thing." She took the handkerchief he offered and mopped at her eyes. "Would you, um, like some coffee or something? It'll only take a minute."

"This is one of those times that I can truly appreciate the human predilection for a good stiff drink. However, since alcohol is neither beneficial nor detrimental to *Earthbound*s …in other words, it won't do a damn thing for me unless I consume enough to float a barge …coffee sounds good."

****

It didn't take any time at all to make the coffee, and when it was done, Kat poured them both a hefty mugful and sat at her kitchen table across from her brother…*her brother*…thoughtfully stirring a fourth spoonful of sugar into her coffee; so preoccupied that she forgot she'd been drinking it black for years.

"Luca, do you have any idea how surreal this all is to me? In a matter of days I discover an entire world I could never have imagined and a brother who looks like he should be posing for the cover of steamy romance novels. I know you've got me by a few…um, decades…but in five or ten years, I'll look older than you do." She absently took a sip of her coffee and gagged on the unexpected sweetness. Luca laughed at her expression and then looked thoughtful.

"Well, I wouldn't worry too much about the aging thing…you're *Earthbound*… you'll look pretty much the way you do now for at least the next couple of decades."

Kat choked again, completely unrelated to the coffee this time, and fixed him with an appalled gaze; how was she going to explain that to people, especially Elle? Although she had to admit there was something to be said for the apparent eternal youth thing. Guess she didn't have to worry about running out of moisturizer ever again.

"But I'm only half *Earthbound*."

"Still, it's a dominant gene. Then, of course, there's your mother. Witches tend to age more slowly than humans, as well."

"Witches?" Kat choked, wide eyed.

"You didn't know?" Luca looked as shocked as she felt.

"Strangely enough, it never came up. You know what?" She held up her palm in his direction and continued as he opened his mouth to elaborate. "Talk to the hand…I'm not sure my nerves are up to any more revelations today. You aren't the only one beginning to understand the predilection for a good stiff drink…any chance it would have the desired effect on me?"

"Not likely," he shrugged, but his lips twitched impishly.

"All these years of abstinence for nothing," she shook her head. "What a waste."

"Lilly really never told you?"

"She really never did. I knew that she was psychic, of course. But I have a sinking feeling you're going to enlighten me even further, aren't you?" Kat sighed in weary resignation. She pushed the undrinkable coffee away, folded her arms on the table, and dropped her forehead on them. She and her mother had been so close. How could Lilly have kept something this life altering from her? She felt as if she didn't know the truth about anything or anyone anymore. She wondered if a person could die from information overload. "Go ahead then…let me have it."

"Well, Lilly was from a long and powerful line of witches," he began slowly, leaning back in his chair and propping his Gucci loafers on the corner of the table. "She didn't practice the craft, but she was a strong empath, too. That's probably where you get it…no one in my family has ever had that particular talent. The only gifts I inherited were the typical *Earthbound* telepathy and a bad attitude," he laughed.

"Why wouldn't she have told me, Luca? And get your feet off of the table. Do you have any idea where your shoes have been? I have to eat there, you know."

"I don't really know and I wouldn't presume to answer for her, but maybe like you, she didn't relish being different. Miranda is another story…she's devoted her life to seeking power." His tone changed completely when he mentioned her cousin.

"Miranda?" she mumbled. If Kat had been asked to use one word to describe her taciturn cousin, it would have definitely rhymed with witch. Somehow, the fact that Miranda was a witch didn't surprise her nearly as much as learning that her mother was. "I can't believe Mom never told me."

He shrugged. "Maybe she would have, if she'd lived… I'm sure she thought she had more time. Doesn't everyone? By rights, she should have had several more centuries. Maybe she thought you had enough to contend with already and was waiting for the right time." She'd been too emotionally overwrought earlier to even attempt keeping him out of her head. Kat knew he'd seen her memories and understood what a struggle she'd had to learn to control her abilities and protect herself from the constant emotional battery.

"I'm surprised you didn't find something among her things that would have clued you in, or at least made you wonder."

"Well, to tell you the truth …I've only ever gotten as far as the things in her room. I finally moved in there a couple of years ago and I didn't find anything that screamed 'Hey, look at me, I'm a witch.' That's where I found the locket with the picture of my…our…father." But then Kat had a thought. The unusual symbols engraved on her locket. She'd always assumed they were some kind of antique Victorian design. She pulled a chain from the neck of her sweater revealing the heavy gold oval. "I've never been able to bring myself to start on the attic or the basement. It always seemed so overwhelming to tackle it alone.

Miranda was more than happy to offer her assistance," Kat's expression grew tense. "So much so that she took it upon herself to start without me when I told her not to; that was when I asked her to leave. But I do have this; Mom always wore it, and I found it in her nightstand after the accident. Do these symbols mean anything?"

Luca's gaze locked on the pendant. "It was my mother's," he said in a tight voice. "The symbols are *sigil*s, a sort of ancient angelic language. Those particular *sigil*s are a protection spell." His tone was grim, and she glanced at him with a worried look.

She started to pull the chain over her head. "I didn't know. If it was your mother's then you should have it." With a visible effort, he cleared his expression and forced a smile. He grabbed her hands and pulled them away from the chain.

"My mother has been dead a long time, so she doesn't need it. You, on the other hand, need all the protection you can get until we get Rapier. I think it's a good idea to leave it right where it is."

"Okay, I'll wear it if you want me to." It had always been a bit ornate for her taste, but it was her mother's, as well as his, and it seemed important to Luca that she wear it. "What about the numbers? Are they *sigil*s, too?"

Luca frowned in confusion. "What numbers?"

"The ones inside the locket under the picture. I took it out thinking maybe there was a name on the back…" She opened the locket and flipped the photo free with her thumb. Luca leaned in for a closer look at the series of numbers engraved into the inside of the locket.

"I have no idea what they mean. They weren't there when my mother had it. Either my father had them added at some point or your mother did." He shrugged and tucked the photo back inside, snapping the locket shut.

Kat sensed his hesitation as he continued. "Kat, maybe it's time to go through your mom's things… it's been years…in fact, maybe you should consider moving out of here altogether? I could give you a hand with the heavy stuff."

"Maybe…I don't know. I really love this house." This was her home, had always been her home, her refuge. She could still feel her mother here. Even though she was upset with her mother at the moment for the many secrets she'd kept she was reluctant to let that go. "You don't think I'm safe here anymore." It wasn't a question. Kat sighed, and pushed back her chair. She gathered up the empty coffee cups and rinsed them in the sink. How had her nice orderly life gotten so out of control in such a short period of time? She turned and leaned back against the counter and examined Luca from across the room.

"I'm not sure you ever were," he admitted reluctantly. "I can see what the place means to you, *cara*. But, I think maybe we were just damn lucky until now. You were off the radar until you met Mac."

"You look so much like him, you know, at least judging from the picture. Whenever I thought about what my father might be like, I guess I pictured someone more along the lines of Ward Cleaver or Mike Brady than Brad Pitt." Her lips twitched as she cocked her head to the side.

"I'm sorry if you're disappointed." He shrugged.

"I didn't say I was disappointed. I'm trying to figure out how I'm going to explain you to Elle." She laughed and he flashed an answering grin. "She'll want to put you on one of her book covers."

Luca visibly shivered and then joined in her laugh. "Kat...I'll admit this whole thing...you...is a shock.... I see so much of Lilly and Dad in you I can't believe I didn't spot it the moment I laid eyes on you. Then again, I guess I had no reason to be looking for it. I haven't had a family in a long time. I never expected I'd have one again. There will be times...a lot of times... I'm sure I won't always act like a brother. I'm not sure I'll ever really get the hang of it...but I'm willing to try if you'll have me."

If she'd have him? Was he kidding? He was so stuck with her, he had no idea!

"I can deal with that," she smiled, her eyes filling. "Look, if we're confessing our shortcomings here, I haven't exactly been the model sister either. I think I might actually have been a little...er...hostile toward you at first."

"Really? I hadn't noticed." He was unable to suppress a smirk at the blatant lie.

"Oh pul-eeze...admit it, I was a total bitch. Honestly, given the way I've been acting, I was surprised to find you here."

"You didn't think I'd come?" His brows rose nearly to his hairline.

"McAllister seemed to think you wouldn't want anything to do with me," she said in a small voice. Her life and everything she'd ever believed had been turned upside down in the last few days. Though she tried, she couldn't completely hide her lingering uncertainty, her need for reassurance.

Luca sighed. "I guess I can see how he might have thought that. And I'll admit, I'm kind of glad you took off and weren't there to see my initial reaction. But the bottom line is that family, to an *Earthbound*, is everything; at least that's usually the case. Mac knew what the situation between my father and Lilly did to me. It cost me what little family I had. I was…angry for a long time, and I blamed your mother. But, I finally realize that my father made his own decisions. He chose to let the loss control him, and ultimately, destroy him. I wasn't enough to hold him to this world. And," he smiled, "as it turns out, I do still have family, after all. There's no way in hell I would walk away from that. Katrina…I am not going anywhere, and if I do, from this moment on you will always know where to find me. I harbor no illusions that I'll ever be anyone's idea of a perfect brother, or anything close to it, but you can always count on me if you need me. I doubt we will ever have a typical or traditional relationship…we'll both have to work at this."

"Well, I'm willing if you are. It makes me sad that we've already missed so much. Luca, what happened between them? All Mom would ever say was that it didn't work out."

His expression became shadowed and he didn't answer right away. She felt his reluctance to revisit the painful episode. "They seemed happy enough. I thought everything was fine, and then one day, out of the blue she decided his life as a *Defensori* was too dangerous and she wanted out. She must have realized by then that she was carrying you, and maybe it was fear for your safety more than her own, I don't know. He would have done anything, given up anything for her. She should have known that. He wasn't...thrilled with her decision." His lips twisted in a rueful smile. "But, I think maybe now I can understand it a little better. Only took a quarter century...not so long in the greater scheme of things, but I'm usually a little quicker on the uptake."

"Ironic, isn't it, that I seem to have ended up right in the middle of the kind of situation she gave up so much to protect me from," Kat mused sadly. "Karma is a bitch."

"Karma is a bitch." He agreed. "Anyway...when she wouldn't see him, he went on a bit of a bender...and then he came back to tell her that he would give it up...leave the *Defensori*...he'd become a businessman or a shopkeeper, bartender, street sweeper; anything she wanted. There are a lot of ways to work against the *Fallen* that don't necessarily involve hand to hand combat. But he was too late."

"Did he mean it?"

"What?"

"That he would give it up? Do something less dangerous. Would you?"

His eyes widened in surprise and he drew a deep, contemplative breath and blew it out slowly. "Are you asking me to?" She felt it. He would do it. He would hate it, but he would give it up...for her; for no other reason than to make her happy, though he hardly knew her; yet. Because she was his family. He'd already accepted her completely. She flashed him a blinding, hundred-watt smile.

"No, I'm not asking. A warrior is who you are, Luca; I could never ask you to change. You might find a way to be content with it, but you would never be really happy. And eventually you would come to resent it...and me. I would never ask it of you...and I suspect that was exactly how my mom felt, too."

"You know, *carissima*..." His voice was suspiciously hoarse. "You're pretty smart for such a youngster. Maybe you're right. She couldn't live with the danger; and she knew he couldn't be happy without it."

"Well, it still isn't fair." Kat's heart was in her voice. "That they had to lose each other...that we had to lose each other."

"Most of life isn't fair, *cara*, but at least we have each other, beginning now....so tell me, what's your plan?" His eyes suddenly sparkled with mischievous anticipation.

"My plan?" She regarded him blankly, disoriented by the sudden change in topic.

"There's no way in hell Mac is about to give you up or leave you unprotected, so the way I see it, you can play this one of two ways. You can let me take you back to Mac's place, or you can come back with me to my place...which will make Mac very, uh, tense." He grinned fiendishly.

"Oh! Er, I hadn't really thought about it. I guess I figured I'd stay here."

"Not an option. It's too isolated, too hard to protect. But you should probably decide..."

Before he could finish there was a tremendous crash that shook the house and rattled the windows. Sid yowled and flew behind the stove for cover as a slow, satisfied smile spread over Luca's face. When it happened a second time, his grin stretched even wider.

Kat clapped her hands to her ears.

"What in the hell is that?"

Luca twitched back his cuff and consulted his watch.

"Mac always was a punctual sonofabitch."

"What on earth is he doing?" She didn't know what was worse, the rattling of the house or the pathetic caterwauling coming from behind the stove. She tried to coax Sid out, but he was having none of it, squeezing his bulk as far back into the darkened corner as he could.

"My guess is he's trying to fade into your living room." Luca smiled complacently. "My bad…I guess I forgot to mention I put up *sigils*."

Chapter 10

Kat ran to the front window and tore back the curtain. She felt the house shudder and groan again before Kassian appeared in a blue flash as he hit the ground several feet beyond the porch as though tossed there by some giant, hostile hand. Blood trickled from the corner of his mouth, his right eye was puffy and turning blue, and the look in his eyes was deadly. She spun to face her brother with a look of alarm.

"Luca, stop it! He's hurt!"

Luca strolled casually from the kitchen, flicked back the curtain, looked out, and smiled coldly. He turned to Kat and pushed up her sleeve, exposing the dark, purplish fingerprints around her wrist.

"So are you."

Kat's face softened, and she raised a hand to Luca's cheek.

"That was an accident. I startled him and he reacted on instinct; it wasn't deliberate. I appreciate the thought, Luca, but don't go all Rambo-Bro on me, okay?"

"I wasn't referring only to the bruise, Katrina," he replied tightly.

"What did he tell you?" She suddenly felt like a naughty schoolgirl caught playing hooky and her stomach did a nervous little flip.

Luca shrugged right on cue. "Enough."

The house rocked again and Sid streaked through the hall and up the stairs, presumably to hide under Kat's bed.

"Kat, you have to remember that Mac and I have been friends for almost six hundred years…we've had each other's backs for a long time. We tell each other… things. Old habits die hard."

"Did you say six hundred…" she whispered faintly. Dear Lord, she couldn't possibly have heard him right! "Well, I always wanted an older brother…guess I should have been a little more specific."

"McAllister, stop… you're cracking my plaster!"

"I am coming in, Kat, and we are going to talk even if I have to keep this up for the rest of the day."

"I really don't want to talk to you right now."

"I know you don't, baby, but I'm coming in anyway."

"I'm not your baby…can you please just park it on the porch and chill for a minute…I can't think…I need to think… give me…ten minutes?"

She risked a peek out the window and saw that Kassian had picked himself up and was hobbling stiffly toward the porch. He lowered himself gingerly into one of the rockers and propped his booted feet on the banister.

"Ten minutes, Kat…then I'm coming in."

Kat raked a trembling hand through her hair and twirled a lock frantically around her forefinger over and over while she paced the confines of the living room. Luca propped a shoulder against the mantel and crossed his arms over his chest, his eyes following her agitated movements silently.

"Okay, Luca...here's your big chance...how about some brotherly advice? What do I do?"

His brow went up. "Sorry, *dolcezza*...I am not getting in the middle of this."

She spun around to glare at him in disbelief.

"Not getting in the middle? What the hell do you call all this?" She waved her arms around wildly gesturing at the house.

"I call this teaching someone a lesson. Besides, he's spent the last hundred or so years focused solely on revenge; it does my heart good to see his attention fixated on something else for a change."

She released a long, deep breath, unaware that she had been holding it and collapsed onto the sofa. Okay, time for an alternate approach.

"You know him probably better than anyone, right?"

"Right."

"So, what do I do?"

"What do you want to do?"

"Do you always answer a question with a question? That isn't particularly helpful, you know. He doesn't trust me."

"He does trust you. He's an insecure ass sometimes...but he figures it out eventually."

"McAllister, insecure? Ha! You're a funny guy. He can be the most arrogant sonofabitch I've ever met! So, you're saying I should let him in?"

"Actually, the most arrogant sonofabitch you've ever met would be me, but I've been on my best behavior so you probably haven't noticed." He winked. "I'm saying you should do what makes you happy."

"Whose side are you on, anyway?" Her eyes

narrowed to slits. Although truthfully, how could she blame him? He and McAllister had been friends for…gulp…six hundred years whereas she and Luca had slightly less history, even if he was her brother.

****

Luca chuckled and came to sit beside her on the sofa. It was old and sagged in the middle so that when he sat down she slid right against him. He put an arm around her shoulders and felt his heart expand to bursting when she snuggled against him. Without hesitation, she accepted him completely. He closed his eyes briefly, and for the first time in a long time he allowed himself a moment of grief for the loss of what little family he'd had. Lilly should have trusted Nicola enough to stay the course, or at least to tell him the truth about Kat. But Kat's reasoning echoed in his head…and maybe she was right; maybe in the long run Nicola would have become resentful and they would have ended up destroying each other. He'd mourned the past for so long, but ultimately, nothing could change it. Now, by some grace, he'd been given a second chance of sorts. He hoped he could live up to it. And he found he could finally let go of the pain, most of it, anyway. He put his fingers under Kat's chin and looked into her eyes, her gaze so similar to his own that he marveled again that neither he nor Mac had suspected anything sooner.

"I told you, I'm not taking sides. I'm only telling you what I know…"

"It's just that you and McAllister have been bosom buddies for…" She swallowed hard. "…six hundred years, and you've known I'm your sister for, what? An hour and a half, tops?"

"An hour or a century…it's all the same, Katrina. You're my family. And I think, as a…big brother—" He was still struggling with the concept. "I'm supposed to believe there is no one good enough for you. But, if there was any man I thought was remotely good enough for you, it's Mac. I trust him with my life and I trust him with yours. And you're good for him, really good for him. You give him back something that he lost a long time ago. He may be too thick to appreciate it yet, but you are his miracle, kiddo. Yeah, he screwed up…and he'll probably screw up again. Hell, I know he'll screw up again. Even we angels aren't perfect, *cara*."

"He feels responsible for me," she mumbled and Luca could hardly miss the misery in her voice.

"Of course he does…he got you into this mess by bringing you home that night. And I should kick his ass for that alone. But, I might never have found you otherwise so I can't really beat him up too much about it. But you're wrong if you think this is Mac feeling responsible and nothing more. I've known him a long time, *cara*."

"Yeah, the six hundred years thing is still freaking me out a little, so could you refrain from mentioning it for a while?" Luca laughed and dropped a kiss on her head.

"Three minutes, Kat."

"Well, I hope he's not bucking for canonization," she grumbled. "He would definitely flunk the 'patience of a saint' requirement."

"You've got that right, sweetness," Luca laughed. "So, tell me…what do you want to do? You want to talk to him, I'm outta here…you don't want to talk to him, I guess we could watch a movie or play Monopoly or something and let him wear himself out."

"I guess I'll talk to him, though I don't like him very much at the moment. Otherwise he'll keep beating his stubborn head against the walls. He's already got a black eye, the idiot!"

"Oh, that isn't from trying to get in," Luca said mildly. The corners of his mouth looked as though they were fighting a smile.

"What do you mean?" she asked. The gaze she turned to Luca was filled with suspicion. Luca raised a brow and ultimately lost the battle against the smile, though it turned out to be more of a smirk than anything. "Luca, you didn't!"

"He'll get over it." He shrugged. "Probably. I can't say I'm sorry. Mac needed to get his head out of his ass and if I was the one who had to provide him with the crowbar to pry it free, so be it."

"You're as bad as he is!" she cried, but it turned into a laugh at his unruffled expression.

"Probably worse. Okay, *cara*, remember, my door is open if you would rather stay with me. As for lover boy out there, whenever you're ready, he can come in through the front door, which, by the way, was free and clear the entire time if he'd bothered to try the polite and civilized route." Luca smirked. "You know what, *cara*? It's true what they say; payback really is a satisfying bitch."

****

Kat tugged at Luca's sleeve as he began to rise from the sofa. "Oh! I have one more question before you go…"

"You have one minute, Kat."

"Don't get your boxers in a twist, McAllister, I'll be there in a sec."

"What makes you think I'm wearing any?"

She chose to ignore him; but she was hard pressed not to smile even though she was still totally pissed; he was completely incorrigible!

"What's the question?" Luca sat back down and patted Kat's thigh.

"Well, since I'm...you know, part *Earthbound*...can I snap, crackle, and pop like you do? It would sure save on time and gas money," she laughed nervously.

Luca's eyes widened. "Honey, you already did!"

"Time's up, baby...I'm coming in."

"Oh, for the love of Pete!" She jumped from the sofa and stomped to the door. She threw it open and glared daggers at the impatient warrior lounging in the doorway. "Get in here before you destroy the place. I don't have construction work factored into my budget this month."

"That shouldn't be an issue," Kassian smirked as he limped in and closed the door. "Didn't Luca provide you with a printout of his net worth? Maybe you'll let *him* buy you a car."

"Maybe I *will*," she scowled back. She spun on her heel and left him standing in the hall while she went back to where Luca waited in the parlor.

"Luca, what are you talking about? I'm pretty sure I would remember if I...what do you call it...faded...dematerialized."

Luca took a deep breath and placed a hand on either of her shoulders looking directly into her eyes.

"You do remember it, *cara*... I guess you didn't

realize what it was. The accident…it's how you got out of the car." He'd seen it in her mind earlier when she was so distressed.

Kat was stunned. She remembered the blinding blue light and then suddenly being at the side of the road. No one, including Kat, had ever understood how she'd survived at all, let alone without a scratch. She closed her eyes and swallowed hard.

"Luca…please tell me that I didn't save myself and leave my mother there to die."

"Ah, *cara*…you couldn't have saved her. You did it unconsciously; it must have been like some kind of defense mechanism…you had no control over it." He smiled faintly and pulled her into his arms for a quick hug.

"Well, boys and girls," he announced dramatically. "I'm outta here." He held Kat away from him. "I'll talk to you later…call me if you need me, huh? And remember what I said; my door is always open."

He brushed his lips awkwardly across her forehead. Now that the initial excess of pent-up emotion had subsided, the familiarity felt a little strange to both of them, especially with Kassian glaring at them from across the room. Kat noticed his eye looked remarkably better already, but there was still enough swelling to remind her that Luca cared enough to defend her to a man who had been like a brother to him for hundreds of years. While she had no desire to cause friction between them, she couldn't help the warmth already surrounding her heart and invading her soul toward this brother she was only beginning to know.

"Wait!" Kat impulsively crossed to the mantel and picked up the photo of her and her mother. She walked back to Luca and uncertainly held it out to him.

"Would you...like to have this?" She held her breath, unsure of how he would react.

"Are you sure?" Kat nodded and Luca reached for the photo with one hand, brushing the back of his fingers along her cheek with the other. He stared at the picture for a long moment, a muscle working in his jaw.

"Thank you, *cara*," he said simply and tucked it inside his jacket.

Luca moved to the door, whacking Kassian in the shoulder as he walked by.

"We good?"

"Yeah, we're good." Kassian punched him in the bicep. "Talk to you later."

"Don't screw this up," Luca said.

"Buh-bye, Luca."

Luca's laughter drifted in from the porch until it was cut off by a sharp crack leaving them alone. Kat drifted back over to the couch and sank down, leaving Kassian to remain standing in the doorway, or not. Now that the house had stopped shaking, Sid delicately picked his way across the room from the foot of the stairs and leapt to the back of the sofa near Kat, stretching out across the top as if he owned it.

"So...how did it go with you and Luca?" Kassian lowered himself stiffly into the armchair. The swelling in his eye was almost completely gone, and the blue black shine was already fading fast.

"Okay...good, I guess...a little strange for both of us, I think, but good."

"I'm glad."

"Are you?" She raised a brow.

"Of course I am...what kind of question is that?"

he groused irritably.

"An obvious one, I think, considering what you said earlier."

She felt the pulsating waves of his discomfort and regret. He was making no attempt to contain his emotions behind a shield. Clearly he wasn't used to apologizing and she suspected he hoped she would sense his remorse without his having to put it into words. She wasn't about to make it that easy for him. He'd cut her to the quick; she wanted the words.

"Yeah…" He sighed. "About that…I guess I'm a thoughtless ass sometimes."

"Oh, I think we've established that, McAllister."

"I'm sorry, Kat."

"I know."

"You *know*?" His brows shot up to his hairline.

"Of course, I know…I'm an empath, you idiot…I can feel that you're sorry."

"So you understand?" His face cleared and he straightened in the chair. "You understand why I…thought…what I thought? It was only for a second and it really wasn't about you, honey…it was about me."

Kat rolled her eyes. "Please tell me you did not just use the 'it's not you, it's me' line… it's older than you are, and that's saying something," she scoffed. "And no, I don't know how you *feel*. I can sense what you are *feeling*…and I know you are feeling sorry right at the moment. I want the words, McAllister…it isn't enough for me to know you're sorry …I want to know how you could even think such a thing in the first place. And I'm not about to let you off the hook even though I know you are sitting there hoping I'll save you the trouble. I want you to look me in the eyes and tell me."

****

Kassian continued to stare at her, his eyes wide. She was really going to make him do it? This could not end well. He had never been good at verbalizing his feelings and he was hundreds of years out of practice. Asking for forgiveness wasn't really in his repertoire.

"I could use my mad skills in mind control and wipe your memory, then plant a suggestion that I'm the best thing since sliced bread," he threatened with a mock frown.

"Ha! Well, if you think you're up to trying," she snorted. "Of course, Luca might think it's strange if I suddenly don't remember anything."

It had been an empty threat, of course. Kassian was really trying to buy himself a little time until he could work up the nerve to get the words out. But that was hardly the response he'd expected! In fact, it hadn't even occurred to him.

"Besides, McAllister," she added in a minutely friendlier tone, "you're an ass, not a bastard."

"Is that supposed to be a good thing?" he replied blankly.

"It could be worse."

"You aren't going to give me a break, are you?"

"Nope."

"But you are going to forgive me, right?

"Possibly…I'll reserve judgment until I hear the explanation."

"I'm not good at this, Kat…it'll probably come out all wrong and make things worse," he muttered miserably.

"You're the one who likes to live dangerously,

169

McAllister." Kat waved a hand in his direction. "Go for it."

He leaned forward, clasping his hands between his knees and bowing his head. He wasn't sure if he should be figuring out what to say or praying he lived through it. He'd left his hair loose and it fell around his face like raven's wings. He risked a glance through the dark strands. Nope. Didn't look like she was going to make this easy. Then again, why should she? When he finally managed to speak, he barely recognized his own voice.

"Ah hell, Kat I'm *really* no good at this..." he forked a hand through his hair and jumped to his feet, only to begin pacing in circles. "I've spent years feeling next to nothing. I had one goal; to make Rapier pay for my sister and all those other women. There was no room in my life for a woman, for a relationship, for anything. I vowed I would never put that on anyone. And then, at the party, there you were, beautiful, interesting, and not the least bit impressed by the legendary Kassian McAllister. You were like a sudden shaft of sunlight breaking through a dusty window that had been locked tight forever. I knew I should walk away and I didn't. When I took you out of there and brought you home I told myself I didn't have a choice, but I did. I put you in danger, and I appropriated your life, and I never gave you a choice. My only excuse is that for the first time in over a century, I felt something that wasn't ugly. You touched me in a way no one ever has, and I was selfish enough to want to feel that again. Something about you made me want to be a person I hardly remembered and forgot how to be. And you know what? I kind of missed being that guy. When I realized Luca was your brother, well, we both know he can protect you as well as I can. I thought that if you didn't need my protection you wouldn't need *me* anymore; you would have no reason to stay." He stopped directly in front of her and paused for breath. She met his gaze squarely and he dared to hope her eyes had softened. "And I wanted you to stay. More than that, I wanted you to *want* to stay. I know it was a stupid reaction, I know I hurt you…I wish I could take it back but I can't. I can't promise I won't ever hurt you again, but I can promise it won't be intentional. I'm a warrior, Kat. It's the only thing I know. I'm stubborn and maybe a little arrogant, and I like my own way. I know I sure as hell don't deserve you. I can't promise I'll always choose the safer path. And I don't have any right to expect you to accept that or any of this. But, I look at you and every other woman I've ever known fades into obscurity. You're the only one I can see, Kat, because you're the only one that matters."

Kassian thought it might have been the longest speech he'd ever made. He'd put his life on the line hundreds, maybe thousands of times, but he'd never put his heart so completely on the line. Battle had never caused this dry, sandy feeling in his mouth, this cold sweat, or this peculiar ache in the region of his heart. Yeah, Kassian decided he would take a good fight over this any day. At least in battle the outcome was relatively predictable. He knew Kat's empathy would sense some of his discomfort, but he wondered if she really appreciated how incredibly difficult those few sentences had been for him. He really *had* been hoping she might take pity on him and let him off the hook. But she hadn't. And he knew he would do it again; for her. She was worth it.

****

Kat watched his struggle in silence; considering every word, every inflection, every hesitation. Maybe she was a fool, but she'd already forgiven him before he ever opened his mouth. Yes, he'd hurt her, but she could feel that his regret was genuine. And he was right; now it wasn't a question of protection. Luca could protect her as easily.

Kassian didn't have to feel responsible for her anymore. He could have merely let her go. But he was here, uncomfortable as hell, but still trying to apologize. She felt the anxiety he experienced at humbling himself. She felt his uncertainty. It was a feeling she could relate to and she finally took pity on him and held out a hand. He pulled her to her feet and she moved right into his arms. She wrapped her arms around his waist and buried her face in his chest.

"McAllister," she mumbled into his shirtfront. "I should not forgive you this easily. You don't get a second chance, so don't ever do that to me again. You really are an ass."

"Oh, I think we've established that." She heard the smile in his voice and the relief. She tilted her head back to look at him.

"Has it ever occurred to you that the only one that's been holding you back from being happy...is you? You really never give yourself a break. And you were wrong about two things; one, you aren't bad at that at all. In fact, you are really very, very good."

"I'd prefer to not make a habit of it."

"Oh, I don't know," she announced airily. "I think I could get used to it."

"Don't bother," he warned, but the growl lost its

bite when he bent to plant a quick peck on her mouth. That wasn't satisfying enough for either of them and so he returned for a longer kiss. His mouth was firm and warm against hers; and it wasn't long before his even warmer tongue slipped between her parted lips and stroked deep and urgently. Her bones turned to rubber and those damn butterflies were back. The man certainly could kiss. He turned her slightly giving him a better angle, and it was a long time before either of them spoke again.

"And two?" He kissed the end of her nose.

"What?" She had completely lost her train of thought.

"You said I was wrong about two things." He reminded her with a chuckle.

"Oh…right! You said now that I had Luca I wouldn't need you anymore." She buried her fingers in his hair and pulled his face down to her to show him how much she, in fact, did.

"Luca thinks maybe I should consider selling the house." Kat wore a contented and slightly bemused expression when they finally came up for air.

"Did he say why?"

"He thinks I'm not safe here."

"Well, I have to agree with him, but you don't have to make any decisions right this minute."

She sighed and slipped from his embrace, backing up a step. "Kassian, actually I was thinking about staying with Luca for a while. It would give us a chance to get to know one another better, and it would leave you free to do what you need to do without worrying about me all the time." She saw every muscle in his body tense. Yeah, he didn't take that idea well, at all.

"I see." He forced through tight lips in a tone that clearly said he didn't see at all. She tried to remember if he'd always had that strange little tic in his cheek.

"Well, unless you think that's a problem? I mean with Alec at your place and everything, I thought…"

"Alec will be moving downstairs later today. I, uh, thought maybe you'd like your privacy."

"Oh, really," she drawled coyly. "So you were that confident I was coming back? Pretty sure of yourself, aren't you?"

"Not really. I just couldn't contemplate the alternative," he replied with simple honesty.

"And people think you're such a bad-ass." She stood on tiptoe and saucily planted a kiss on his chin.

"I am *so* bad-ass," he replied arrogantly.

"Save it for the *animorti*, McAllister, I know better. Let me get some work to take with me and then we can go."

"Work wasn't exactly what I had in mind."

"Mmm…yes, well, nonetheless, all play and no work means Katrina misses her deadline," she laughed.

Kat crossed to the table and dragged her pink paisley computer bag from under the chair. She stuffed her laptop and cables, a dog-eared thesaurus, and a set of earbuds into one side. She balanced the bag against the arm of the chair with her leg and tried to shove her no longer neat pile of notes into the other pocket, but half of them ended up on the floor. She dropped the bag on the chair and bent to shuffle everything back together.

Kassian wandered over and started to gather up the papers that had fallen.

"No…I've got it." She hurried to push the telltale

sheaf into her bag, but Kassian had managed to grab a few stragglers that had floated out into the middle of the floor. He glanced at them briefly. Then he stopped and leafed through them more slowly, his eyes widening and his lips twitching as comprehension dawned.

"Kat, honey…do you have any other little secrets you'd like to confess today?" he drawled slowly.

"Is there really any point? I assume you've already figured it out," she sighed resignedly.

"*You* are K.L. Brookes?"

She quirked a brow and shrugged.

"McAllister Publishing has been trying to sign her…you… for over a year!"'

"Um, yeah, that doesn't come as a big newsflash to me," she laughed.

"What do you have against McAllister? I know it was an extremely lucrative offer. I oversaw the contracts myself."

"Should I be flattered?" she teased. "Seriously, Kassian, Apple House Press has been very good to me. They gave me my first break and over the years my books have been very good sellers for them. As a small indie publisher, that's revenue that allows them to keep their head above water while providing opportunities for unique new voices that the big boys like McAllister aren't prepared to take a risk on."

"That contract would have allowed you to live quite comfortably, Kat."

"Maybe," she shrugged. "But, I do okay between my writing and my graphic design work; some things are more important than money."

He shook his head. "You never cease to amaze me. At least I know you aren't interested in me for my bankroll. That's a novel experience. Well, I'm determined that McAllister will get you under contract, so I guess we'll have to work on hammering out the sticking points."

Kat shook her head with a smile and finished stuffing her papers into her bag.

"Okay, do you have everything? Where's your duffle?"

"Yeah, I'm ready." She picked Sid up and rubbed her face against his neck. Sid batted playfully at her locket, tangling his paw in the chain, and tugging hard against her neck. "Hey," she laughed, working the chain free. "Let go, you stinker!" Kassian reached out with a look of blatant distaste to help her untangle the cat and set him back on the floor at her feet.

"What's this?" He turned the locket over in his fingers with a frown. "It has *sigil*s engraved on it."

"Apparently it does," Kat confirmed. "It was my mother's. Actually, Luca said it had been *his* mother's so Nicola must have given it to my mom. Luca said it carries protection and that I should wear it. We couldn't figure out what the numbers were, though."

"What numbers?"

Kat retrieved the locket from his grasp, opened it, and popped out the photo, revealing the engraved numbers beneath. Kassian leaned forward, his brows still drawn together.

"Maybe the combination to a safe? But that doesn't seem quite right, either."

"Really? How odd!"

"Is there a safe in the house?"

"Not that I know of," she shrugged, "but there could be one hidden away in the attic or the basement somewhere. I've never really gone through everything since Mom died."

"Well, once we take care of Rapier, Luca and I will help you."

"Whatever, there's no rush." Kat smiled tucking the locket back into her sweater. "I highly doubt Mom had millions socked away somewhere. C'mon, I think my duffle is still in the car."

"Oh, God," he groaned. "We have to take your car?"

"Unless you can give me a crash course in that snap, crackle, pop thing," she teased.

"Yeah, maybe I'll leave those lessons up to your *brother*."

Kassian contorted himself behind the wheel and turned the key while Kat worked her magic with the screwdriver. She spent the first ten minutes of the drive trying to convince him that given the choice between teaching her to fade and driving back, her car was the lesser of two evils. Judging by the constant grumbling under his breath occasionally punctuated by a vast array of colorful curses, she was fairly sure she hadn't won the argument.

****

Sid watched them through the glass with wide, unblinking amber eyes, waiting until the car had backed out of the drive and headed off toward the interstate. He jumped down from his seat in the bay window and the air around him began to shimmer as he hit the floor. His whiskers and claws retracted, his face and body began stretching, shifting, contorting, and growing, his fur dissolving. In seconds, a sinewy naked man lay stretched on the living room rug where the cat had been. He stretched languidly, joints popping and creaking free of their confinement, then jumped to his feet, pulled the curtains against prying eyes, and headed for the phone.

Chapter 11

On the way back to the penthouse, Kassian decided to make a quick stop at the shelter to determine whether Rapier's latest victim was connected to them in any way. Kat found that the place wasn't anything like she'd expected. The building was old and unexceptional; the mortar crumbling between the bricks in places, but once inside everything was bright, modern and cheerful. To the left of the long hallway off of the entry was a cozy sitting room and opposite that, a room containing long tables with computers and rows and rows of books. A bulletin board in the hall listed the dates and times of available classes ranging from GEDs to college level business courses, and everything in between. The House of Angels didn't merely provide a roof and a bed; it provided the tools for positive life changes. She was impressed with the concept and wondered how much of the actual operations had been Kassian's idea.

Just beyond the foyer was a tasteful reception area. The woman behind the desk had a huge mass of perfectly coiffed hair, in the most unnatural shade of red that Kat had ever seen. Violet reading glasses studded with rhinestones perched daringly on the end of her long, thin nose, which she'd buried in the pages of a thick romance novel. Kat was amused to see that it was one of Elle's. The woman didn't bother to look up as she turned the page; Kat assumed this was the "Estelle" that Dimitri had referred to the previous evening.

"I'm sorry, we're completely filled for tonight." She blindly reached for a sheet from neat pile and held it out. "Here is a list of alternate shelters that may have something available."

"Is Estelle in?" Kassian asked politely.

With an exaggerated sigh, the receptionist plunked the book face down being careful to keep her place, pushed the glasses up, and poised grotesquely long acrylic nails over the computer keyboard. She still hadn't looked up.

"Do you have an appointment?" She prompted icily, raising heavily charcoaled brows, which contrasted clownishly with the artificially bright hair.

"Oh, I think she'll see me, Vidalia," Kassian returned dryly.

That finally caught the woman's attention and she glanced up. Her gaze passed over Kat, dismissing her without a second thought, but her eyes flashed with definite interest as they came to rest on Kassian. She surreptitiously inched the hunky hero and buxom beauty locked in book cover lust under some papers until they could no longer be seen from the visitor's side of the desk, and then leaned forward providing Kat and Kassian with more than an eyeful of foundation-garment-assisted cleavage.

"Why, hello, Mr. McAllister," she purred in a low, husky voice, pouting comically in a spot on imitation of the heaving heroine on the book's cover. "We weren't expecting you. As I said, we are completely filled, but I'm sure we could find something for your little friend here." She favored him with an exaggerated wink that caused her lethally mascara-ed lashes to stick together. The resultant contortions to get her eye open completely negated any flirtatious effect.

"Don't get up, Vidalia," Kassian said. "I know the way."

"I think you have an admirer, McAllister," Kat said once they were out of earshot.

"It's a curse…sometimes I have to beat them off with a stick." He smirked.

"Oh, brother!" Kat rolled her eyes and pulled her hand free to dig in her purse.

"What are you looking for?"

"A pen…I wanted to add modesty to the list of your virtues."

Kassian burst out laughing and recaptured her hand. He planted a kiss on her knuckles that she felt all the way to her toes, and pulled her down the long hallway. He stopped in front of the last door on the left and rapped once before turning the knob and dragging her into the room behind him.

The tall brunette who stood from behind the desk when they entered could have walked straight out of every man's fantasy. Long and lean in a designer wrap dress that hugged her ample curves in all of the right places, her dark, almond shaped eyes lit up at the sight of Kassian and her generous lips curved in a welcoming smile that revealed a set of perfectly matched white teeth. Kat felt at a distinct disadvantage in the grubby jeans and sweater she'd thrown on earlier. Kassian released her hand as Estelle came around the desk to embrace him.

"Darling! We don't see you nearly often enough these days." Kat didn't miss the casual way the woman's lacquered nails brushed across Kassian's high, firm butt before she drew back from the embrace. It was an obvious and familiar gesture and it immediately set Kat's teeth on edge. The woman's curious gaze swept up and down Kat's smaller form then dismissed her as completely inconsequential. Kat felt the initial flash of jealousy followed closely by complete disinterest.

"What brings you here to our little neck of the woods, Kassian?"

Kat was gratified to feel the annoyance swirling around Kassian. At least she knew he wasn't any happier than she was about that less than subtle little sweep of Estelle's hand. Estelle wore her sensuality like she wore her clothes, bright, bold, and obvious. Sure, it was probably appealing to men, but Kat found it generally didn't go over really well with women. And it definitely wasn't going over really well with her. Not when it was directed at Kassian. Kassian reached back to pull her up beside him, cupping his hand possessively around the nape of her neck under her hair, his long fingers discreetly massaging the tight knots that had begun to form there.

"Estelle, I'd like you to meet Katrina Shephard...Kat, this is Estelle Townsend. She's the director of the shelter."

"Nice to meet you, Estelle," Kat bit out shortly.

"Oh, er...yes, nice to meet you too...Kitty, was it?" she returned her attention to Kassian. "My mistake, I'd rather thought that you were bringing her here for...oh, never mind...a misunderstanding." She unleashed the full effect of her smile. Kat knew it was for her benefit as much as McAllister's. She was willing to bet that

Estelle was just being Estelle. It had probably never bothered Kassian before, but the increased pressure of his fingers on her neck indicated that it might be bothering him now. Kat's smile was even bigger and brighter than Estelle's at the thought.

"Actually, her name is Kat. And she's with me," Kassian returned amicably enough but in a tone that left no doubt as to his meaning.

"I see," Estelle replied in a voice that was shade cooler. "So, what can I do for you, Kassian?"

"You've heard Rapier is in the area?"

Estelle's perfect face was not as perfect when it screwed up in a little moue of distaste.

"Of course; bad news travels fast."

"This last girl…any connections to us?"

"No, none. The one before her, though, the night of your party…that one was staying here, as you know. There was a younger brother, Brian. He's still here. Can't be more than seven or eight. He hasn't spoken a word since it happened. I'm not sure he even realizes his sister is gone. I've tried reading him, but his thoughts are so scattered and so chaotic I can't make any sense of them. We'll have to alert Children and Youth soon…we haven't been able to determine if there is any other family."

Kassian nodded stiffly; Kat knew it was one more tragedy that Rapier would have to answer for.

"McAllister…" Kat began hesitantly. She remembered exactly how it felt to be left suddenly and irrevocably alone, and she'd had a few years on this poor child. "Could I see him? Maybe I could help?"

"You?" Estelle spat out doubtfully then reddened and snapped her lips together. Kassian's glare could have melted glaciers. She quickly added in a friendlier tone. "Do you, uh, have experience with children?"

"Kat is an empath."

Estelle's cool gaze warmed with slightly more interest. "I see...how unusual. Well, at this point, anything is worth a try. No one here has been able to get through to him. Come this way."

They followed the authoritative tap of her Manolo Blahniks to the elevator. Kassian's soothing fingers never left Kat's neck. She concentrated on the hypnotic rotation of his fingertips and gripped her locket tightly, like a talisman. She felt hope in this place, but such an undercurrent of despair that she had difficulty tuning it out. They got off at the second floor and followed Estelle down the hallway, past bright, cheerful rooms set up with multiple twin beds, dormitory style. Each bed had a small trunk at the foot; some covered with colorful blankets and children's toys. At the end of the hall, Estelle stopped and gestured inside. A young boy sat alone on a bed near the window. He stared blankly into space and rocked slightly back and forth, humming quietly to himself. There were no blankets or toys piled on the trunk at the foot of his bed, and the bed linens were obviously those provided by the shelter. They observed him in silence for a few moments. He didn't acknowledge their arrival.

"Could he be autistic?" Kassian said in a low voice.

"That's the problem...we don't know. They'd only arrived that morning and no one really noticed him until afterwards. The sister gave very little information on the intake form, and now that she's gone..." Estelle shrugged.

Kat barely heard them. She was focused solely on the boy as she approached him cautiously. Fear and misery radiated from him in waves and Kat knew immediately that he wasn't autistic; his rocking and humming were his way of blocking out the world, the way she sometimes used music and poetry when she was feeling overwhelmed. When she was about a foot away, she squatted down to his eye level. Then she lowered herself slowly and cautiously to sit cross-legged beside the bed, being careful not to startle him.

"Hi Brian...my name is Kat." She fought to maintain a calm, neutral tone, as his anguish threatened to engulf her. He didn't look at her, but he stopped humming, though the rocking continued. "I wondered if maybe I could talk to you for a little while? I guess things have been kind of tough lately, huh? Some pretty scary stuff going on."

The boy's eyes flickered to her face, quickly, furtively, and then returned to the window. Well, at least she had his attention. She touched his mind, briefly, and got a private Technicolor show of horrors that no one should ever have to see, let alone a child. She blanched and swallowed hard, working to stay focused and not become overwhelmed by the pain. She hadn't been able to hide her reaction and she felt it when Kassian's mind touched and followed hers.

"Estelle, you didn't tell me he'd witnessed the murder," he whispered.

"We weren't sure," she replied quietly. "They went out together, but he returned alone. I guess he didn't know where else to go. We didn't know how much he'd seen or what he knew. That poor kid."

"Brian," Kat continued gently, tuning out their

whispered exchange. "I know you've seen some awful things. There are very bad people in the world, and sometimes they do terrible things, but there are a lot of good people too, and they want to help you. What happened to your sister was an awful thing, but she's safe now. No one can hurt her ever again. That's why she brought you here…so you would be safe and cared for. Miss Townsend and the other nice people here can make sure that nothing bad ever happens to you again. They can find you a place where you'll be safe and loved and no one can ever hurt you. Won't you let us help you, Brian? It's okay to be afraid and sad, but you're safe now. I promise you that you're safe."

The tears were pouring down Kat's pale face as she absorbed the young boy's agony. She held up a hand as she saw Kassian moving toward her from the corner of her eye. The boy had stopped rocking and now stared directly at Kat. She'd knew she'd gotten through to him as the empty look left his eyes and they overflowed with tears. He reached out to touch Kat's face with shaking hands.

"Lissy told me to stay here, but I didn't…and then the man came and I knew he was a bad man…and …and then she told me to run away…so I hid…and he hurt her…he hurt her and even when she stopped screaming he kept hurting her."

He gasped the words over deep gut-wrenching sobs and Kat wrapped her arms around herself and nearly doubled over from his pain. But as he finally got the words out, Kat simply opened her arms and he threw himself into them sobbing as though his heart would break. Through her own tears, Kat looked over his head toward the doorway. Estelle stood with a hand pressed to her mouth and a river of mascara running down her cheeks. Even Kassian's eyes were moist and his jaw clenched as tightly as she'd ever seen it. She held the little boy and rocked him in her arms for what seemed like hours until they both were spent, his breath coming in strangled hiccoughs, and then she motioned Estelle into the room and introduced her to Brian.

"Brian, Miss Townsend is in charge here, and she is going to make sure that you're safe and happy…and my friend, Mac, over there, he's going to make sure that the man who hurt your sister is punished. You don't have to be afraid anymore, do you understand?"

"What about…my dad? He'll find me…he'll make me go back," he said nervously. Kat looked at Estelle and Kassian, who both nodded shortly. They understood one another completely. Estelle would make sure that the father's rights were terminated one way or another. If not, Kassian would make sure that the father never got near this child again.

"He can't hurt you anymore either, Brian. It's over. None of it was your fault, do you hear me? None of it. Your sister made her own choice; you couldn't stop her and you couldn't save her. It wasn't your fault." As she said this, she looked over his head again at Kassian. Her words were as much for him as for the suffering little boy. She guided the child toward Estelle in her designer duds, who to her credit, did not shrink away and wrapped her arms around the shaking child.

Kassian crossed the room in two strides and swept Kat from the floor and into his arms. Her whole body trembled from the strain and exhaustion weighed her down to the point of near collapse. She wasn't sure her legs would hold her, but she felt like an idiot being held like a child while Estelle looked on with interest.

"Kassian, put me down, I'm fine."

"You're not fine."

"Okay, I'm not fine, but I feel like a fool so put me down. You can hold me up if it will make you feel like a hero."

Kassian smiled and lowered her feet to the floor. But he was right, she wasn't fine, at least not yet, and hero that he was he held her upright on her feet as she leaned against him with an arm wrapped around his waist.

"Why don't you take Miss Shephard back down to my office? There's coffee there, or some tea if you'd rather...and there's a fridge with cold drinks, too. And if I'm not mistaken, there might be a package of cookies hidden somewhere. Please help yourselves. You look like you could use something." The smile she gave Kat was far more genuine this time. "I'm going to talk with Brian for a few minutes and then I'll join you."

"Thank you, Estelle." Kat smiled tiredly. "And please call me Kat. I vastly prefer that to either Miss Shephard or Kitty." Estelle colored immediately, and Kat gave her a quick wink to let her know that there were no hard feelings. Anyone who could overlook a child rubbing tears and snot all over her five hundred dollar silk dress couldn't be all bad.

****

"C'mon, baby, drink this," Kassian coaxed gently, pouring hot tea heavily laced with sugar down her throat. Kat nearly gagged. Between the sickening sweetness and the scalding temperature, his attempts at playing nursemaid were painful.

"McAllister, I know you are trying to be helpful, but could you please stop before you kill me?" she laughed, sucking in cool air to soothe her burnt tongue. He fussed around her like an old maid and given his massive size and his usual macho-er-than-thou attitude, it was almost comical. He handed her a half a bag of peanut M&Ms that he'd found tucked behind the coffee filters in the small cabinet, remembering that she liked them, and plopped down beside her hauling her possessively against his side. She felt remarkably better, but Kat wasn't complaining about the close contact. Knowing what Rapier was capable of was bad enough, but it couldn't begin to compare to reliving the actual murder through Brian's eyes. So that was Rapier, Jack the Ripper, the Whitechapel murderer. She wished Brian's memories of Rapier were clearer; he'd naturally been more absorbed in his sister. It would have been nice to be able to put a face to her threat. The experience had shaken her deeply, leaving her feeling drained and vulnerable.

"You were amazing in there." He pressed his lips to her temple.

"Kassian, isn't there anything you can do for him? Erase his memory or something? I remember Dimitri saying something about erasing a girl's memory before bringing her to Estelle. Ordinarily I'd never condone such a thing, but I'm not sure that this child will ever heal with the trauma he's carrying around in his head."

He shook his head slowly. "Not completely, too much time has passed. I may be able to soften the worst of it, though."

"Then do it...do whatever you can. No child

should have to live with that if we can help it," Kat responded wearily. "You know, I think that this might be the first time that I actually felt like what I can do might be a gift instead of a curse. Up until now it never seemed like it was good for much of anything beyond causing me misery." She shook the last few candies into her mouth and crunched contentedly. "I guess I owe Estelle a bag of these."

"Maybe you'd consider it payment in full?" Estelle breezed in with a smile. "It's the least I can do."

"Fair enough," Kat smiled back.

"You wouldn't be interested in volunteering down here once in a while, would you? We get some really tough cases, especially the kids. I think they would benefit from your...er, talents," Estelle smiled hopefully.

"Not a chance in hell, Estelle," Kassian answered for her before she was able to formulate a response.

"Um, hey look at me, over here." Kat waved a hand in the air. "Last time I checked, I can still speak for myself."

Kassian's brows drew together in a dark frown.

"We'll talk about it later," he pronounced.

"There isn't anything to talk about," she returned. "I'll give you a call, Estelle, and we'll set something up?"

Estelle's eyes didn't leave Kassian's face. His expression said he wouldn't be happy if she took Kat up on the offer.

"That would be fine. But, please don't feel obligated if you change your mind. I'll understand completely."

"We should get going. Galen or Dimitri will be

outside during the night if there are any problems, and you know how to get hold of me." Kassian pulled Kat to her feet and kept an arm securely around her shoulders. Estelle rose, as well, and moved around the desk offering Kat her hand.

Kat took Estelle's manicured fingers in her own. "Seriously, call me. I'd really like to help." Estelle simply smiled and looked to Kassian who shook his head. Kat elbowed him and frowned.

"We'll discuss it later," he said to Kat.

"There's nothing to discuss, McAllister." Kat smiled tightly. "I'm perfectly capable of making my own decisions."

****

Kassian forked a hand through his hair in frustration. She must have missed the part in his little speech earlier about his being stubborn, arrogant, and liking his own way. He would never let her risk herself like that again. He was glad she'd been able to help the child, but he was not about to let her put herself through that on a regular basis for anyone. It had taken everything he had to stand back and let her do it this one time. He knew what it cost her to open herself up and absorb all of those negative emotions. He had been so tempted to put her out to spare her the pain as he had at the party. She was lucky that she had him to take care of her. She didn't even realize how draining it had been for her.

Kassian had always assumed that if he ever found a woman to share his life, she would be obedient and biddable; well, at least that's what he thought when he bothered to think of it at all. It hadn't been his priority in more years than he cared to remember. He spared a fond thought for his empty but fairly mundane former life, pre-Kat, where he was in charge and there were few surprises. Maybe boredom hadn't been such a bad thing, after all. Battle, anger, remorse, there was a predictable flow and consistency; he knew precisely what to expect every day. Maybe he was too old for this.

Kassian turned to look at her. She could barely stand on her own at the moment and she was hell-bent on doing it again no matter what he said. She sure as hell wasn't obedient and biddable. He wanted her so much he felt like a ticking time bomb with a faulty detonator. But at the moment she looked so small, lost, and tired; she looked so damned tired. Connecting with the boy had drained her; yet she stayed upright by sheer will and volunteered to come back for more. He gave himself a mental kick in the ass. If he was feeling blindsided by all of the recent changes in his life, what about Kat? Given the things she'd seen and learned over the past few days, most women would have run away screaming; but he'd known from the moment he met her that she wasn't most women. She absorbed everything she learned, processed it, and then sat there gazing at him with those amazing silver eyes, trusting him. She believed in him when he wasn't sure he believed in himself. He wanted to be what she needed. He pulled her against him, pressing his lips to her hair. He'd forgotten that he could actually be sensitive, yet another surprise. He could tell himself that he was in charge, but he would move heaven and earth to make her happy. He was going to have to learn how to compromise. That should be interesting.

"Well, I think you've done enough for today,

anyway," he allowed noncommittally. "Estelle, you know how to find me if you need me." He leaned forward and kissed her on the cheek, then turned and led Kat out of the building.

The drive back to the apartment was conducted mostly in silence, each of them lost in their own thoughts. They pulled into the underground parking garage and he clicked off the ignition, turning to look at her.

"You okay?" he asked gently, resting a hand on her jean clad thigh. He swore he could feel the heat from her skin through the worn denim, burning his palm like a brand.

Yeah," she smiled back, "just incredibly tired."

Kassian climbed out of the car and came around to open her door and pull her to her feet. He grabbed her duffle from the back and tucked her into his side, leading her toward the elevator.

"You're awfully quiet," he whispered into her hair.

"I'm thinking." She smiled up at him. He didn't doubt that for a minute. He wondered if anyone had ever had to process as much unexpected and bizarre information in such a short time in the history of the world.

"About?"

"Right now, I'm thinking those M&Ms didn't really do it for me, and you haven't eaten all day either…pizza?"

"Sounds good to me, but I thought you could cook?" he teased.

"I can cook when there's something to cook." She groused. "Your kitchen is like Old Mother Hubbard's cupboard. Even scrounging up that omelet was a challenge."

"Yeah, I guess you're right…we'll make a list later and I'll send someone shopping."

"You send someone to do your grocery shopping? That is just wrong on so many levels, McAllister," she laughed. "What about specials, sales, impulse buying? You don't know what you're missing!"

"Hmmm…well, I do, actually. Been there, done that…and you're forgetting senior citizens, coupon clippers, long lines, and whining kids…nope, sending an assistant." He poked a finger at himself. "Billionaire, remember?"

She shook her head. "You're a spoiled brat! I'll help you make a list, but you and I are going shopping, so prepare yourself."

"I think I'd rather take on a hundred *animorti* singlehandedly," he shuddered with a grin as the elevator opened on the top floor outside the apartment door.

"Yeah, well don't let it worry you, McAllister, you may be the warrior in this scenario, but I have a few talents of my own. I'll protect you from the big, bad grannies and their nasty shopping carts when the time comes," she laughed. "For now, go order the pizza."

Chapter 12

Kassian punched in the number for the pizza delivery while Kat took her duffle and dropped it, along with her computer bag, inside the bedroom door. Alec arrived before the pizza did and practically beamed when he saw she was back. Kassian called back and ordered a second pie and a couple of dozen wings when it turned out Luca wasn't far behind. He greeted Kat with an affectionate hug. They made short work of the food, the three men nursing beers, while Kat settled for the tail end of a bottle of cranberry juice she found in the fridge.

"I thought alcohol didn't affect *Earthbound*s," she remarked to no one in particular.

"It doesn't; but who doesn't enjoy the taste of a cold beer with their pizza?" Alec laughed.

"Me." She clinked her glass against his bottle with a smile.

Kassian offered no response other than to haul her across his lap and wrap his arms around her. She snuggled against him, stifling a yawn. She was reasonably sure she had never had such a long day in her life, and it was catching up with her despite her best efforts. She felt like she could fall asleep and spend the rest of the night exactly where she was. Kassian pressed his lips to her hair.

"Can I assume that you've given up on the idea of

using Kat as bait to draw Rapier out?" Luca drawled. Kat's eyes snapped open.

Kassian's face darkened dangerously. "That was never a serious consideration, Luca, and you know it," he muttered quietly.

"Bait? You planned to use me as bait?"

"Not exactly," Kassian replied uncomfortably with an evil look at Luca whose smirk had become more pronounced. "The morning after I brought you home, Luca and I vaguely discussed that Rapier was unlikely to go back into hiding as long as he thought I had something to lose."

Kat struggled to a sitting position and pushed her heavy mass of hair out of her eyes. "Really?" she replied slowly looking from one to the other. "You know, McAllister, the idea might have some merit. I mean, I know that you wouldn't let him actually get his hands on me, and maybe it would help to get this thing over and done with once and for all."

"No," replied all three men in one emphatic voice.

Kat shrugged and slumped back against Kassian with an enormous yawn. "Only trying to help."

"I was busting his balls, Kat. Putting you in danger won't help anyone," Luca said firmly. "It's not even a consideration...end of story."

"Go to sleep, Kat."

"It would be incredibly rude of me."

"No one will mind if you go to sleep, Kat," he said aloud. "You're exhausted and the boys were just leaving. Weren't you boys? I'll catch up with you later."

"And Mom always said you were the subtle one," Alec laughed. "Kass, why don't you take a night off?

Luca and I can head out and sniff around to see if we come up with anything. We'll call you if anything goes down."

"I don't know, I think I should go with you," Kassian began slowly. Kat snuggled closer. "Yeah, okay…thanks. But make sure you call if anything looks promising."

"Agreed," Luca said. "C'mon, Alec, we aren't going to accomplish anything sitting around here eating pizza and nursing our beer guts."

Kat was too tired to stir, but she sent a quiet laugh across the common pathway to all three of them; if there was anyone on the planet less in danger of acquiring beer guts it was them. She had never been in the company of three more perfect specimens of masculinity in her life.

"Night, Luca."

"*Notte,* Katrina. Mac, unless we come up with anything, I'll talk to you tomorrow. Alec can crash at my place tonight."

"Only if you put *sigil*s up, my brother," Kassian warned. "You may not give a damn about your own ass, but you will protect Alec's."

"Whatever," Luca agreed. But Kat hadn't missed the exchange.

"Wait a minute…" she murmured, struggling to sit up. "Do you mean that you don't protect yourself at home? Are you trying to get yourself killed when something snap, crackle, pops in on you while you're sleeping? After all of the lectures I've had to endure about my safety, I think a little self-preservation should be in order on your end, too!"

Her voice was getting louder and more agitated by

the minute.

"I think all in all I've done a pretty good job of dealing with all of this and staying relatively calm, but I swear to God if something happens to one of you, I won't be calm, and if something happens because of arrogance or stupidity, I won't only be upset, I will be totally pissed, so be forewarned. Luca, you will put those *sigil*s up and keep them up whether Alec is there or not, do you understand me?"

Luca didn't meet her eyes; he was busy staring at her hands.

"Luca, are you hearing me?" she demanded hotly. Golden sparks were spewing from Kat's fingertips like sparkers on a birthday cake.

"Sure, *cara*, the *sigil*s…whatever you want, kiddo," he replied mildly. "Kat, can you take a deep breath before you set the sofa on fire?"

"Damn!" As tired as she was, she hopped up quickly, her eyes roving worriedly over Kassian to make sure that he hadn't gotten burned.

"Apparently, her ability to manifest her powers is tied to her emotions," Luca observed dryly.

"Gee, ya think, Captain Obvious?" Kat groused sarcastically. "What's the big deal anyway? You all do that blue light special thing, right?" She felt like a bug under a microscope the way they were all looking at her. She self-consciously shoved her hands into the pockets of her jeans.

"True," Luca shrugged. "But ours is controlled. Then again, we've been doing it longer. We'll work on it."

Luca dropped a kiss on her head and gave her an affectionate squeeze, admonished her to get some rest, then he and Alec left while Kassian busied himself clearing up the remnants of the impromptu pizza party. Kat dragged herself into the bedroom to change.

Kassian had stretched out on the sofa and was clicking through the channels when Kat came back into the living room. He shifted over to make room for her. As exhausted as she was, she still felt a bit too restless and distracted to get comfortable.

"I was thinking maybe I'd soak in the tub for a while to relax. Do you mind?"

Kassian's brows went up. "Sure, baby, whatever you want. Are you okay?"

"Yeah, I'm fine, maybe a little antsy, I guess. It's been a long day." She offered him a small half smile.

****

Kassian felt a twinge of guilt when he decided to stay home rather than go out hunting with Luca and Alec. But when he compared the thrill of the hunt with the warm weight of Kat dozing against his side, he realized that for the first time in as long as he could remember, something seemed more important to him than personally being the one to kill Rapier. Luca and Alec were perfectly capable. But now, looking at Kat, the guilt he felt earlier was minuscule in comparison. There were dark smudges under her clear, gray eyes, and a slight tremor in her hands. He'd been contemplating seduction. She was dead on her feet. Dealing with the boy had wiped out what little she'd had left after dealing with everything else she'd been handed today. He knew she fully intended to volunteer at the shelter. He thought it might be better to wait until another time to tell her that he was never letting her do that again. She didn't realize how fragile she really was.

It was a good thing she had him to remind her.

Kassian unfolded his long frame from the couch and strode toward the bedroom, scooping her off of her feet as he went by. He set her down on the bed and continued on into the bathroom. He turned the faucet on full blast and cranked up the heat. When the water reached the level of the jets, he turned those on and then rummaged around in the cabinet beneath the sink until he located an extra bottle of shower gel. Women liked that stuff, right? He shook a generous portion into the tub, where it immediately began to fizz and foam. He hit a couple of buttons on the wall and the soothing sounds of Mozart wafted through the steamy space. With a wave of his hand, the scented candles in the wall sconces burst into flame. He stacked a bath sheet and a pile of thick, soft towels on the side of the tub. Satisfied, he returned to the bedroom where he found Kat curled in a ball on the bed, already sound asleep. A soothing warmth uncurled deep within his very bone marrow at the realization that she actually wanted to be here, with him, even knowing who and what he was. He'd never expected to find peace, aside from finally making Rapier pay. He sure hadn't expected to find it in a silver eyed nymph of a woman. She made him want things he hadn't allowed himself to want in more years than he could count. Her poetry had resonated deep within his soul before he'd ever known her, and now that he did, he felt a vague stirring of anger at everyone and anyone who had ever caused her to feel that she deserved less than everything. She shifted in her sleep and something sharp and profound twisted in his gut. He wanted nothing more than to curl himself around her and hold her against him for the rest of the night...or forever. But that was him being a selfish bastard, again. He sat carefully on the side of the bed and gently stroked her hair away from her face. Merely looking at her gave him a feeling of peace he hadn't known in generations, if ever. He bent to press his lips to the tender spot where her neck met her shoulder and she stirred awake. Her heavy lashes lifted slowly, and he was nearly undone by the look of unconscious invitation in her eyes as they met his.

"I ran you a bath if you're still up for it?" He smiled gently, taking her hand and pulling her into a sitting position. She let out a sexy little moan and stretched like a contented kitten. Kassian's nostrils flared and he felt his body's immediate response. Okay, down boy, that was not what she needed right now! He pulled her to her feet and then grabbed his thick terry robe from the closet before pushing her before him into the bathroom. Because he always took showers he'd misjudged how quickly the tub would fill. A few minutes longer and the water would have been pouring over the sides. As it was, he was afraid Kat might disappear under the mound of foam once she got in. He dropped the robe next to the towels and quickly switched off the jets with a muffled curse, swiping ineffectually at the fluffy, white clouds of fragrant bubbles clinging to his chest. Kat bit her lip and giggled.

"Guess maybe I used too much of that stuff," he muttered.

"Well, I'm not sure it was meant to be used in a Jacuzzi," she smiled. "Kassian McAllister, this is quite possibly the sweetest thing anyone has ever done for me."

Kassian felt the heat rise into his face. Sweet was not a description that he was used to hearing in reference to himself. If Luca could see him now he'd never live it down. Big tough guy, yeah right! Well, maybe in the boardroom or in a fight, but apparently not here with Kat. Then again, here with Kat, maybe he didn't need to be.

"Well, I'll get lost so you can relax. Be careful not to fall asleep in here...I probably wouldn't be able to find you in all...this." He waved his arms vaguely toward the marshmallow-y mounds of white froth.

"You're probably right," she agreed and stood on tip toe to plant a kiss on his jaw, brushing away a clump of bubbles from his cheek. "Thank you."

"You're welcome...yell if you need anything." Kassian closed the door with a soft click and went back into the bedroom. He stripped out of his damp shirt and tossed it over the chair. He stretched out on the bed and hit the remote that raised the flat screen from behind the chest of drawers. Keeping the volume muted, he flicked mindlessly through the channels wanting to be nearby in case Kat called out.

****

Kat slowly pulled off her clothes and dropped them in a heap in front of the vanity. She twisted her hair into a towel on top of her head and slipped into the hot water with a contented sigh, rolling another towel behind her neck. Her heart was so full she thought it might burst. A big, sword-packing, evil-slaying, angel warrior had run her a bubble bath, complete with soft music and candlelight. She'd always been an independent girl who took care of herself, by necessity if not by choice. Maybe being pampered really *was* all it was cracked up to be, at least once in a while, especially by Kassian McAllister. Intellectually, she knew there was a side of him that was cold, calculating, and lethal; that was who he needed to be to function as a *Defensori*. But the side he shared with her, the one that touched her, was selfless, thoughtful, and gentle. She hadn't felt this safe and cared for in a long time.

Damn, what a day! She'd found out more about herself in the last twenty-four hours than she had in the last twenty-four years. She wasn't exactly sure how she felt about some of it yet, but helping the child at the center had been incredibly rewarding, at least. Maybe her abilities didn't have to be such a curse, after all. She'd prayed her entire life that one day she would simply wake up normal. In this world, she was normal. She indulged in a jaw-cracking yawn and slid further down in the hot, soothing water until it reached her chin. She couldn't remember the last time a bath had felt this good. She closed her eyes and sighed.

"Kat, wake up!" The command entered her mind with the sharp crack of a bullet and her eyes flew open. They immediately began to tear and burn from the soap suds covering her face. Kassian burst into the bathroom, right as she emerged from the mountain of bubbles, covered with foam, sputtering and swiping at her eyes. Her hair had tumbled from the towel and fell loosely around her shoulders, skimming the tops of her breasts where they disappeared into the suds. Feeling the blood rush into her cheeks, she glanced in his direction, very, very ill at ease to find him standing in the doorway. She probably looked like a drowned rat.

"Thanks for waking me up," she mumbled, eyes down, face flaming. "I think I'd better get out now."

Kassian leaned forward and picked up the enormous bath sheet and held it open for her.

"Well, c'mon." He laughed at the expression on her face as her eyes flew to his in embarrassed alarm. "I promise I won't look…much. I don't want you to slip…that bubble stuff is all over the floor and the marble is really slick." He dutifully tipped his head back toward the ceiling and closed his eyes. Kat eyed him warily, and then slowly climbed out of the water, stepping carefully. She backed into the towel and reached out to pull it around herself, but Kassian folded it around her first, and he kept his arms wrapped around her snugly, before she had a chance to protest. He buried his face in the curve of her neck and she felt his chest expand against her back as he breathed her in. Kat relaxed against him, bringing their bodies into full length contact with nothing but her towel and his jeans between them. She could feel the hard evidence of his desire pressed insistently against her buttocks. She turned her head and rubbed her cheek against the warm silk of his chest in a silent gesture of longing. Barely aware of it for what it was, she reacted purely on instinct.

"You are so tired, baby. You should get dried off and get some rest." He mumbled against her neck.

He turned her in his arms. Her eyes darted to his straining jeans and returned quickly to his face. She might be inexperienced, but she'd been around enough to recognize a man's desire when it stood at attention and saluted. Her eyes dropped to his chest, but that didn't help much, as he had bright drops of water glistening there and she felt a peculiar desire to lean forward and catch them on her tongue. She settled for tracing the path of one with her finger and felt more than heard his indrawn breath.

"I, um…well, I know I don't have much experience," she whispered so quietly that he had to lean forward to hear her. "But do you think maybe I could learn to, um, please you?" Good Lord, had she really said that? Maybe she could give classes in seduction. What hot-blooded male wouldn't want a piece of that? Well, she'd gone ahead and put it out there and there was no taking it back. She waited for his reaction with a mixture of embarrassment and anticipation. If he rejected her now, she would never be able to face him again.

****

Kassian took a half step back and stared down at the vision in his arms. The minute he'd turned her toward him he understood his mistake as the sight of her wet, warm, and wide-eyed, wearing nothing but a towel, had a violent effect on his control. He rubbed his big hands briskly up and down her arms, pulling away slightly. He took a deep breath in an attempt to curb his lust. She'd already been through hell today. His gaze moved over her body slowly, hotly, committing every inch of her to memory. She was glorious, and innocent, and so very, sweetly, vulnerable. And she was deadly serious. So much so that he weighed his response carefully, knowing that one wrong word, one wrong move could hurt her terribly.

"Katrina, look at me," he ordered quietly. She raised her eyes to his as he struggled to keep a straight face.

"Oh, God, please don't laugh..." she began, tightening her fingers on the towel in a death grip and trying to step back.

"Sweetheart, I am about as far from laughing at you as I have ever been." He pulled her back against him. "Everything you do pleases me, honey, it's only that I expected to be the one doing the seducing. You've had a hell of a day and you're tired. I was trying to be considerate. Trust me, it's a stretch. I'm a little out of practice."

"You were planning to seduce me?" she asked uncertainly.

"Oh, I most definitely was," he assured her. His gaze moved over her towel clad body with slow, deliberate heat, his eyes devouring every inch of her. She was so damned enticing.

"Oh," she replied breathlessly.

He felt her trembling and saw the uncertainty on her expressive face. How could he explain it to her? He could barely understand it himself. He wanted to wrap her in his arms and hold her with everything he had, everything he ever was or ever would be. He wanted to shelter and protect her so that nothing could ever touch her.

"Just breathe, honey," he whispered as he lowered his head and slowly rubbed his lips on hers, one hand cupping the back of her neck, and the other sliding to rest possessively on her rounded buttocks and pull her more closely against him. Kassian's lips and tongue burned a feathery trail along her throat and shoulders that were still damp with heat and steam. He lifted her easily, the towel somehow falling away, and he let his mouth roam freely as he slowly moved them out of the bathroom and toward the bed. He felt Kat's fingers on him, as soft as raindrops as she did her own exploring, learning the feel of him, becoming bolder when she felt his breath hitch and his desire spike at her slightest touch. Moonlight spilled across the black satin sheets and the lights of the city twinkled beyond the window glass like garlands of Christmas lights in the night, but he was blind to everything but her.

****

Kat felt the smooth, cool caress of the satin against her heated skin as Kassian tucked her beneath him in one smooth movement before again reclaiming her mouth. She opened her lips to his sweet invasion, tangling her tongue with his, memorizing his taste. Pressing against him, she felt her taut nipples graze his smooth chest, the feeling so exquisite it was nearly pain. He pulled away for a moment and when he returned to her there was no longer anything between them. He lavished his attention on her sweetly curved breasts, teasing and taunting, feathering light kisses on first one and then the other, before finally taking a nipple into his mouth and suckling the tender peak with an ardor and expertise that Kat felt all the way to her toes. He licked and kissed and suckled nearly every inch of her until she felt as though she might go up in flames. His long hair brushed against her skin as his lips moved over her and that, too, felt incredibly erotic. The hard, muscular length of him was pressed tightly against her belly and she moved her legs restlessly along the outside of his long, hard thighs where they rested between hers. Fully concentrated on Kassian and the glorious, unfamiliar sensations, there were no distractions, no thought in her mind but the delicious pleasure that was building until the urgency became nearly overwhelming. She could hardly breathe with wanting him. Her common sense tried to intrude, but she knew that her heart was already lost. Kat was done thinking, done worrying; for now she was giving herself up to what her heart and body wanted. If there were consequences, she'd worry about them later. Even so, when Kassian slid a hand between their sweat slick bodies toward the moist heart of her she tensed automatically.

"Kat, open up," he commanded softly. "What am I feeling right now?"

She lifted her gaze to his and opened herself fully to his emotions. It was then that she felt it, raw, primal desire, but something more, so much more she was nearly swamped by the strength of his feelings. Her breath caught in her throat.

"Kassian…" she whispered.

He smiled tenderly and swooped to capture her mouth. This time when she felt his clever fingers seeking her core, she opened for him readily. He continued to plunder her mouth as his fingers teased her with a slow, intimate massage that nearly sent her over the edge. She bucked against his hand with a stifled scream of pleasure as he slid first one long finger, and then another into her slick, wet heat while his thumb continued to stroke her sensitive nub.

"Honey, are you sure? There's no going back after this, not for either of us." Sweat beaded his forehead as he held his weight off of her and waited for her answer. "I don't want to hurt you, Kat. Not now, not ever."

"Kassian," she gasped. "Yes, I want…please…now." Her voice was hungry and the strength of her desire shook them both. He came to his knees and nudged her thighs apart. He fisted his hot, swollen flesh, guiding it to her moist cleft, and slowly eased himself inside her tight, tight warmth, his eyes locked on her face.

His mind was open to her and though he didn't say the words, there was no mistaking the deep emotion pouring from him. Kat's eyes filled with tears and she thought her heart might burst as she reached to pull him down to her, feeling the odd but strangely right sensation of invisible ties binding them together heart, mind, and soul as his lips closed over hers. She wasn't sure whose desire was the driving force now that their minds were joined, but she knew that if she didn't have him inside of her right now, she would go mad with wanting. She discarded caution and uncertainty and her hips rose to meet him, obeying an instinct she hadn't known she possessed, accepting all that he offered in one deep thrust. She froze and cried out at the unexpected pain and burning fullness. He stilled instantly.

****

"Baby, you should have told me," he groaned. "If I'd known it was your first time I could have made it easier for you." His every nerve ending sang with need, his blood running hot and fast, but he clenched his jaw and remained unmoving. He knew that she didn't understand the significance of the step they were taking. This was more than desire, more than sex; it was a blending of two souls that had been created for one another. He would never let her go. Now that he had finally accepted and given in to his feelings for her, there was no other option for him. It was the *Earthbound* way. He thought it might very well kill him if she asked him to stop now, but he would do it rather than cause her an ounce of discomfort or a moment of regret. It wouldn't really have mattered, but somewhere deep inside he was arrogantly pleased that he was her first; and he was just as arrogantly sure that he would be her last. She might never know how great a gift she was to him. She took a shuddering breath and he felt her muscles begin to relax around him.

"I've …well, it never seemed right before; it was never…like this," she panted. She stroked his hair back from his damp forehead. "I can hear what you're thinking, feel what you're feeling, and it's… I want this, Kassian, I want you. I think I must have been waiting for you my whole life."

He couldn't think with needing her and she didn't have to tell him twice. He began moving, slowly at first, allowing time for her body to adjust to his. As he felt her relax and move with him, he gripped her rounded bottom possessively and brought her more closely against him, driving deeper, guiding her hips until they found a perfect rhythm. As they moved together, their hearts and minds melding as closely and intimately as their bodies, he felt something stir inside, something deep and hot and aching. He experienced an indescribable awareness as they became part of one another, completely encompassed, heart to heart, soul to soul, and intertwined at a cellular level. He watched her face as Kat fought for breath, fought for control, but he knew that both were beyond her. He was all but strangling on the riot of emotions that he could not voice, but she could read them in his mind, just as he could read them in hers. When at last they fell apart in each other's arms, Kassian felt the missing pieces of his soul knitting themselves back together.

Much later, with a well-loved and exhausted Kat curled warmly against him in sleep, Kassian held her close, stared into the darkness and swallowed past the lump in his throat. Only now did he truly realize how alone he'd been, how isolated. It had been a conscious choice, one he'd hoped would give him some measure of absolution. He'd all but cut himself off from his family, reluctant to face them, though they'd never even hinted at blame. But now that Kat had come into his life and opened his heart, somewhere deep down he was finally able to face and accept the truth about that night. He had done what he had to do; and Calli had known better. It didn't make it hurt any less; it didn't make it any less tragic; it didn't mean that his vendetta against Rapier was over; in fact, now that he had Kat to consider, it was even more imperative that Rapier be dealt with. But a little of the pressure that he had carried in his chest for longer than he could remember finally eased, and with Kat's arms wrapped around him, he slept peacefully for the first time in years.

Chapter 13

Kassian rose early and was in the middle of making a pot of coffee after reluctantly detaching himself from the warmth of Kat's body. He'd been painfully tempted to waken her with another round of lovemaking, but knew she would be both tired and sore after last night. He figured gluttony wasn't an unusual side effect given his years of starvation, and he was still working on rediscovering his capacity for consideration, not an easy task. When the call came, it was completely unexpected.

"McAllister," he snapped into the phone. The news conveyed by the nearly incoherent voice of his assistant on the other end was both alarming and unwelcome. One of his warehouses near the harbor was in flames. What Kassian found even more concerning was that the mutilated body of a young woman had been discovered near the loading docks soon after the fire department arrived. Rapier's calling card. He assured the nearly hysterical woman that he was on his way, and then punched in a number to let Alec and Luca know what was going on. They could get into places that the firefighters couldn't in an effort to locate and rescue any men who might still be trapped inside, and who knew what Rapier's next move might be. He couldn't allow more innocent people to get in the middle of this private war.

Hurrying back to the bedroom, he quickly and efficiently pulled on his clothes as quietly as possible and grabbed his car keys from a porcelain dish on the dresser. He chafed at the delay of having to drive, but it would cause more than a sensation if he suddenly faded to the scene using *Earthbound* methods. He hesitated, debating whether or not to waken Kat, finally deciding that he didn't want her to wake up alone after the night they'd shared. After fighting the urge for precious minutes, he finally pressed his lips to Kat's bare shoulder where it peeked from beneath the sheets. Once she woke up he knew it would be a struggle to leave her, but Rapier had upped the ante, both by striking in daylight and by attacking Kassian through his human employees. He had an uneasy feeling that the *Fallen* might only be getting started and had something even more sinister in the offing; it was time to end this, for everyone's sake. And now that he'd found something besides vengeance to live for, he was more anxious than ever to rid the world of Rapier's threat.

****

Kat awoke with a start, disoriented, with her heart pounding wildly. For a split second, she wondered if she'd imagined the whole night. Then she became aware of Kassian's sizzling lips tracing a path from her collarbone to her ear and a satisfied smile curled her lips. She shoved her heavy mane of hair out of her face and struggled to a sitting position, stretching contentedly. The movement induced delightful aches in regions she hadn't previously been aware of, convincing her that last night really hadn't been a dream, though she doubted she could have dreamt anything half as spectacular if she tried.

"Hey," she whispered softly, reaching up to bury her hand in his thick, dark hair and pull him closer. He pressed his lips firmly to her jaw then pulled back to sit on the side of the bed facing her. His hand rested on the rounded curve of her hip through the satin, and she noticed he couldn't seem to stop touching her. She wasn't complaining. With a final lingering caress, he stood and stepped back from the bed.

"I have to go out for a while," he said gently. "I'm not sure how long I'll be, but I don't want you to leave the apartment. I'll leave a man outside in case you need anything."

Kat blinked the sleep from her eyes and came completely awake. Her hopes of waking up in his arms for a repeat performance of last night's bliss were dashed for the moment, so she slid from the bed and reached around him to grab the tee shirt that he'd tossed over the chair last night after the battle of the bubbles. She pulled it over her head hugging it to her and wrapping herself in his scent. Though she'd been initially worried that it was only about the sex for him, the look in his eyes and the emotions pouring off of him this morning assured her that she wasn't mistaken in thinking that last night had bound them together in some profound and lasting way. For maybe the first time in her life, she felt accepted, normal, and complete. It was a good way to start the day.

"Where are you going?" she asked, coming to stand in front of him and placing her hands on either side of his trim waist.

"There's a fire at one of my warehouses and I need to get down there," he replied, tucking a strand of hair behind her ear.

"Don't you have 'people' for that?" She smiled lazily, leaning her face into his hand, mildly surprised that the light touch was enough to start the flames flickering in her very core all over again.

"Ordinarily." He returned her smile and rubbed his thumb along the corner of her full lips. "But there may be men still trapped inside and there's…a possibility that Rapier is behind it."

"What if it's a trap?" Her brow furrowed and a hint of worry crept into her voice. "Maybe…"

"Kat, I have to go," he said firmly. "Luca and Alec will be there and everything will be fine. I'll be back as soon as I can and we'll go out later and do something. If you play your cards right, maybe I'll even let you take me grocery shopping."

She let herself be reassured by his playful grin and stood on tiptoe to plant a kiss on his chin. "Don't be surprised when I hold you to that, McAllister. For your information, I have a vast collection of coupons in my purse."

"You have a mean streak, woman," he laughed. "I'll see you later." He dropped a kiss on the top of her head and strode from the room.

"Be careful," she called after him in a worried voice.

"Come back to me," she added, sending the thought to his mind.

"Always," came the reply as she heard the door click shut.

When he was gone, Kat padded barefoot into the bathroom and took a long, hot shower, letting the water work its magic on her deliciously sore muscles. After drying her hair, she pulled on a pair of jeans and a soft, beige turtleneck. She dropped her mother's locket over her head and tucked it inside her sweater, then grabbed her laptop bag and plunked it on the couch while she went into the kitchen for a cup of coffee. She was sorting through her disorganized stack of notes, waiting for her laptop to boot up, when her cell phone jangled from her purse. Thinking it might be Kassian, she jumped up, tripping on the end table and stubbing her toe painfully. Cursing under her breath, she hurriedly limped around the couch and grabbed her bag from behind it, digging her phone out before it could stop ringing. She didn't bother to check the display as she flipped it open.

"Hello?" she panted.

"Katrina?" The female voice was definitely not McAllister. "Are you all right? You sound…winded."

"Miranda? Oh, yes, I'm fine…banged my foot getting to the phone. How are you?"

"I'm fine, dear. I'm in the city for an auction and thought I might stop out at your place on the way back home and see you. It's been ages."

And it could be several more ages as far as Kat was concerned. Then it occurred to her that Miranda was the one person who might know the truth about her mother. Finding out how much her mother had kept hidden from her was still a dull ache that she had temporarily pushed to the back of her mind. Miranda was her mother's only living family; if anyone might have the answers, it would be her.

"Actually, Miranda, I'm in the city myself. I've been staying with a…friend for a few days. Maybe we could meet somewhere for coffee? In fact, I'd like to talk to you about something."

"Oh really? Like what?"

"Like the fact that my mother was a witch." Kat would have sworn the woman stopped breathing.

"I see," she replied carefully. "Well, I suppose you were bound to find out sooner or later. Lilly never understood that some things are an obligation, not a choice."

"Of course," replied Kat, implying that she understood the somewhat cryptic remark although, of course, she didn't. Miranda indicated that the items she was waiting for were going on the block within the next five minutes and then she would be free. She named a place and time. Kat glanced at her watch. It was now a little after eleven. She didn't know what time to expect McAllister, but the coffee shop Miranda suggested was helpfully only a block or two away. She could meet Miranda for coffee and be back before he ever knew she was gone. Her stomach did a funny little flip when she contemplated his reaction to her leaving the apartment after he'd specifically told her not to. But the chances were good that he would be tied up for most of the day and she would be back before he ever knew she'd left. By then she'd be parked behind her computer and he would see how ridiculously overprotective he was being. It was the middle of the day and there were people everywhere. Oh, he'd be pissed, all right, but he would get over it once he saw that she was fine. There was no reason she shouldn't be perfectly safe for an hour or so. She needed to know more about her mother and why she had kept her in the dark. The one person she had believed in completely had lied to her for her entire life, by omission, at least. It might be easier to accept if she could understand why.

In case McAllister returned before she did, Kat left a note telling him that she was meeting Miranda and the name of the coffee shop and propped it against a small brass lamp on the table inside the front door. After she tugged a pair of socks over her still smarting toes, she slipped her feet into her tennis shoes and stuffed her phone into her back pocket. She pulled a couple of crumpled bills out of her wallet, pulled on her vest, and threw open the door. She almost knocked herself unconscious as she barreled headfirst into a broad back that was as solid and unforgiving as granite. Galen, the bald giant with the shuriken tattoos, was standing right outside. She'd completely forgotten that Kassian had said he would be leaving a guard; she should have realized McAllister would never have left her unprotected. He turned slowly, crossing his arms over his massive chest, and cocked a brow as the corners of his lips turned up.

"Going somewhere?" If he wasn't so big and scary, Kat realized he was actually quite an attractive man. Assuming you could get past the big and scary. Her head barely reached his nipple line and his black tee strained across a chest nearly as wide as the doorway. But he had a beautiful smile, and with his shockingly green eyes twinkling in amusement, he wasn't quite as intimidating as he might otherwise have been.

"Um, yes, I am actually," Kat smiled back trying unsuccessfully to edge around him. "I'm, uh, meeting my cousin for coffee down the street. She's in town for the day and I haven't seen her in ages. I won't be long."

"You're right about that," he grinned. "You won't be long at all. Go back inside."

"Look, Galen, right? This is important. It's about

my mother. I really have to go. McAllister doesn't have to know. Trust me, my lips are sealed." She smiled conspiratorially.

"Nope." He widened his stance slightly to take up even more room in the doorway. "I have my orders. You are to be guarded at all times when you aren't with Mac or Luca. I like my head right where it is."

"For heaven's sake, you're twice the size of either of them! You don't mean to tell me that you're afraid of McAllister?" She was hoping to shame him into letting her pass.

"You've obviously never seen either of them in a fight." The inked giant laughed, not rising to the bait. "Besides, it has very little to do with fear and everything to do with respect. I gave my word I would keep you safe until Mac returns, and that's exactly what I plan to do." He reached for Kat's shoulders and spun her around to face back into the apartment. "In you go."

Kat's mind was spinning. She needed to get to that coffee shop. Miranda was the only one who could answer her questions and she wanted to talk to her face to face. She'd never been able to read Miranda well, so she wanted to be able to at least observe her and allow her empathy a chance to assess her reactions. She felt the amusement rolling off of the big man at her frustration and she became more incensed. She peered around Galen at the elevator and knew she could never reach it before he stopped her. Dammit! She wasn't a helpless child and they all needed to stop treating her as though she was. She needed to get to that elevator! She pictured herself standing inside waving merrily to Galen as he tried to catch her. The blue white flash caught her completely by surprise, but not nearly as much as finding herself actually in the elevator with the doors sliding closed as Galen roared and started toward her. Funny, he didn't seem all that amused now.

Kat burst out laughing as the elevator began to descend. She'd done it! She'd managed to snap, crackle, pop without even knowing how. And it couldn't have happened at a better time! She knew Galen couldn't risk fading into the lobby of the building, but she guessed that he would probably pop himself into the stairwell on the ground floor and be standing in front of the elevator doors when they slid open. She laughed again, picturing the look on his face, but quickly sobered when she realized it was nothing compared to the look that McAllister would be wearing if she didn't get back to the apartment before he did. She had no doubt that Galen would be reporting her little stunt, but she might be able to mitigate McAllister's anger if she could explain herself first. She got off of the elevator on the third floor, and pressed the button for the tenth, sending the elevator back up. She jogged lightly down the stairs, carefully bypassing the lobby and heading straight for the basement. She planned to leave via the parking garage while Galen cooled his heels waiting for the elevator in the lobby.

Kat was momentarily blinded by the bright, mid-day sun as she emerged from the relative darkness of the underground edifice and didn't notice the large man lounging against the building next to the front door underneath the burgundy fabric awning until he reached out and grabbed her arm. She squeaked in alarm, her heart climbing into her throat, until she realized that the man tugging her into the shadows was Galen. Then her heart sank. She had been so close.

He held her upper arm firmly in one large hand and reached for the door with the other.

"Nice try," he growled. She felt the waves of annoyance; he definitely was no longer amused. Kat dug in her heels and looked up, way up, at the frowning *Earthbound*.

"Look, I'm sorry, okay? I don't know how I did that, honest. But I really need to talk to my cousin, and I don't want to invite her here. The less she knows about my life, the better I like it. What if you go with me?" Kat tried a tentative smile and batted her eyelashes. "It's only down the street. That way, you'd still be guarding me like you promised McAllister, and I could maybe get the answers I need. I won't be long, and if you sense one little thing that seems off and say we need to go, I will get right up and leave with you. I promise."

Kat held her breath and tried to sort through the waves of indecision he was throwing off and gauge which way he was going to go. He didn't like the idea; of that much she was certain. She dropped her shields and let him read her, finally convincing him she really meant what she said.

"Look, I'm really not trying to give you any trouble, Galen. If McAllister or Luca were here I would ask them to take me, but they aren't and I have no idea how long they'll be tied up. Miranda is only here for a short time, so it's now or never. I can't feel her over the phone so I'd really like to talk to her face to face."

Galen blew out a long, slow breath and loosened his hold, though he didn't release her right away. "So, it's true, you really are an empath?" he asked.

Kat nodded. "I am. And if it makes you feel any

better, I picked up on the presence of evil before even Kassian did, twice now, in fact, so between the two of us, we'll definitely feel if something wicked this way comes and we can hightail it out of there," she coaxed.

"Fine," he grumbled. "This is against my better judgment, and if I say move, you move, got it?"

"Got it," she replied in relief as he let go of her arm and turned to walk beside her toward the coffee shop. "I really appreciate it."

"Yeah, well you should," he groused. "I'm gonna get my ass chewed off for this."

"Not if we get back first," Kat laughed. "Then it will be a moot point."

The tattooed giant rolled his eyes comically and pulled her arm through his, keeping her close. Kat assumed the heavy jolt of resignation that hit her meant that he didn't exactly agree.

They reached the coffee shop in record time, Kat practically running to keep up with Galen's long strides and too winded by the effort to carry on a conversation even if she'd been so inclined. The place was small, dimly lit, and already crowded this close to lunchtime. The air was thick with the rich scent of freshly ground coffee and a background chorus of conversation, clinking glass, and cutlery. Kat carefully opened herself to the cacophony of thoughts and emotions swirling around her and sensed no evil, only the usual discordance of sensation that she typically felt in a crowd. Galen appeared alert, but unruffled so she guessed he hadn't picked up on anything concerning either. From the doorway, she noticed Miranda at a small booth in the back, waving her in.

"Maybe you should wait here," she whispered to

Galen. "I have a feeling she won't be very talkative if you're hanging over my shoulder like a big, hulking Guardian Angel."

"I don't like it," he hissed back.

"You're less than twenty feet away, what could possibly happen? Anyway, if anyone or anything tries to come at me, you'll feel them, plus they'll have to walk right past you to do it, right?"

"I guess, but I still don't like it. Make this quick, huh? I'll feel a hell of a lot better when we're outta here."

"I'll be as quick as I can…thanks, Galen." She offered him her most charming smile.

"You feel one twitch of uneasiness, you get to me pronto, got it?"

"Got it."

Galen leaned against the wall near the doorway, his eyes vigilantly scanning the crowd as people came and went and milled around inside. Kat weaved her way through the crushing throng standing around the counter waiting for tables, to the booth where Miranda waited. The older woman stood and hugged Kat awkwardly on arrival and then slid back into her seat.

"I hope you don't mind, I already ordered for you since it was so busy and I don't have much time." She pushed a heavy mug of steaming coffee in Kat's direction. She followed that with a small, aluminum pitcher of cream and a couple of sugar packets. "I wasn't sure how you take it."

"Black is fine, thanks," Kat smiled, taking a large sip. "So, how have you been, Miranda."

"Oh, you know." Miranda waved a hand airily. "Same old thing, different day. With the holidays coming up, business at the shop has been pretty brisk, so when I saw the listing for this auction, I thought it was a good chance to replenish some stock and get a chance to see you at the same time. It's been ages."

"Yeah, I guess it has," Kat allowed, taking another hefty sip of the fresh, dark brew. It was a darker roast than she would have ordered for herself, and had far more bitterness than she preferred, but she had to admit that if Miranda hadn't ordered, they probably would have waited forever to be served in the standing room only crowd and the hot liquid warmed and soothed her after the brisk, cold walk from the apartment. Miranda was nervous. Kat could feel the anxiety swirling like an opaque cloud all around her, but even without the benefit of her empathic abilities, it didn't escape her notice that her cousin was perspiring rather profusely and was careful to avoid meeting her eyes. She glanced toward the door and saw that Galen was manfully struggling to maintain his surveillance while pretending to be polite to a blonde, in a short skirt and stilettoes, who had practically attached herself to his side. He did not look happy and with a frown in Kat's direction, he stepped back into the small vestibule to give himself some breathing space. The new position put Kat out of his direct line of vision, but he was still between her and the front door.

"Look, Miranda," Kat gulped half of the cup and set it back on the table decisively. "I know you don't have much time and frankly, neither do I. Why don't we get to the point? Why didn't my mother tell me that she was a witch? And after she was gone, why didn't you?"

Miranda opened her mouth to speak, but as Kat

stared, her cousin's face became cloudy and contorted. Her lips moved, but Kat couldn't understand the words and the room felt like it was closing in on her at an alarming rate. She felt heavy and weightless at the same time and she fought the overwhelming nausea that rose up to choke her as everything around her began to spin. Too late, she realized the coffee owed its bitterness to more than a dark roast. She wanted to scream, but her voice was snagged in her throat and her mind felt thick, like concrete setting. She wanted to wave her arms to get Galen's attention, but her movements were dulled and her body felt slow and heavy as if trapped in the cold, black water of a bottomless well, numb and drowning. Miranda towered over her, her lips still mouthing words that Kat couldn't decipher. Kat tried in vain to reach for Miranda's throat as the witch came closer.

"Bitch," she hissed viciously as everything went dark.

Chapter 14

Smoke hung heavy in the early afternoon air, blocking the watery winter sun, and the choking scent of charred wood and blackened steel was thick enough to make Kassian's eyes water. Burnt and curled paper scraps skittered along the ground in the chill breeze toward the water's edge like a frightened flock of small, black birds. The fire was finally out, though the fire department would be on site for hours yet, soaking down the skeletal remains to preclude another flare-up, while the fire marshal poked through the ruins searching for a cause. Thankfully, none of the warehouse workers had perished thanks to Luca and Alec's ability to scan and locate them and then direct the thoughts of the rescuers to the right locations to ensure they would be found. None of the injuries that did occur appeared to be serious and Kassian was thankful it hadn't been worse. He surveyed the devastated area with a practiced eye. Insurance would cover the building and contents; there was nothing that was irreplaceable from a material standpoint. The body of Jacques's latest victim was another matter, and as he expected would happen sooner or later, a man in a rumpled polyester suit and an equally disreputable looking taupe trench coat detached himself from the knot of investigators gathered around the remains with cameras flashing and pencils scribbling. He ducked awkwardly under the yellow crime-taped border, and headed in Kassian's direction, scratching his head and doing an impressively uncanny impersonation of Columbo. Kassian waited patiently as the man approached; the policeman was broadcasting his thoughts loud and clear and Kassian knew exactly what to expect. The disheveled man flashed a badge in one hand while sticking out the other in a faux friendly greeting.

"Mr. McAllister? Detective Frank Barnes, Homicide," he offered. Kassian clasped the outstretched hand in a firm, but brief grip after running his palm down the side of his jeans in a futile attempt to remove the worst of the soot.

"Detective," he returned easily, "what can I do for you?"

Barnes scanned the smoldering ruins through narrowed eyes. "I assume you're well insured?"

"Of course."

"Well, thank God everyone managed to get out." He paused. "Funny how these murdered women keep turning up in your vicinity though, isn't it?" Barnes asked as casually as though he was inquiring about Kassian's opinion on the chance of snow.

"It *is* disturbing," Kassian replied in an equally mild voice. Two of the three recent murders might be perceived as pointing toward a connection to Kassian. There was little to no chance of his actually being held accountable for them, but it could be damned inconvenient, which he was sure was part of Rapier's plan. He hadn't intended on moving back to Europe for several years yet, and now there was Kat to consider. He nearly gasped aloud as that thought occurred to him.

He'd never bothered to consult with anyone regarding his actions and decisions; it was a completely foreign concept. Just one of the many things he hadn't stopped to consider. He had no idea how she would feel about relocating every few decades. In fact, he had no real idea how she felt about a lot of things. He pushed the concern aside; he knew the important things, and as for the rest, they had all the time in the world to learn about one another.

"One could almost hypothesize that the fire was set to cover up the murder," Barnes continued thoughtfully, rocking back and forth on his heels.

"One could," Kassian smiled his agreement, "but if that were the case, don't you think it would have made more sense to put the body *inside* the warehouse first?" He could easily read the detective's annoyance. He was fishing, pure and simple, and had expected Kassian to be far more anxious about both the fire and the murders.

"Perhaps," the detective returned stiffly. "I'll need a phone number and address in case I need to talk to you again, Mr. McAllister."

Kassian chuckled with absolutely no discernible trace of concern, his white teeth flashing against his soot streaked face. He fished his wallet out of his back pocket and flipped it open, pulling out a business card and handing it to Barnes.

"Here you are, Detective, but frankly, I'm pretty easy to find." Kassian heard, as much as felt, Luca and Alec coming up behind him. Detective Barnes tucked the card inside his breast pocket and turned to leave.

"I'll be in touch" was his parting remark.

"I'll look forward to it, Detective."

Something struck the back of Kassian's knee causing his leg to nearly buckle. Kassian turned around quickly and swung at Alec's shoulder. He grinned when he caught nothing but empty air. The kid had reflexes.

"What was that all about?" Luca asked, jerking his chin in the direction of the retreating policeman.

"The good detective is looking for someone to pin a couple of murders on," Kassian replied dryly.

"Yeah, well he's not the only one…difference is, we know who we're looking for," Luca observed. "You about done? I could use a shower, a beer, and a great big steak."

"Yeah," Kassian sighed wearily. "It's all a matter of paperwork from here. Let's…" Suddenly he stopped and became eerily still. His muscles tightened with a strange sense of foreboding and a ribbon of dread snaked through his bones. He felt an urgent and overwhelming desire to talk to Kat, to assure himself that she was safe. Of course, he'd left Galen to protect her so there really should be no reason for concern. Still, he couldn't shake the uneasy feeling. He needed to get home.

"What?" Luca looked around tensely.

"I'm not sure," Kassian began slowly. "It's like I'm picking up on Kat, but not her thoughts exactly. I can't seem to touch her mind….but something. Something doesn't feel right."

"You're picking up on Kat?" Luca sucked in a breath. "Damn, Mac, you bonded her? Does she even know what that means?"

"You object?" Kassian's brows lowered ominously. Kat might be Luca's sister, but she was now Kassian's mate and that trumped everything as far as

Kassian was concerned. Sure, he should have explained it to her better, or given her a choice, or, well, or something…but sometimes you couldn't play by the rules; sometimes you had to make them up as you went along.

Luca stared him down for what seemed like hours but was, in fact, brief seconds. "No, of course I don't object, exactly…hell, Mac, you should know better. I'm surprised, is all. I thought you'd give her more time."

"Yeah, well, sometimes you gotta go with the flow, my brother. Why postpone the inevitable? Now, let's get back to my place and make sure that she's okay, we're done here."

Kassian walked quickly to his car with Luca and Alec close behind. With so many people milling around the fire scene, it was nearly impossible to find a spot from which to fade. Ten minutes later, Kassian swung the car into his parking spot beneath the building. He hadn't been able to shake the feeling of unease, and his increasing disquiet had communicated itself to the other two *Earthbound*s. After climbing out of the car, with a quick look around to make sure that they were unobserved, the three quickly faded into the hallway outside of Kassian's apartment. All of them noticed two things simultaneously; there was no sign of Galen, and none of them could detect a trace of Kat. She wasn't here.

"Dammit," hissed McAllister as he stormed through the door. He refused to acknowledge the clawing fingers of fear that were working their way into his throat making it hard to breathe. The note Kat left for him sailed from the table and fluttered to the floor from the force of the door flying open. Luca scooped it up and quickly scanned the contents.

"Sonofabitch." He held the missive out to McAllister. "Miranda...she's gone to meet her cousin for coffee."

"Well, hey, that's good news, right?" interjected Alec with a puzzled look. "I mean, Galen is with her, and she's with her family."

"I don't trust Miranda as far as I can throw her," Luca growled, "and from the little Kat told me, I strongly suspect that Kat has something Miranda wants. Call Galen and see where they are and then let's go get her."

Kassian had his phone out and was punching in Galen's number before Luca had finished speaking. Luca and Alec watched as the color left Kassian's face completely then rushed back like a tsunami as the rage kicked in.

"Don't move," Kassian snarled at Galen, snapping the phone closed and shoving it in his back pocket. He started for the door without a word.

"Mac?"

"She's gone," Kassian threw back over his shoulder. "Galen lost sight of her for a few minutes and when he looked back, she was gone." Kassian was fighting to keep his anger in the forefront and not let the unfamiliar taste of fear override it. He knew that he'd been very clear; Kat was to stay inside the apartment until he returned. The minute he was gone, she'd charmed her guard and sneaked away. *Just like Calli.*

****

The three warriors materialized in the alley behind the coffee shop. Galen waited, pale and tense, a slinky blonde in heels pinned against the building by his massive body. The woman looked frightened and confused and the appearance of the three angry looking giants did nothing to reassure her.

"Speak," McAllister growled in a clipped tone.

"Mac, I…, Galen began in a stilted voice. Kassian held up a hand for him to stop.

"Later, Galen…just tell us what happened, and who the hell this is." He gestured at the quivering blonde.

Galen's brows drew together in a dark frown. The blonde shrank against the rough brick of the coffee shop's back wall. "Someone paid her to distract me. I'm ashamed to admit that it worked…only for a minute, but I guess that's all it took." The big man dropped his head. "Hell, Mac, I'm sorry. I should have never let her talk me into this. Even though she faded into the elevator, I had her outside the building, I should have marched her right back upstairs."

Luca's brows rose. "She faded? Without any training? *Merda*, we Fiorelli's are a talented lot."

"So not the issue, right now, Luca," Kassian said shortly. Pushing Galen aside, he leaned forward and addressed the girl. "Who put you up to this?"

Surrounded by four of the biggest and most menacing looking men she'd ever seen, the blonde's eyes were so wide with alarm that they nearly rolled back in her head. "I…I can't remember." Her features screwed up in confusion. "It was a man…I remember that, but I can't see his face. He gave me a hundred bucks to distract your friend here for five minutes. A girl's gotta eat. Seemed like easy money to me."

Kassian leaned forward and captured her gaze, staring hard and quickly shuffling though her recollection of the morning's events. Someone had altered her memory leaving gaping holes. He couldn't see the man's face, but the voice he knew as well as his own and his jaw clenched tightly enough to shatter teeth. The girl had been approached at least two blocks from the coffee shop which would explain why neither Galen nor Kat had felt any inkling of a threat. He turned from the woman with a moan and punched a fist into the unforgiving façade of the building with an anguished roar that echoed through the empty alleyway and beyond.

"Alec," Luca commanded tightly. "Find out where she lives. You and Galen get her home and make sure she doesn't remember anything that happened today, including her conversation with us, got it?"

"But…" Alec began.

"Just do it, Alec." Alec didn't look happy and Galen had yet to meet anyone's eyes. They each took the girl by an arm and led her down the alley and out toward the street.

"The bastard knew he couldn't get close to her without someone picking up on him." Kassian hissed. "How in the hell did he get to her cousin?"

"Only two ways that I can think of…a promise or a threat."

"What now?" Both anger at himself and fear for Kat threatened to overwhelm Kassian. He knew he had to swallow both and think logically if they were going to find her and get her back. And they were going to get her back. He would not even contemplate the alternative. He should never have left her alone, especially after last night. He should have seen through Rapier's plot to get him out of the apartment. If that bastard laid one finger on her…

****

Kat woke in utter darkness to the damp, earthy smell of confined spaces and buried secrets. Her senses were immediately assaulted by anger, despair, and desperation all swirling together in an overstimulating vortex. She couldn't differentiate how much of it was her own. Combined with the aftereffects of whatever drug Miranda had slipped into her coffee, her head felt like an overplayed bongo drum and she struggled to gather her shields around her and block out the emotions. The air was dank and murky, thick with the scent of mold and decay, and it took a few minutes for her eyes to adjust. When they did, she knew exactly where she was. Behind her home, where the trees and brush began to climb toward the mountains, there was a series of caves. In the basement of her house, there was a tunnel connecting the house to the caves. Her mother said they'd been used by whiskey runners in the days of prohibition. Kat hadn't been down here in years, but had often explored them as a child, much to her mother's consternation. Her mother had finally barricaded the entrance to the tunnel with crates and boxes to keep Kat from wandering. She knew she was in one of the deeper chambers by the steady drip of water echoing eerily and the faint rush from the underground river in another chamber far below. Why on earth would Miranda have brought her here, how did she even know about the caves, and more to the point, what could she be up to that required such extreme measures?

She had no idea how long she'd been unconscious, but it was long enough for the chilling damp to penetrate her jeans and creep into her bones where she rested on the moist ground. She was already cold and stiff and knew it was going to be difficult to muster the agility and energy to escape. She hoped that Galen had pried himself loose from the blonde quickly enough to have seen something. She was worried, but she wasn't particularly terrified, not yet, anyway. Kassian would come for her, she knew he would. He would be as pissed as hell that she'd gotten herself into this mess, but he would come. Coupled with that, she knew these caves like the back of her hand and Miranda was older and slower. Kat figured that even cold and stiff, she had the advantage; at least she thought she did until she realized that her ankle was encased in an iron manacle and chained to the wall. This had obviously not been a spur of the moment decision on Miranda's part.

She detected a scuffling noise from the darkness on the other side of the chamber and realized she wasn't alone in the gloom. The hair on her neck stood on end as she thought first of rats, and then every other manner of creepy, crawly thing, but when she strained her eyes toward the sound and focused, she could barely make out the hunched figure of someone curled up in the far corner wrapped in a blanket that looked more like a fetid ball of dirty rags. She opened herself a bit and realized that the pathetic figure was the source of the overwhelming despair she had felt upon awakening. Before Kat had a chance to call out to whoever was sharing her misery, she felt it, the insidious creep of evil. It crawled over her skin and agitated every nerve ending filling her with a heavy dread that made it difficult to breathe. She recognized it instantly. It was the same evil she'd felt at Elle's party. Oh, God! Rapier was here. She hurriedly swallowed the thick knot of terror that clawed its way into her throat. She thought she'd only need to outsmart Miranda; she never dreamed she'd be up against the evil *Fallen*, as well. The figure in the corner must have felt something, too, since it curled into itself to appear even smaller, as if hoping to go unnoticed. Kat quickly drew on everything that she'd learned by following and observing the minds of Kassian, Luca, and the other *Earthbound* and imitated them as well as she could in an attempt to block the worst of the malevolence and protect her own thoughts from anyone who might be trying to read her. As terrified as she was at the thought of coming face to face with Jack the Ripper, she knew that her only hope for staying alive until Kassian could find her was to use her head.

****

Kassian's phone buzzed from the inside pocket of his jacket. He fished it out and glanced at the display. His heart leapt in his chest. Was it possible that they'd been wrong and she'd simply slipped out the back door with Miranda to get out from under Galen's watchful eye? He quickly hit accept and raised the phone to his ear.

"Kat?" he barked hoarsely, his heart pounding.

"Ah, McAllister! It has been far too long, *mon ami, c'est vrai?*"

"If you touch a single hair on her head, you piece of shit, I swear to God I'll…"

"You'll what?" Jacques interrupted in a hard, bored voice. "I'm the one running the show. Exactly as it's always been."

"Let her go, Jacques. We both know it's me you

want. You can have me. Let her go and I'm all yours." Kassian knew that it was pointless to reason with a madman, still he had to try.

"You? Oh, you silly, silly man. I don't want you. Oh, no, McAllister…I want you very much alive…alive and suffering the loss of those you love. The way I have suffered the pain of losing my beloved Jean-Marc all these years."

"That was war, Rapier, not personal. You already got your payback when you took Callista. Kat did nothing to deserve this."

"Ah, but who is to say what someone deserves? She brings you happiness, *non*? In my book, that is reason enough to die. But to prove that I am not the animal you think I am, I have called to let you say *au revoir*. Quite magnanimous of me, *c'est vrai*?"

Kassian could hear the phone being jostled and Rapier's warning growl. Then he heard a small, breathless voice.

"McAllister?"

"Kat, baby, are you all right? Do you know where you are?" She sounded terrified and the pain of her fear cut him like a knife. This was his fault; again.

"Say your goodbyes, McAllister. My patience is not limitless," Rapier broke in, letting Kassian know he had Kat's cell on speaker. Kassian hit the speaker on his phone so that Luca could hear, as well. Maybe he would hear something that Kassian didn't, pick up a clue that Kassian missed.

"Kat, I'll find you, baby. Don't be afraid." Whatever happened, he didn't want her last moments to be filled with fear. He had no idea how they would find her, but he had to make her believe that they would.

Hell, he had to believe it, too, or he was going to fall apart right here in the street.

"McAllister..." Her voice caught on a sob. "Please don't forget to check on my fairies and gnomes."

He saw the puzzled look Luca gave him, but he smiled slowly with the first glimmer of hope he dared to feel. She was as brilliant as she was beautiful. The smile didn't last long as he heard Kat's muffled exclamation of pain. Rapier fed on fear and pain. They didn't have much time.

"Ah, *l'amour*...it makes my heart feel all warm and fuzzy!" came the raspy voice once more. "Nevertheless, our lovely chat must come to an end now. Other matters demand my attention."

"Get your affairs in order, Jacques. Today is the day you die."

"Ah, but first you must find me, *mon ami.* I look forward to it," Jacques maniacal cackle was the last sound they heard before the line went dead.

Kassian's smile was chilling as he turned to Luca. "And I know exactly where to start looking."

Chapter 15

Kat lifted her chin with her jaw tightly clenched to hide the trembling. She stared at Jacques Rapier with far more defiance than she actually felt as he dropped her cell into the pocket of his jacket. She understood now how he had been able to lure his victims. It should be illegal for insanity to look so good. He was a man most women would find compelling with his dark hair and eyes, classically chiseled features, and lean, muscular physique. But unlike most women, Kat felt the evil that swirled around him like a cold, dark cloud, obscuring any semblance of charm or appeal. As she regarded him boldly, the corners of his mouth quirked upwards in a slight grin, but Kat saw only that the smile was cruel and his eyes were dead pools. No light, no emotion, and most assuredly, no mercy. Kat sent up a silent prayer to whoever might be listening that Kassian understood her reference to the gnomes and fairies and figured out it was her way of telling him she was being held near her home. She readily acknowledged that she'd gotten herself into this mess, but she wasn't altogether convinced she was going to be able to get herself out of it. It didn't help her state of mind to know that Kassian was, no doubt, blaming himself exactly as he had with Calli. She desperately hoped she lived long enough to convince him that neither of them being captured by Rapier was his fault. Miranda hovered slightly behind Rapier, watching his every movement with a rapt gaze, oblivious to the true nature of the monster with whom she'd obviously aligned herself.

Rapier reached back and drew Miranda to his side, wrapping an arm about her shoulders to draw her close. The infatuated look on her face turned Kat's stomach. She felt the thick desire rolling off of Miranda; the woman was gone on Rapier, hook, line, and sinker. Miranda had no clue that her feelings were unreciprocated. Kat thought he must be one hell of an actor to inspire such utter adoration; she felt nothing from him but unadulterated evil, mixed with a healthy dose of irritation and revulsion.

"I will leave you to catch up with your cousin, *ma cher*," Rapier rasped. "I must prepare for McAllister's arrival. She led him right to us, *ma cherie*, as you predicted she would."

Oh, God! Somehow they knew she had given Kassian a clue! He was headed into a trap and it was because of her. She had to warn him somehow. She sent her thoughts out on the common channel hoping if she couldn't yet reach Kassian, she could at least reach some other nearby *Earthbound* who could get word to him and warn him.

"He'll suspect a trap, he always does. But, he'll come anyway, no matter what you say or do. He's tenacious like that."

Kat swallowed a gasp. The voice that came into her head was female, and it had come from the bundle of rags in the corner. Whoever the woman was, she obviously knew Kassian, and knew him well. Kat hardly dared to hope; was it possible?

"Callista?"

"So you've heard of me. I should have known my stubborn brother would still be looking. I've spent over a hundred years terrified that my stupidity would be the instrument of his death."

"He thinks you're dead. He's mourned you all these years, but never stopped trying to avenge you. How is it possible you're still alive?"

"Jacques has his own twisted reasons for keeping me alive. For now, don't let them know we can communicate. Play along with your cousin, sick bitch that she is, and if an opportunity presents itself, I'll help you if I can. Maybe getting you out of here alive will make up to my brother for some of the grief I've caused him."

"We get out together, or not at all," Kat replied firmly, turning her attention to Miranda, who had stepped between them, blocking Kat's view of Kassian's sister. She felt the anger and frustration that rose from Callista's huddled form as she made that pronouncement, but there was no way in hell Kat could escape this place if the opportunity arose and leave the other woman behind. She would never be able to face Kassian and Alec, nor would she be able to live with herself. She gazed up at Miranda, eyes narrowed, making no attempt to disguise the hatred and disgust she felt.

"Why, Miranda?" she demanded. "If nothing else, we're family. Why would you betray me like this and hand me over to that soulless murderer? He cares nothing for you and you're too blind to see it."

"Family," Miranda spat as she leaned down into Kat's face. "What would you know of family? Your mother betrayed both of us and everything we stood for.

She let that do-gooder convince her to turn her back on her heritage and lock away the source of our family's power."

"I have no idea what you're talking about, Miranda, and you know it," Kat hissed. "My mother may have hidden things from me, but she would never betray me."

"Wouldn't she? Did she tell you what she was? What you were? Did she ever give you a choice of becoming all that you had the potential to be? She was so worried the power would corrupt her as it had so many others that she refused to accept the power for herself and she made damn sure I couldn't have it either. Well, I'll have it now! Give me the locket, Katrina."

Miranda held out her hand, but Kat noticed that she didn't make a move to physically take it. Kat remembered the *sigil*s and Luca's reference to a protection spell. Like the Wicked Witch of the West and the Ruby Slippers, maybe Miranda couldn't simply take it. Maybe Kat had to hand it over willingly? Not happening; not in this lifetime.

"You want me to believe this harmless little locket holds the power of an entire lineage of witches? Please, Miranda, how naïve do you think I am?" Kat procrastinated. Actually, Kat realized that until recently she'd been a lot more naïve than she would have ever believed possible, but she also knew she had to keep Miranda talking. The longer she could postpone giving her what she wanted, the greater the chance she could warn Kassian of the trap and keep him safe

"Not the locket, you little fool, the ring," Miranda screeched impatiently. "The locket contains the directions that will lead me to it!"

"What ring?" Kat's confusion was genuine. Her mother had never owned a ring, aside from the wedding band from her short and ill-fated marriage to Roger Shephard. Lilly had pawned that years ago when money was tight.

"You really don't know anything, do you? Lilly really was determined that our line would end with her. She locked the ring away and buried it. And that bastard Fiorelli helped, I know it! Well, I took care of him," she snorted. "I may not have had the ring, but I did have the grimoiré."

"You bitch!" Kat hissed angrily. Magic. Miranda had somehow used magic to come between her parents. This woman's singular quest for power had caused so much misery. Kat felt her anger rising. Unbidden, her fingertips began to glow and spark and she quickly put them behind her so Miranda wouldn't notice. She felt the metal ring that held her to the wall, and keeping her fingers on the seam where the metal was joined, she concentrated on using her mind to slowly and quietly widen the gap in the link, waiting for a chance to her to free herself.

"Sticks and stones, Katrina," Miranda sighed impatiently. "Now hand it over nicely and maybe I can convince Jacques to spare your life. You are my cousin, after all." Miranda leaned closer and held out a hand.

"You didn't have to drug me and turn me over to a sick masochist, Miranda. I know nothing about this ring or this power you speak of. Why would I want it? Did it ever, at any time, occur to you that you could merely ask me for the locket?"

Miranda straightened up and blinked. "No."

"No wonder you're so attracted to Rapier. You're as crazy as he is." Kat spat out. "Fine. If you want the locket, you loony bitch, then come and get it," Miranda leaned forward again and as she did, Kat brought the loose end of the heavy chain up and swung it with everything she had into the side of Miranda's head, sending her to the floor with a satisfying thud. Heart pounding, Kat quickly ran her hands down her leg to feel for the shackle and loosened it the same way. She pulled it free from her own ankle and locked it around Miranda's. Then she resealed the gap in the link to secure her cousin to the wall. She pulled a short dagger in a sheath from Miranda's belt and tucked it into the waistband at the back of her jeans, tugging her sweater down to cover it. Kat had never killed so much as a fly, and she wasn't sure she could actually use the thing, but self-preservation was a strong motivator.

"Impressive," said a soft voice, hoarse with disuse. Kat awkwardly scrambled across the uneven floor of the cave to the other woman and began feeling for the chains that bound her. In the dim light, Kat could see that Kassian's sister was thinner, though still as strikingly beautiful as the photograph in his album. Her dark hair was tangled and matted, but hung well past her hips in a thick braid. Callista's lips were pressed together and she slapped Kat away from her.

"There's no time for this," Callista whispered. "Get yourself out. If you make it, then worry about me later. Jacques won't kill me. Somewhere in his sick, twisted mind he thinks that my love is the key to saving his soul. It's a completely misguided notion, of course, but one I make no effort to dispute as it's kept me alive this long. Now go!"

"But, I can't just leave..." Kat began while furiously feeling for the gap in the chain and breathing a sigh when she finally felt it and began to manipulate it free.

"Kat?"

She nearly collapsed with relief at the sound of his voice in her head. The feeling was quickly followed by fear for his safety. Callista again pushed her away.

"The witch has spelled the caves," she whispered in a desperate voice. "He can't get in and they'll be waiting for him to try. But, there is nothing keeping you from getting out. The fools underestimated you." Callista forced a smile. "It seems women have become much more resourceful over the last hundred years."

"You've managed to stay alive while being held captive by a sociopathic serial killer for over a hundred years. I'd say you're pretty resourceful yourself," Kat returned the smile.

"McAllister? Where are you?"

"Kat?" The relief in his voice was so apparent to her. *"I'm in your basement. Sid led us down here and keeps pacing in front of a pile of crates on the west wall."*

"Don't tell him I'm here," Callista warned quietly, "not yet. It will only distract him."

Kat hated to admit it, but she knew the other woman was right. She couldn't tell him Callista was alive; not yet. And Callista was too weak; she would only slow her down. The best chance for both of them lay in Kat reaching the tunnel to her basement and finding a way to lead the others back to Callista.

"Move the crates and get the door open so I can get through, but stay where you are, Kassian. I think I

can make it out on my own."

"*Like hell!*"

"*As if!*"

"*No way!*"

Kat heard the emphatic denials of Kassian, Luca, and Alec in her head simultaneously. Great! Just what she needed; triple testosterone. Suddenly she felt the familiar creep of evil approaching. It was now or never. She reached out and quickly pulled the other woman into her arms, surprising them both.

"I'll be back for you," Kat whispered hoarsely against the thick, matted hair. Callista hugged her back weakly and nodded. Kat felt her hopelessness. She expected nothing. "I promise."

Callista nodded again and pushed her away with more strength than Kat would have expected. "He's coming. Go."

With a last look that she hoped was reassuring Kat pulled the knife from its hiding place at her back and moved quickly into the dark passage at the back of the cave. She heard Callista's voice in her head one last time as the deeper darkness engulfed her.

"*The dagger is a mortal weapon and it won't kill a Fallen. Only his own weapon or one of ours can...*"

The voice stopped abruptly and Kat heard a cry of pain behind her in the cave, but couldn't discern whose it was. She prayed it was Miranda's. It had nearly broken her heart to leave Kassian's sister behind, but she realized that the only chance for either of them was for one of them to escape. Kat was surprised to find that despite the number of years since she'd been here, she remembered the layout of the caves as though it was yesterday. She moved slowly and carefully, keeping a hand on the rough, damp walls since, unlike the times she had played here as a child, she had no Power Rangers flashlight to guide her. The sense of evil still crawled through her and her heart beat painfully in her throat as she realized that Rapier must be following her. It felt like hours before she approached the fork in the tunnel leading to her basement. She heard a dull, rhythmic pounding ahead and immediately suspected what it was.

"McAllister? I'm almost there ...stop the pounding."

"Kat." McAllister sounded almost, well, frantic. But that couldn't be right because it would mean that he was worried. And if he was worried…no, she couldn't allow her mind to go there or she would become paralyzed with fear.

"Stop where you are. There are animorti in the tunnel...we can see them but we can't get to them. You must be headed right for them. Is there another way out?"

"No, and I think Rapier is right behind me."

****

Kassian knew he was in danger of letting his fear for Kat control him. He couldn't begin to fathom how she'd managed to escape, but she was walking right into a potential ambush and Rapier was close behind her. He could feel it. And if they couldn't find a way to bring the barrier down, he knew he would be forced to stand by helplessly and watch her die through the impenetrable window keeping them out. Luca knew it too, and wasn't in much better shape. Only Alec seemed objective enough to still able to reason and he stood in front of the doorway with his head cocked to the side, sizing up the barrier and finally turning to them with a hint of a crooked smile lighting his face.

"Gentlemen, we've been going about this all wrong. We've been trying to go through this thing. What we need to do is go around it."

"What?"

"The witch spelled the entrances, not the entire tunnel system. We blast through the wall next to the doorway, open a space parallel to the tunnel and come in from the side."

Kassian released a breath he hadn't realized he'd been holding and turned to Luca. "What do you think?"

"I think it could work and it's better than nothing, which is what we have at the moment," Luca replied grimly as he set his daggers on the floor, stepped to the side, and began rubbing his hands together. He directed a blast of blue white energy at the cinderblock wall to the side of the doorway and gave a satisfied grunt as it began to give way. Kassian and Alec added their energy and within minutes they had carved a parallel passage several feet into the earth next to the tunnel.

"McAllister? I can see the light from the basement. I'm close. How many animorti did you see?"

"At least two...and they're armed. Stay where you are and sit tight, Kat. I think we've found a way in."

"He's closer, Kassian. I don't only feel him now, I hear him. I have to keep moving. Will a mortal weapon kill an animorti?"

"What? Cara, don't do something stupid...give us a minute..."

"No time, brother...in case this doesn't work, I want you both to know these last few days have

been...well, you know what I mean."

"Kat!"

****

The anguish in both Luca and McAllister's voice bounced around in her head, but she forced herself to block them out and swallow the sobs that threatened to overtake and incapacitate her when she felt how close Rapier was and realized she might never see McAllister or her brother again. She could hear the increasing ferocity with which the *Earthbound* were blasting through the rock to get to her, but she knew they would be too late. The *animorti* were now directly in front of her and Rapier was close behind. Luckily, the *animorti* were uneasy and preoccupied with the continuous explosions rattling the walls around them and the first one was an oily puddle at her feet before he even realized she was there. She picked up her pace until she was running full out now that she could literally see the light at the end of the tunnel. The second *animorti* barely had a chance to turn and raise his sword when she plunged the dagger into his chest with all the force afforded her by her forward momentum. The creature exploded into a mass of foul, oily glop that covered her from head to toe as she pitched through it and forward toward the doorway, landing with a painful crash on the hard, concrete floor of her basement.

"Ouch," she cried, struggling to rise from the floor and slipping in the greasy slime. The three *Earthbound* turned and regarded her with comical expressions of amazement and disbelief as she finally gained her feet and looked down at herself. "Oh, and also, ewww."

Her second exclamation was muffled in Kassian's broad chest as he pulled her against him with enough forced to crack ribs. She was shocked to find that he was trembling from head to toe and put it down to the energy he'd expended to pulverize the rock. She knew she must be right when Luca pulled her away from Kassian and into his arms and she realized that he was suffering from the same affliction. She risked a glance at Alec who merely flashed his dimples, but his Adam's apple bobbed with an unusual amount of force as he swallowed before turning away.

They all felt it at the same moment; Rapier was near. Kat pulled out of Luca's arms and reached for Kassian's hand.

"McAllister, there's something I have to tell…" Her words were cut off in midstream by the angry roar that echoed from the passage. Kassian pushed her behind him as they all turned to face the threat. Jacques Rapier stood not ten feet beyond the barrier, jet black wings spread ominously behind him, blocking the passage beyond. Miranda sat slumped at his feet panting, held upright only by the length of her hair wrapped in the *Fallen*'s fist. In his other hand, he held a length of heavy chain that reached to the floor and then trailed off behind him into the darkness.

"So, the witch still wears the locket," Rapier roared. "Can you do nothing right, *cherie*?" He gave a brutal tug on Miranda's hair. "*I* arranged her capture, *I* carried her soft and lifeless body to the cave, *and I* chained her to the wall." Kat felt Kassian stiffen and clench his fists with rage. "I did all of the work, it seems, and left you such a simple task, *ma coeur*…and yet you failed me. What am I to do with you?"

Miranda raised a tear streaked face in supplication. "Please, Jacques…you don't understand. The locket is protected. I couldn't just take it from her...I..." Suddenly, Jacques dropped the chain to the floor of the cave and secured it with a booted foot. With his free hand, he reached to stroke Miranda's cheek.

"There, there, *ma petite*," he crooned. "I know that you tried your best." Miranda gazed at him with a hope and adoration that caused Kat's stomach to churn. "But your best was not good enough," he sighed as he grabbed her chin and jerked her head sharply up and to the side with a loud crack, breaking her neck in one quick movement and letting her body drop heavily to the floor.

The moment Miranda's lifeless body hit the dirt, her magic became null and void and the barrier wavered and fell. While Kassian, Kat, and Luca watched the macabre scene unfolding in front of them, Alec remained slightly behind them using their bodies for cover as his hands wove intricate patterns in the direction of the tunnel entrance creating his own barrier made up of *sigils*. Jacques yanked a wicked looking dagger from his boot and sent it sailing, full force, directly at Kat's chest. Before anyone even had a chance to breathe, the dagger hit an invisible wall and bounced back at Rapier with equal force. Kat immediately gathered her wits and used her mind to turn the dagger in midair until it pointed directly at Rapier's heart. He shifted to the side at the last moment and the blade sliced through his still outstretched wing, its momentum slowing as it sliced through the thick, fibrous membrane. Jacques' roar of pain and outrage was drowned out by the ear splitting scream that came from behind him.

"No!" Kat screamed, falling to her knees as

Rapier's wings collapsed. He spun to catch Callista as she fell. Kassian and Alec were stunned immobile at the sight of their sister with Rapier's blade protruding from her chest, but Luca showed no such hesitation. One minute he was standing at Kat's side, the next he had faded and appeared directly behind Jacques. His daggers were still on the floor of the basement, so he pulled the blade from Callista's chest and buried it in Rapier's back.

Rapier's eyes widened in shock as he dropped heavily to his knees with Callista still cradled in his arms. She opened her eyes and looked at him and an expression that was almost peace came to the madman's face.

"If only you could have loved me..." he gasped, laying her on the ground as gently as he could before his strength left him and he fell to his side. "If only..."

To everyone's astonishment, Callista reached out and grasped his hand. "Perhaps I could have loved the man, Jacques, if only you could have stopped. Perhaps I could have loved the man, but I could have never loved the beast that possessed you."

Rapier smiled serenely. "In that case, *ma couer,* perhaps I am saved, after all."

"Doubtful," Luca muttered coldly as he shoved the *Fallen*'s body away and bent to lift Callista into his arms.

****

Kat was still on her knees, and dropped her face into her hands, sobbing brokenly. Kassian tried to get a grip on her slime covered arms and pull her to her feet. Finally, he simply scooped her up bodily and held her against him, stinking *animorti* guts and all. He thought he might actually love her more in that moment than he ever would have believed it was possible to love anyone. Rapier was dead, Calli was alive, and Kat was safe in his arms, right where she belonged. None of it thanks to him and surprisingly, he was okay with that. He'd spent what felt like a lifetime convinced that the only thing that could bring him peace was being the instrument of Rapier's demise. In the end, he hadn't been able to control Kat any more than he'd been able to control Calli, but he finally understood that while he might love them both, he couldn't make their decisions for them, nor was he responsible for the consequences of the decisions they made. The only thing he could hope for was that he would always be able to protect them from whatever those consequences might be; or at least hope that they were strong enough to protect themselves. And while Rapier's death finally gave him release, it was the woman in his arms who'd finally given him peace.

****

Kat couldn't understand the overwhelming emotions rolling off of Kassian. They seemed to be directed at her, but that wasn't possible. Not after what she'd done. She took a deep breath and tried to speak, but no words came out. It would be so much easier to communicate without the words, but that was a coward's way out. She'd made him give her the words once, knowing how difficult it was for him. She owed him no less. She peeked between her fingers and her heart broke into a million pieces when she saw the tears tracking down his cheeks; tears she mistook for grief.

"Kassian," she whispered in a small choked voice. "I'm so sorry...I tried...I ..."

253

Kassian pulled one tiny hand away from her face and looked for one area free of slime to kiss. He failed. Instead, he put his lips as close to her ear as he could without getting a faceful of *animorti*.

"I love you, Katrina Shephard," he whispered. "But if you ever scare me like that again I will smack your ass until you beg for mercy." He glanced up as Luca stepped into the basement with Callista in his arms.

"But, I...Callista..." Hearing her name, Callista opened one eye and quirked a brow at Luca's worried gaze.

"Took you long enough," she sniffed.

"Cheer up, Kat," Luca chuckled. "She's fine."

Epilogue

Callista's convalescence was trying, for everyone around her. Kat had been astounded to discover that Dimitri was a bona fide doctor and thanks to his medical skills, Calli's recovery was relatively swift. Still, it involved a good deal of complaining and demanding. Luca was the only one immune to her whining, and she did seem to do a lot less of it when he was around. For the first few days, she actually seemed to be mourning for Rapier. Kat took Kassian aside and worriedly suggested Stockholm syndrome, but Callista finally explained that though she could never have loved Jacques the way he wanted, over the years she had come to understand and develop a certain fondness for the man he could have been if only he'd been able to overcome his demons. He'd loved her in his way. It saddened her that he hadn't been strong enough to keep the depravity at bay, but she took comfort in the fact that perhaps death had finally ended his struggle. She acknowledged the horrible things he'd done, but maintained her conviction that they had been beyond his control. Not one of them agreed with her assessment, but whatever her faults, Callista clearly had a tender heart.

While she healed, she spent her days voraciously reading popular magazines and glued to the television, working hard to acclimate herself to this new century to which she'd had little exposure during her captivity, and trying to stifle her shock at how much everything had changed. Once she was feeling a little more human, or at least the *Earthbound* equivalent, she was able to fill in some of the gaps for the rest of them. After a hundred or so years of captivity, Jacques took it for granted that she wasn't going anywhere and was less guarded around her, less concerned with what she might overhear. When Kat learned that Sid was in fact, Miranda's *Familiar*, and he'd reported back to her on a regular basis, she became physically ill. Having spent the lion's share of the last five years in Sid's company, Kat was appalled to realize exactly how familiar the *Familiar* must have been with every private aspect of her life. Kassian ungallantly reminded her that he'd never liked cats, and gleefully offered to fade to Kat's house and wring the animal's neck, but not surprisingly, Sid was nowhere to be found. The numbers in Kat's locket turned out to be map coordinates that indicated the spot where Nicola and Lilly had hidden the ring Miranda had been so desperate to find. When Kassian and Luca returned from retrieving it, the looks on their faces sent Callista into gales of laughter that brought tears to her eyes even as she grimaced and pressed her palms against the sudden pain the unexpected mirth exacerbated in her healing chest.

"You knew," Kassian accused, wearing an expression that made it clear he found no humor in the situation whatsoever.

"Of course, I knew," Callista swiped at the tears gathered in the corners of her eyes, "but, it was worth keeping it to myself just to see the looks on your faces." At that, she launched into another fit of laughter, clutching at her chest until Luca wordlessly handed her a throw pillow from the sofa to use as a splint.

"Can someone let me in on the joke?" Kat looked from one to the other.

"You're an Archangel," Kassian mumbled in a voice that sounded almost pitiful.

"Say what?" Kat asked, sure she must have misheard. "I'm *Earthbound*; well half of me, anyway. How could I possibly be an Archangel?"

"This is the Ring of Aandalena," he said, holding up a thick gold band engraved with *sigil*s and embedded with colorful gemstones.

"Your family apparently descended from Aandalena," Luca clarified. "That means you are part Archangel. On your mother's side."

"Which means you outrank both of them," Calli cackled delightedly.

"Shut up, Calli," Kassian and Luca said in unison, which only sent her into further fits of giggles. Kat was quickly learning that despite her sweet nature and generous heart, Callista McAllister could be quite the nudge.

"Aandalena may have been an Archangel, but she married a human, as has nearly every successive generation of her line since then." Kassian raked his fingers through his dark hair, which Kat had convinced him to wear loose more often than not. "Kat can't have inherited more than a few drops of Archangel blood after all these centuries, if there's even *any* left."

"Apparently a few drops are all it takes…the ring is spelled to recognize its own and feed their power," Luca pronounced, pinching the bridge of his nose between a thumb and forefinger. "Honestly, Mac, doesn't it sound like something Michael would create? He was devastated when his daughter chose a human mate, but he loved her too much to deny her. He had no choice but to revoke her immortality, but he designed the ring to ensure that her descendants, *his* descendants, would never be powerless as the Archangel blood became more and more diluted. Through the centuries, witches married into the line, adding even more power, and someone, sometime must have gotten greedy and become corrupted by the power, much as I suspect Miranda would have had she gotten her hands on it. Not to mention the chaos that would have ensued if Miranda was under Jacques's influence when she obtained it. Lilly, knowing Miranda as she did, must have feared just such corruption and decided to take the ring out of circulation for good."

"But what does it do?" Kat asked fearfully. "My mother was afraid of it, Miranda was willing to kill for it, and Jacques lusted for it. It doesn't sound like anything I want to be responsible for."

"Tradition says that it gives the wearer control over demons," Callista interjected softly. "Jacques hoped it might cure him."

"Michael is the only one that would still know for sure what power the ring truly has," Luca replied.

"I don't want it."

"*Cara...*" Luca came and put a comforting arm around her shoulders. "I know this is a shock, but think this through..."

"No," she nearly shouted, twisting from his embrace. "I don't want it! I've spent a lifetime trying to figure out where I belong and I finally have. I finally know who I am and what I want. And I don't want that…that thing!" She spun to face Kassian. Maybe this ring had some power that could help them in their fight against the *Fallen*. Maybe she was being selfish? "Do you want me to keep it?"

Kassian crooked a finger at her and she walked slowly across the room to stand in front of where he sat on the sofa. He reached out and tugged her hand until she fell into his lap. He cupped her face in his hands and gazed into her tear bright eyes.

"It's your decision and I won't try to influence you one way or the other, baby. I think we should find out what power the ring has and what you might be giving up before you decide. Heck, maybe the ring entitles you to wings," he smiled. She didn't. "Kat, I want whatever makes you happy. What do you want?"

"I don't care about the power," she whispered, shaking her head slowly. "I've spent a lifetime struggling with powers I didn't understand." She held up a hand when he opened his mouth to speak. "And while I'll admit, they've occasionally come in handy and I guess I can live with the ones I already have, it's more than enough. I want the ring gone. I want you." She reached for Luca's hand. "I want my family. I don't want to be an Archangel."

Kassian leaned his forehead against hers. "You can't change what you are, Kat, but you'll always be who you are; and who you are is who I want, always."

"Give the ring back to this Michael character," she said firmly. "He created it, let it be his problem."

"Can I please be there when she tells him that?" Luca laughed.

Gossip among the *Fallen* was that Michael now spent his time on earth holed up in the Castel

Sant'Angelo, admiring his statue on the parapet, and the more accurate likeness by Raphael in the courtyard, watching satellite TV, and finding endless amusement in the Discovery Channel's attempts to discredit the Divine. The *Defensori*, for whom Michael served as Commander in Chief, knew better. Michael wielded as much power as he ever had, if not more, and his temper was legendary. He wouldn't be happy to have his lone descendant refuse his gift.

****

Kassian planted a kiss on Kat's nose and looked around the room at four of the five people who meant the most to him. The fifth was in Rome, and that's where they'd need to go to return the ring to Michael, anyway. He'd almost missed this. He'd almost let anger and regret make him oblivious to the good things life still had to offer. He hadn't been home in over fifty years and suddenly he was anxious to see his mother. She'd cried for over an hour when she learned Calli was alive and he had no doubt that she was going to love Kat. He stood so quickly that he nearly dumped Kat on the floor, and then he pulled her into his arms and dropped his mouth to hers. The kiss held the promise of what he had planned when they were finally alone. And in case she hadn't picked up on that, he sent a few suggestive scenes into her mind along with it. When he finally lifted his head, Kat looked dazed, Luca was rolling his eyes, Alec was grinning lasciviously, and Callista, unused to the sexual freedom of this new century, was blushing furiously.

"Okay, it's settled." Kassian stepped back and clapped his hands together. "Get packed. Alec, call Mom and make sure the villa's ready. We're going to

Italy."

"Tonight," Kat replied with a frown.

"What?"

"You said we were going tonight. We have other plans this afternoon," Kat reminded him. "And don't try telling me you forgot; it won't work this time."

"Well, no…" Kassian looked uncomfortable as hell. "No, I didn't forget, honey. But wouldn't you rather go to Italy?"

"We *are* going to Italy…tonight," Kat's brows were drawn together in the most threatening expression. "You promised Elle she could go with us on the corporate jet. Trust me, after dangling that carrot in front of her, you do *not* want to tell her we're leaving this afternoon before she's finished at the conference and abandoning her to fly coach. They only allow one checked bag now, you know. Elle isn't a one bag kind of girl; not even for a simple weekend at my house."

"Besides, if we leave now, we'll land at *Fiumicino* in the middle of the night," Luca argued. "You'll be dragging your mother out of bed and she isn't as young as she used to be. Besides, I doubt she'll get much sleep once she gets you all together under one roof again. Not to mention the wedding preparations, so you really should let her get some rest before we descend on her like a plague of locusts."

"Whose side are you on, anyway?" Kassian narrowed his eyes at Luca.

Luca shrugged. "Me? I'm Switzerland, my brother."

"Luca's right, Kass," Callista whispered quietly. "I'm as anxious to see Mother as you are, but as soon as she gets over her initial relief and excitement, I'm in for the lecture to end all lectures. I, uh, don't mind waiting a few more hours."

"Then it's settled!" Kat crowed triumphantly. "Besides, McAllister, everyone is tired of pizza and wings. I know I am."

"Heaven help me," he groaned, adding an eye roll for good measure.

"Don't waste your time calling for help. Heaven has more important things to worry about than your unreasonable little phobias...now move, McAllister," she demanded.

"Oh, fine!" he huffed, then strode to the door and yanked it open. Kat did smile then.

"*Cara*...where are you going, anyway?" Luca finally called when she was nearly out the door.

Kat looked at him over her shoulder and waggled her brows like the villain in a silent movie.

"Grocery shopping."

A word about the author...

Sharon Saracino resides in the anthracite coal country of Pennsylvania with her long-suffering husband, funny and talented son, and two insane dogs. When she is not reading, writing, or enjoying photography and genealogy, she brews limoncello, dreams of living in Italy, and works as a Certified Registered Rehabilitation Nurse.

Thank you for purchasing
this publication of The Wild Rose Press, Inc.
For other wonderful stories of romance,
please visit our on-line bookstore at
www.thewildrosepress.com.

For questions or more information
contact us at
info@thewildrosepress.com.

The Wild Rose Press, Inc.
www.thewildrosepress.com

To visit with authors of
The Wild Rose Press, Inc.
join our yahoo loop at
http://groups.yahoo.com/group/thewildrosepress/